Feast for the Ravens

Feast for the Ravens

A Bradecote
and Catchpoll Mystery

SARAH HAWKSWOOD

Allison & Busby Limited
11 Wardour Mews
London W1F 8AN
allisonandbusby.com

First published in Great Britain by Allison & Busby in 2025

A CIP catalogue record for this book is available from
the British Library.

10 9 8 7 6 5 4 3 2 1

ISBN 978-0-7490-3258-6

Typeset in 11/16pt Adobe Garamond Pro by
Allison & Busby Ltd.

FSC
www.fsc.org
MIX
Paper | Supporting
responsible forestry
FSC® C018072

Printed and bound in Great Britain by Clays Ltd. Elcograf S.p.A

EU GPSR Authorised Representative
LOGOS EUROPE, 9 rue Nicolas Poussin, 17000, LA ROCHELLE, France
E-mail: Contact@logoseurope.eu

For H. J. B.

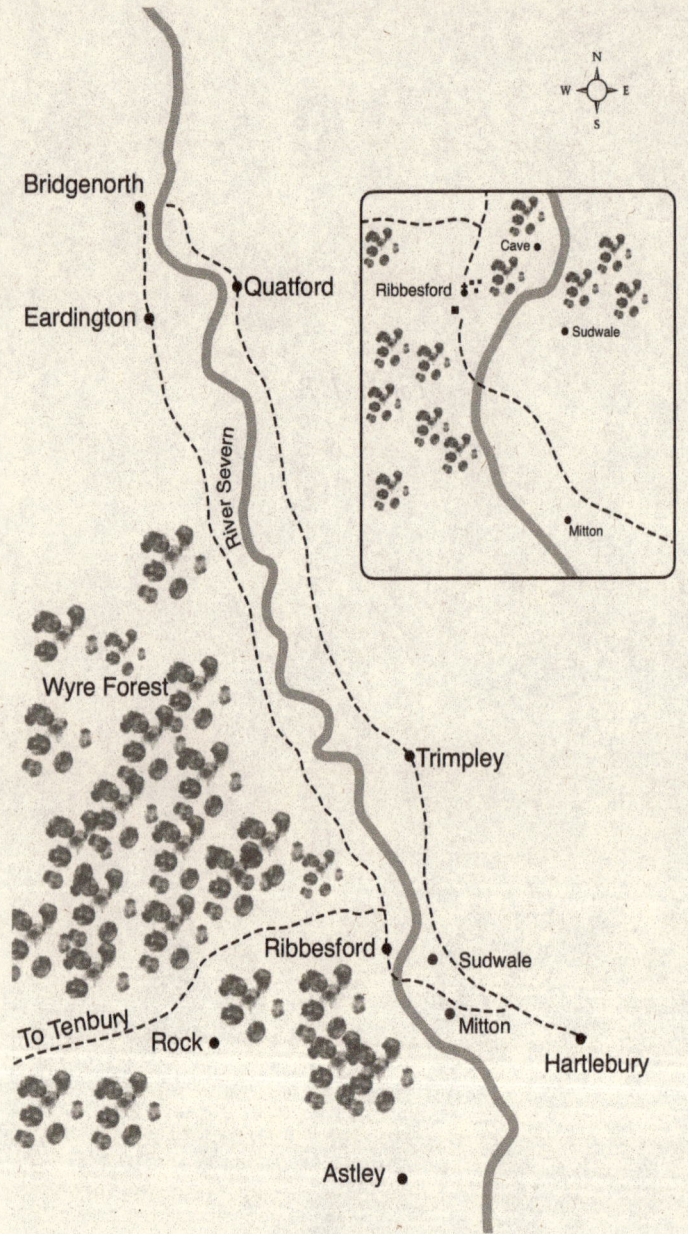

Letan him behindan hræw bryttian
saluwigpadan, þone sweartan hræfn,
hyrnednebban, and þane hasewanpadan,
earn æftan hwit, æses brucan,

They left behind them, to enjoy the corpses,
The dark-plumaged, swarthy raven,
Horny beaked, and the ash-plumaged
Eagle, white behind, to partake of the carrion

From 'The Battle of Brunanburh', Old English poem

Chapter One

Two days after the feast of St Gregory the Great,
September 1145

The knight rode slowly, on a loose rein and clearly lost in his own thoughts. A frown drew his brows together as though they might whisper secretively of what was going on in his mind, but he looked otherwise impassive. He was trying to remember topography from his youth, though in doing so he was assailed by other memories, mostly of the man who had journeyed with him for over two decades, and was now growing cold and stiff in the clearing where he had left him. He apostrophised himself out loud, and his horse's ears flicked back and forth, perhaps expecting an admonishing pull at the bit. It was foolishness, he told himself, to think of the past, for it was gone and irrelevant. What lay ahead was the future, and one that had more purpose than any in the years of exile. To achieve that he must follow his plan in every detail, but one doubt remained. Did the brook, whose name at present still eluded him, truly mark the shire boundary, and was it recognised by those who lived on either side? Either way, it would be best not to go far, not yet. There was no need for haste, for the body would surely not be discovered for several days at least, since it lay out of sight off the trackway, and any hue and cry would be half-hearted. By the time any report of it reached Worcester the trail would be colder than the corpse.

The track was descending now, and glimpses of the Severn to the right-hand side were spasmodic in the fast-fading daylight. The undergrowth beneath the trees was a little thicker on the left side, and a stunted holly, kept bushy by the overarching branches of oak and beech shading it from the light, would be good cover. He brought his mount to a halt and dismounted, leading it and the spare horse off the trackway and behind the screen of prickly leaves, where he hobbled them. Then he took a roll from behind his saddle, removed both surcoat and, with some grunting, the encumbering mailshirt, and transformed from Templar into anonymous rider. It was a perfectly good place to make camp for the night, so he scuffed an area bare with his boot, and gathered bark and twigs for a small fire. The autumnal display of nuts and berries would supplement the bread and smoked fish he had in his pack, and of course that was now feeding not two but only one. When later he slept, his dreams would not be haunted by ghosts of his own making.

It had been a good summer, with ample sunshine to warm the red earth and ripen the wheat, and sufficient rain to swell the grain. When Herluin the Steward had rubbed the kernels from a golden head of wheat in his weathered palm, he had smiled as he declared the crop ready to harvest, and in the frantic days that followed, the weather had held. Now the last stooks in the great field had been piled onto the ox wagon, the expanse of stubble was silent and empty, and the threshing barn was busy. A huge sense of relief pervaded the manor of Ribbesford, for the granary would be full and the spectre of hunger was banished from the following summer. It was not a large manor, being limited to the east by the flow of the Severn, which flooded its fields in wet winters but made them fertile, and the rising high ground of the Forest of Wyre curling about it, almost protectively, on all other sides. Had it not been for the ford, and the track from it that passed by church, hall and the cluster of lesser dwellings and barns, it would have been a hidden and secret place.

The children, who had toiled from dawn to dusk alongside their mothers during the harvest, gathering the sheaves, had now been released from their labours and given freedom for a couple of days. There were blackberries bejewelling the hedgerows about the harvest-shorn fields, and in the woods the first cobnuts were beginning to fall as the leaves lost their lustre, pattering softly upon the woodland floor. It was a fine late summer morn, warm from the first, for the autumnal chill and change to the scent in the air was still perhaps a week or two away. Edric and Agar's mother had given them each a willow basket and sent them off early, telling them that they should make themselves useful and forage for some of the seasonal bounty when they had finished wasting their time trying to catch fish in their hands in the still summer-shallow water of the ford. The lord of Ribbesford was a fair man, and the depredations of two small boys upon bushes and boughs that were 'his' would not attract his wrath, especially in the aftermath of a successful harvest.

The ford, which would be viable until the late autumn rains in Wales raised the Severn, was a favoured summer haunt for the boys, but almost as soon as they had begun paddling their older cousin, Wulfric, arrived, and began skimming stones aggressively across the water, his dark brows drawn in a scowl that boded ill to anyone who got in his way, especially if they were smaller. Edric and Agar looked at each other and sighed, since even the most sluggish fish would be disturbed, and there was no guarantee that their cousin, in such a mood, might not throw stones at them. After a murmured conversation, the brothers agreed to look in the woods for cobnuts first, so that they could have a competition to see who could collect most nuts and any berries they picked afterwards would not get squashed. They returned up the track, skirting about the barn in case a grown-up came out and decided there was a task for them after all, and past the church, set where the ground began to rise and above any possible flooding. The woods rose more steeply to their left, and were dominated by the 'big trees', sessile oak, ash, yew and beech, with hazel and elderberry scattered thinly. To their right, the high ground descended gradually as it approached the willow-and-alder-edged river, but then veered sharply northward as if shy of the water and the red sandstone crag that faced them from the eastern bank. There were plenty of hazels here, but none had been touched by the manor children for fear of the *Hrafn Wif*, the Raven Woman, a figure perceived more as some evil combination of witch and ghost than a creature of flesh and blood. She had become a fireside tale, and grown more frightening in the telling, and those adults who did not quite believe it were content to use her as a way to deter their children from playing by the river's turn, where the current ran stronger and they would be beyond earshot if they called for aid in difficulties.

'Shall we go that way?' Edric whispered, as if the Raven Woman would hear them.

'I dares not.' Agar was the younger by a year and a half.

'But we need not go too far, and look at that tree just over there. There be big nuts on it. And think – Wulfric will look small when we 'as been brave and done somethin' even 'e dare not.' Edric was trying to boost his own courage as much as that of his sibling.

Agar dithered. 'If we just goes a little way, then mayhap she will not find us?'

'Surely she will not. Come on.' Edric took his little brother's hand, and they stepped aside from the track into the woods. A squirrel, agitated by their arrival, disappeared in a flash of russet accompanied by alarmed churring and quivering twigs, which sent their hearts beating faster, and Agar gripped Edric's hand even more tightly. Edric tried to laugh it off and pretend that he had not been scared at all. The first tree they plundered for fallen bounty and those nuts that they could shake down with sticks provided cobnuts of great size, but too few were quite ripe enough to come loose. Pleased with their initial success, and arguing mildly over who had the most, the boys relaxed, and moved a little lower down the slope and more towards the river, beyond the sight of the track. An even better tree tempted them across a small, sunlit glade, where the gaunt skeleton of an ash that had died and toppled lay prostrate upon the carpet of opportunist grass and flower. Bees buzzed lazily among the woodland blooms of high summer. As they made to step into the light, Edric caught his breath and held his brother back. A large black bird, its wingspan as great as the boy was tall, glided down from somewhere to their left, landed upon the grass beyond the fallen tree and hopped purposefully for a few feet and began to peck at something. It dawned upon Edric that the sound he had heard was not just the buzzing of bees, but also flies. He had not taken in more than the laden hazel and the fallen tree, but now saw that there was something lying in the grass, some carrion that had attracted both fly and raven. He told himself it would be a roe buck or a fox, but his eyes, now looking with purpose, gave the lie to the thought. The shape was too long, and peeping between the stalks of hedge parsley was a booted foot. Edric's hold on Agar tightened as another raven flew in, and, to their horror, laughed. It was definitely a laugh, low and rasping, but a human laugh for all that. The boys had been frozen in their fear, holding their breaths until they felt their lungs would burst, but now Agar let out a strangled cry. The nearer raven hopped onto the top of one of the prostrate ash's skyward-pointing branches. It did not seem particularly afraid of humans, and just stared at them accusingly. Agar felt its beady eyes assess him as another meal. He panicked, and ran, dropping his basket and briefly breaking his handhold with Edric, though the older boy took it again almost immediately to drag him faster than the little legs had ever run in Agar's seven years of life. The raven flapped loudly behind them and they dared not look back. Their speed made them less footsure, and Edric half-stumbled as his foot caught in a shoot of bramble lying treacherously across their way. As he regained his balance he dared to take a single glance behind, and his thumping heart nearly stopped. A figure clothed head to toe in shabby black, the face, if it possessed one, veiled, stood where he had expected to see the raven. He whimpered, and ran faster even though his ankle hurt, and he prayed as he had never prayed before.

It took some considerable time before the two small, ashen-faced boys were able to do more than cry and tremble, even within the comforting hold of their mother. All threshing had ceased in the barn when they had stumbled within, terrified, and it was silent except for the sobbing, with all eyes fixed upon the trio. That something truly terrible had happened to them was not in doubt, and eventually a murmur of 'wolf', in a questioning tone, was heard in a man's low whisper. Herluin the Steward, grim-faced, shook his head. No wolves had been seen in this part of the Wyre Forest since before he had been of tithing age, and, whilst he did not say so, if a wolf had got close enough to the boys that they could be so frightened, it would likely have been stalking them and taken one. The healing woman had slipped out quietly and returned bearing two beakers, and urged both boys to drink. The concoction was nothing more than goat's milk sweetened with honey, rather than any remedy, but her reasoning was that the very normal act of drinking, and something that was sweet and pleasant, would help calm them so that the full tale could be related. She had also brought the priest, who had been saying Matins in the church.

The adults could only wait, but eventually Edric took a deep breath and managed to speak, though in little more than a whisper.

'There's a body, a-lyin' in the clearin' by the white tree. We . . .' Edric's voice faltered and he licked his lips, though without tasting the sweet residue that lingered there. 'We saw Her fly down as a raven and peck at it, and then She saw us and we ran, and when I looked back, She was a woman shape again.' He crossed himself, and many copied the action.

'"Her"?' Herluin knew the answer he would receive, but still sought verification.

'The *Hrafn Wif*, Master Steward. Afore God I swears it. She must 'ave killed 'im and . . .' Edric could not continue and turned his face into his mother's skirts.

'Then we must go and bring the body to the church and report the death.' Herluin's tone ensured nobody thought this merely a suggestion, but he could feel the lack of enthusiasm almost palpably. 'I will take six men and that hurdle as you repaired last week, Odda. Four can carry the body and two will have bill hooks in case of need.'

'But what good is bill 'ooks 'gainst somethin' that be not flesh and blood and can change shape into a bird and attack us from the sky?' Odda, thinking that he would be one of those detailed for the party by virtue of having worked upon the hurdle, sounded very doubtful.

'Because I will come with you also.' The voice was new. The priest, Father Laurentius, had kept silent and a little apart while everyone was focused upon Edric. 'No evil will have power over the Cross, and I will bear our processional cross before us.' The priest did not believe that anything supernatural existed in the wood, but realised that persuading his flock otherwise was a near impossible task, especially in view of the child's honest declaration. He sounded so calm that it gave the faint-hearted hope.

'Thank you, Father.' Herluin cast his eye over the other men within the barn, and selected those who were the younger and fitter.

It did not take very long to reach the clearing, not least because the hurdle weighed very little, unladen, though it looked very much like a religious procession for some sylvan saint, with Father Laurentius holding the wooden cross from the church before him, though his arms eventually trembled so much with the strain that he had to clasp it less ostentatiously against his chest, and mentally apostrophised himself for the sin of pride in thinking how well he had looked before his parishioners.

The arrival of a group of men making no effort to be quiet, and in fact trying to make as much noise as possible to scare off anything nasty, caused the ravens to rise into the air, up well above tree height, and voice their annoyance by means of throaty croaking. There were now three of them, and they continued to circle above the clearing, to the concern of several of the men below. Herluin stepped forward to advance alongside the priest. From a man's height it was easy to see that a body lay, face up, in the grass. It was the corpse of a man, and he did not stare at the sky because he no longer possessed even the unseeing eyes of the dead. The face was bloodied and torn, the sockets raw and empty. Herluin crossed himself, and not just because of the horror of the visage. The man was garbed as a knight, and the chances of him being proved English before the Law were almost nil. The murdrum fine would be levied upon the Hundred for the death of anyone of Norman ancestry, and Ribbesford and its steward 'blamed' for it. Father Laurentius, already intoning prayers for the dead man's soul, was consoling himself with the knowledge that whoever the knight might be, he was a deeply Christian soul, for his white surcoat was emblazoned upon the left breast with a scarlet cross such as the priest had never seen before, though it was not the only scarlet present, for the cloth was spotted with blood below the neck. He wore a mail shirt beneath the garment, but had clearly not been prepared for combat, for his coif had been drawn back, revealing a head of lightly curling, dark hair still full and untainted by grey. His arms were outstretched, and in his right hand he still clasped his sword. Flies, disturbed by their arrival, rose from the already raven-damaged flesh.

'Never 'eard of a raven a-goin' for a man and killin' 'im, but then what flies 'ere be no normal bird. 'Tis sorcery.' Odda spoke softly, not just out of respect for the dead, but because he feared the circling ravens were listening, and he crossed himself nervously.

A muttering of agreement and copying of the action showed that his view was shared. Father Laurentius, crossing himself at the conclusion of his prayer rather than in solidarity with his companions, raised a hand to prevent further comment.

'This we cannot know until he is laid within the church and the body cleaned. It could be he had drawn his sword because he thought he heard a wild animal, a boar mayhap, but in that moment died naturally at God's calling and what we see is just nature at work after he died.'

'Then where be the knight's 'orse?'

'And would such a man travel without servant or squire?'

These questions could have no answer, but Father Laurentius

felt they drew minds away from superstition and back to the explicable, so was glad of them.

'If there is a thought this man was killed by another, the lord Sheriff must be told of the death,' he declared, 'and should not a hue and cry be raised?'

'Waste of time would scourin' the woods be, Father, since the 'orse be gone, and the threshin' only part done, but I must go and tell our lord, and bring 'im back from Rock, and then all can be laid before the lord Sheriff, as you says.' Herluin the Steward was already thinking it would be far better for all this to lie in the hands of William de Ribbesford, who held the manor from the lord of Wigmore. 'Pity it be that 'e should be otherwhere this day.'

This was agreed by all. Herluin then took the sword from the dead man's hand, and directed the body to be picked up and laid upon the hurdle. The corpse was stiff, but not so rigid that the outlying arm could not be moved, with effort, to the side of the body, for which he gave up silent thanks. He then placed the sword upon the knight's chest, respectfully. The four men who were bearers lifted their burden to their shoulders, and the grim procession retraced their steps to Ribbesford and the cool of the church, where they found a board and trestles already laid before the altar, and the healing woman in attendance.

'I thought it best I be ready to wash the body, Father,' she murmured, as the corpse was laid upon the board, 'if'n it be no kin of anyone of us.'

'A good thought.' The priest nodded approvingly, and turned to Herluin, who was quietly dismissing the bearers. 'Will you go to Rock?'

'Aye. Five mile be none so far, though up the Long Bank slows a man on foot, but I should be back early after noontide, God willin'.'

'Let us hope so, indeed. You would not think to take the mule?'

'Well. I doubt it could bear my weight, and besides, I never rode afore now.' Herluin was a big man.

Herluin sent the men back to threshing, though he doubted much labour would take place with both news and imaginings to be passed among all, and set off up the track to then follow the ridge line westward. Father Laurentius and the healing woman, Estrith, were left with the deceased, and the priest did not think it beneath him to assist her in removing the weight of the mailcoat from the body. It was then that they made two discoveries.

Herluin the Steward strode back down into Ribbesford alone, and solemn of face. He had spent much of the return journey contemplating what should happen next, since the decisions now lay with him. He was a little surprised that everyone was in the open, and clearly opinions were being exchanged very freely. He could see Father Laurentius making calming gestures with his hands, though without effect. It meant that his approach was not heard until he was well within range for his voice to carry over the others.

'Does everyone think this another Holy Day when none toil?' He had their attention, and some folk looked guilty and gazed at their feet. 'I leaves for but an hour or so and the manor lies idle.' His disapproval was clear.

'But it needs to be decided.' This was a woman from the back of the group. 'Should the *Hrafn Wif* be hunted down to keep us safe in our beds, or at least our children safe when they be out of our sight?'

'My daughter, there is no proof that the man was killed by other than the evil that men do.' Father Laurentius's voice showed strain. He had been making this point for some time. 'The lord Sheriff's men must come and decide if the killer can be found, and why he died.'

'He died 'cos the *Hrafn Wif* wanted 'is eyes for breakin' 'er fast.'

'But we cannot kill 'er if she be no woman at all.'

'Can the good Father cast 'er away with prayers?'

The three voices spoke at once, and the words tangled in Herluin's brain for a moment.

'Quiet!' It was a command, and was obeyed. 'Father, you are sure this was the act of a man?' Herluin had no doubt of it himself, but thought that if the priest said it was so, no blame could thereafter attach to him if folk acted like headless chickens.

'Assuredly. Come into the church. But where is the lord?'

'Left Rock yesterday, called by the lord de Mortemer to meet him at Brimfield, and 'twere not clear if they would then both go on to Wigmore. It would take too long to walk all the way there to tell 'im and then to return.' Herluin was thinking how sore his feet would have been. ''Twould be late forenoon on the morrow afore the lord Sheriff could be told, and I doubts 'e would like the delay.' He followed the priest into the cool quiet of the church. They approached the altar and the now shrouded body. Both genuflected and then the priest uncovered the face, calm in the absence of a soul within, with a band of cloth bound about it to hold the jaw shut as the death stiffness faded.

'The lord Sheriff needs to be informed, as I have said, Herluin, and not just because we have discovered the man died by violence. There was a message hidden close to his chest, for which I think he died, though I have long forgotten most of my Latin beyond the Offices. Do not go to Worcester yourself. I fear I cannot keep them' – Father Laurentius waved a hand indicating those outside – 'from wanting to scour the forest, which would be wasteful of time, and, I hope, futile. They will listen to you.'

'Aye, Father, they will listen, if I has to knock 'eads together for it to be so.' Herluin looked grim, though he liked the idea that it would not be him having to walk all the way to Worcester. 'I could send Baldric, I suppose.' There was a touch of reluctance, for Baldric was one of William de Ribbesford's men-at-arms, and of the other two one was laid up with a broken hand, and the other had been given leave to visit his dying father in Bridgnorth. Baldric was not a man capable of much thought, but he was strong, looked very intimidating, and was very obedient as long as the command was simple.

'Can the mule take his weight? If it could not take yours?' The questions came to Father Laurentius's lips unbidden.

'At the pace Baldric can manage, yes. I think so. My worry would be 'im explainin' it all.'

'I think the message itself will help with that, Herluin. When I aided Estrith in stripping the body, we found it, as I said, beneath the poor man's coat of mail, a little bloodstained

22

but readable. The lord Sheriff will have clerks who can read every word of it to him.'

'So you do not think he was killed by the *Hrafn Wif*, Father.' Herluin gave a small, twisted smile.

'No, I do not. Nor did he die at the beak of a raven, for Estrith discovered that a blade had been thrust up under his chin and into the mouth and beyond. The body is still rather stiff' – the priest grimaced, for Estrith, in her zeal to discover if what she believed was true, had been very forceful in opening the jaws – 'but you could see for yourself.'

'No need, Father, if Estrith says it is so and you saw also. Someone must 'ave got up close to do that. Must 'ave been the servant or squire as did it.'

'But his sword was in his hand, Herluin.'

'Aye, true enough. 'Tis all too difficult for ordinary folk to unravel' – Herluin shook his head – 'and best left for the lord Sheriff, though at Baldric's pace 'e will not reach Worcester much afore Vespers.'

Baldric was called, and told what he must do and say. After the third attempt at repeating it he got it right, though Herluin and Father Laurentius made him repeat it once again before they finally watched him ride towards the ford with a look of determination upon his slightly vacant face.

'He will be able to find his way to Worcester?' Father Laurentius had a sudden worrying thought.

'I told him to 'ead south, and 'e is able to ask. No more could I do.' Herluin shrugged, and turned his mind to persuading the rest of the manor folk to get back to work and not go hunting for the Raven Woman.

Chapter Two

Hugh Bradecote, a half-smile on his lips, was watching his lady haggle, in a very polite way, over the price of four ells of fine wool cloth to make winter gowns for their infant daughter and an undershirt for little Gilbert, who was about to attain his second birthday and was exploring the boundaries of behaviour. This meant running his nurse ragged, much noise, and the occasional need for paternal intervention. When this was added to the infant demands of baby Edeva, it meant Bradecote's hall was far from quiet. He gave thanks that it was so, but it was also good that he and Christina could have this afternoon away on their own. Now that the harvest was safely gathered in, and it looked likely that there would be an excess to sell, he felt that he could relax a little.

He might not normally have escorted his wife as she made her purchases, and instead remained within the castle, but Bradecote was still aware of being less than the lord Sheriff's favourite vassal. His 'disobedience' in Evesham at midsummer, pursuing lines of enquiry where his overlord had commanded he should leave well alone, had very briefly put his tenure as undersheriff of the shire in doubt, and although it was now clear that he was not to be removed from the office, he had thought it best to lie low and let William de Beauchamp's well-known bad temper reduce to a normal simmer. When he and Christina had ridden into the castle bailey to leave their mounts to be stabled, he had not asked whether the lord Sheriff was in residence, and had left immediately, feeling almost furtive.

'So this where you 'as disappeared to, my lord.'

Bradecote turned, the smile now lengthened, to see Serjeant Catchpoll within three strides of him. The man was very good at 'appearing' almost silently, as the thieves of Worcester would vouch.

'It is not faint-heartedness, Catchpoll, just – caution. I was not avoiding you.'

'I doubts you could do that, my lord, not if'n I wanted to find you in Worcester.' It was stated as a simple fact.

'True enough. I suppose you saw my grey.' Bradecote's steel-grey horse was distinctive.

'Saw its rear end as a lad led it into the stables. I would 'ave caught up with you afore you left the castle foregate, but for the need to give some advice to the guard on the gate who let a stranger walk right into the bailey without so much as a glance, 'is eyes bein' on a shapely maid with two big' – Catchpoll paused for a moment – 'water pails. If I earnt a silver penny for every man-at-arms I showed the error of lettin' 'is eyes wander when on guard, I would be wearin' new boots each winter, no doubt of it.'

'But you told me you liked your boot soles a little thin, the better to feel Worcester beneath you, Catchpoll.'

'That I did, my lord, so a good thing 'tis those pennies was never given.'

This interchange having acted as their mutual greeting, Bradecote asked if anything of note had occurred, even if it had not meant him being called in to duty. Catchpoll did not interpret that as an interest in the thefts and minor assaults that were part and parcel of town life.

'The lord Sheriff 'as stayed back at Elmley mostly, while Worcester's smell would offend 'is nose these last two months, which means life in the castle 'as stayed quiet but for the lord Castellan buzzin' about like an angry wasp, just to make hisself feel important. The lord Sheriff came in the end of last month for three days, and when I gave my report, almost waved me away, sayin' there was far more important things goin' on. I overheard a messenger bein' sent to Earl Roger, and the clerk let slip it were not the first these last weeks.'

'Earl Roger of Hereford? I never heard the lord Sheriff speak much of him before.' Bradecote looked thoughtful for a moment. 'But it might be that Earl Roger is concerned about the Welsh.'

'Hmm, well that 'as always been the case, and they must be keepin' an eye on discord in England, ready to take advantage when eyes is lookin' elsewhere.' Catchpoll's distrust of the Welsh, collectively, was a very personal thing, but in this case did make strategic sense.

Christina now joined them, her purchase laid over her arm, and Catchpoll greeted her politely, removing his cap and asking if she had struck a good bargain.

'Indeed I did, Serjeant. Now, do not tell me you have come to take my lord from me.' She smiled, but was not speaking in jest.

'No, no, my lady. We was just—'

The response was cut short as a man-at-arms, slightly out of breath, turned the corner and then dithered not quite sure whether to address the serjeant or the lord Undersheriff. He glanced between the pair and then opted for Catchpoll.

'Serjeant, you is needed. Underserjeant Walkelin says report 'as been made of the killin' of a knight in the north of the shire, and the lord Castellan is angry.'

'Which probably means I should return also.' Bradecote was addressing Christina more than Catchpoll. She sighed.

'Indeed, my lord. I will visit Roger the Healer to buy more of that salve he made up for Edeva's dry skin, and which worked so well, and then I will return immediately to the castle. I am only concerned that you have nothing with you, not even a change of undershirt if the weather breaks and you get soaked.' She looked at him with wifely concern.

'I doubt I would shrink, my love.' Bradecote smiled at her. 'But if "the north of the shire" means we would be riding in the dark, you have nothing to concern you. I would escort you back to Bradecote, collect all I may need and return to Worcester, ready for an early start.'

'Then, for once, my lord, I hope you are called further from me.' She laid a hand upon his arm for a moment, smiled at Catchpoll and flitted away to seek the apothecary.

Underserjeant Walkelin was looking worried. That a report of a killing had come in was not a concern, but that it had been presented to the lord Castellan made things difficult. Walkelin even thought he preferred the lord Sheriff's bear-like demeanour to that of Simon Furnaux, who disliked Catchpoll and openly loathed the lord Bradecote, and made every effort to get the better of both. He was currently making loud complaint that neither was present to do their duty, as though they knew by instinct when such a report might be made. Walkelin escaped the tirade upon the excuse of sending out more men to locate Serjeant Catchpoll in the streets of Worcester, and went to the gatehouse. As the serjeant and undersheriff approached along the castle foregate he gave a sigh of relief, and only just kept himself from rushing forward. That, however, would demean the position of underserjeant, so he stood his ground. Catchpoll, observing him, silently commended his action.

'My lord Bradecote, I did not know you was in Worcester.' Walkelin gave a nod as his obeisance and then looked at Catchpoll. 'Glad I am you was not far away, Serjeant. A rider came in from Ribbesford, upriver in the Forest of Wyre, nigh on the shire border. Two little lads found the body of a man, a knight with the sign of a scarlet cross upon 'is surcoat, in a clearin' off the track from the ford. The steward sent a man-at-arms from the manor to us, the lord bein' absent, but the messenger could give no more'n the message itself, bein' the sort as leaves thinkin' to others. A vellum message were found beneath the man's clothin', when the body were stripped for washin', and it were sent also. A clerk 'as read it out to the lord Castellan, and only then did 'e send for me, and will not say what lies within it.'

'He might not choose to tell you, but he will tell me.' Bradecote looked grim, and strode purposefully into the castle bailey and thence to the hall. Simon Furnaux was ensconced in the high seat upon the dais at the end of the hall, which was where William de Beauchamp would sit. Catchpoll thought the man did it to make himself feel more important, since he was not a man who looked naturally commanding. At the sight of Bradecote, Furnaux smiled in an unpleasant way.

'Ah, my lord Undersheriff. That means I do not have to send for you and delay further.'

Both Bradecote and Catchpoll strove to hide their annoyance, the one for being treated as a vassal and the other for being ignored.

'It is indeed fortunate, since I will be able to hear exactly what was in the document concealed upon the dead man, and which may be vital to why he was killed and who did it.'

'Well, I can tell you that—' the castellan began, but Bradecote held up a hand and stopped him.

'No. We need to see the vellum itself, and have a clerk read it to us.' Bradecote felt that finding it too difficult for his very basic reading skills and handing it back to a clerk would look worse than asserting that a clerk would read it from the start. He could see Furnaux dithering. The man liked to know things that others did not. 'You command this castle in our lord's stead, but this is about the King's Laws, in which you have no part. We will hear the document, and then speak with the man who brought the news.' It was not a request.

'Very well.' Furnaux sounded petulant. 'You' – he gestured at a servant – 'go and fetch back the clerk and the vellum I told him to place safely.' He then glared at Bradecote. 'I do not think what lies within is for the ears of them.' He nodded towards Catchpoll and Walkelin.

'And I do not much care what you think, my lord Castellan.'

Bradecote saw the tensing in Furnaux's hand upon the arm of the seat. Yes, that hit home. There was an uncomfortable silence.

A clerk scurried back into the hall and bowed to castellan and then undersheriff, to the same degree. Clerks, or at least those in the service of the lord Sheriff of Worcester, learnt how to keep their superiors' displeasure at bay.

'My lords.' He left it at that, and awaited instruction.

'The lord Castellan has heard the contents of the vellum found upon the dead man at Ribbesford and has, correctly, called upon us. He is now free to deal with other . . . things, but we would look closely at the vellum, and also hear what is has to say and to whom it was sent.' Bradecote was rather pleased that he had managed to effectively dismiss Furnaux at the same time as asserting his command of the situation, and heard Furnaux grind his teeth. The clerk looked a little nervously towards the castellan, who controlled himself enough to look casual and wave a hand towards the officers of the law.

'Yes, I have more important matters to attend to. Do as the undersheriff says.' Furnaux omitted giving Bradecote the lordly prefix, but Bradecote still smiled as the man got up and left, head held haughtily, but the tell-tale hand clasped into a fist. There was silence until he had left the chamber.

'Now, let us see the thing first.' Catchpoll's voice was almost convivial. 'You never knows what might also be present other than words.'

'Well, it is obvious enough, for it is bloodstained to the point where some words are no longer readable.' The clerk sounded very highly affronted that such a precious thing as a document should be sullied by a man's blood. He unrolled what was held in his right hand, for it was a small document, no more than a spread hand's width in length, and barely as wide. He placed it, reverently, upon a small table beside the sheriff's seat, smoothed it flat and set a stone as a weight at either end.

The three sheriff's men came forward, leaning to inspect it and looking as if paying homage to it.

'A messenger would not normally carry his message concealed within his clothing unless the contents were very private, and possibly dangerous. Whoever killed this man either did not look for it, or was disturbed before he could do so.' Bradecote was thinking out loud. 'Read it to us, without haste.'

'As you desire, my lord.' The clerk cleared his throat, more as an habitual mannerism than from necessity, and began.

'"To the lord Hugh de Mortemer, lord of Wig—"' The clerk pursed his lips and then continued, 'The rest of that word and the next are unreadable, but obviously "Wigmore" and followed by the standard salutation "greeting". There are then four or five damaged words, the last of which is most likely "of" and a place beginning "Fari—". It then continues "we are still resolute in our plan and hope to draw the Usurper Stephen, who ought never to have been crowned, northward, which will allow our Lady's forces in the south to gather more securely. We rely upon the fulfilment of your treaty with us to begin as if loyal to him and then, when your men form a major part of his force, show yourself for the Just Cause." There is then a seal' – the clerk pointed at the bottom of the message – 'and the name, which reads—'

'W, I,' Bradecote could not help murmuring phonetically,

31

peering at each letter individually, and the clerk, approving of the attempt but eager to end its tortuous nature, broke in.

'William fitzAlan, lord of Oswestry, my lord.'

'FitzAlan fled England after Shrewsbury fell to King Stephen when the Empress mustered her supporters. It sounds as if he has returned.' Bradecote spoke softly, almost to himself. 'And Hugh de Mortemer has always been a loyal supporter of King Stephen.'

'Until now,' added Catchpoll.

'Mmm.' Bradecote was thinking. 'This gives us a reason why the messenger was killed, but I wonder if the lord Sheriff is aware of this change in allegiance.' Bradecote looked at the clerk. 'I want you to write a message to the lord Sheriff and send it with this to his castle at Elmley. Bring ink and write as I dictate.'

The clerk bowed and went swiftly to find the tools of his craft.

'Always gets difficult when we deals with power that great, my lord. The business of the kingdom – 'tis a big knot.' Catchpoll pulled a face.

'Indeed, Catchpoll, and I am sure that this information, if new to the lord Sheriff, will be important, but we must come to an answer, even if thereafter the King's Justice is not served.' Bradecote wondered whether he might find himself once again delving where William de Beauchamp would prefer him not to go. The politics of power was complicated, as Catchpoll said. As hereditary lord Sheriff of Worcester, William de Beauchamp gathered the King's taxes and saw his laws obeyed, though he, and now his overlord, Earl Waleran, had taken a position on the side of the Empress Maud when King Stephen had been captured after the Battle of Lincoln. De Beauchamp was performing the difficult feat of keeping close enough to both sides that neither sought his blood. Bradecote did not think his overlord a man of strongly held moral belief, other than in the success of the line of de Beauchamp, and was pragmatic enough to follow whichever side gave most to him and least to his enemies. It was possible that de Beauchamp already knew of this plan, but if he did not, he would not thank his subordinate if he kept it from him.

The clerk returned, and settled himself to write what he was told. Bradecote thought for a moment and then began.

'Write thus. "My lord, this was found upon the body of a knight at Ribbesford, one bearing a red cross upon his white surcoat, and shown to have been killed by intent. The vellum was sent to Worcester and has been read first to the lord Castellan, in your absence, and now to me. It appears important and so I send it swiftly onward to you. I head north with Serjeant Catchpoll and Underserjeant Walkelin to find out the name of the dead man, if possible, who killed him, and why." That is the message. I will put my mark upon it, not being possessor of a seal, and you underwrite "Hugh Bradecote, Undersheriff".'

'Yes, my lord.' The quill scratched across the vellum and then paused, and the clerk handed it to Bradecote, who, very carefully, formed an irregular H with three distinct lines, and an approximation of a B. He felt the clerk watching him, no doubt critical of his meagre penmanship, though he commended him out loud.

'Thank you. Now have this taken straight to Elmley.'

'At once, my lord.' The clerk bowed low and left, bearing both documents, and Bradecote sighed.

'Now we can speak with the man who brought the news.'

'And be more like usual, my lord.' Walkelin was very aware of being at the edge of something so far above his rank as to be beyond imagining. 'Shall I go and bring him in?'

'Yes, do that, Walkelin.'

As Walkelin exited, Bradecote looked at Serjeant Catchpoll.

'I wish this had been a "simple" case of jealousy or greed, Catchpoll. I can see us treading where the lord Sheriff would not have us go in this.'

'Mayhap, my lord, but sometimes the simple proves the answer after all. We can but pray for it.'

'Most fervently, Catchpoll. Most fervently.'

The man who entered the hall behind Walkelin looked overawed. He already clasped his cap in both his hands before him and was leaning forward as if caught in the act of bowing.

'This is Baldric, from Ribbesford, my lord.' Walkelin announced the man, who raised his round and slightly vacuous face to nod agreement to the statement and then lowered his gaze once more.

'You have had a long ride, Baldric.' Bradecote tried to begin without making the man feel more nervous.

'Set off 'bout two hours after noontide, my lord. I could not ride faster, bein' a bit big for the beast.' Baldric addressed Bradecote's feet, and the undersheriff wondered if his lord was a hard taskmaster.

'Then give me your message as you gave it to the lord Castellan.'

'As best I can, my lord.' Baldric did not think he could match the words exactly. He stumbled through the clearly memorised message, which gave no more than what Walkelin had passed on. At its conclusion he gave a sigh of relief.

'So that was the report itself but what can you tell us?' Catchpoll took over the questioning, seeing that Baldric was so overawed, or possibly tired.

''Twas not me as found the knight. Two little lads went foraging for cobnuts, and went where they was told not to go, up where the *Hrafn Wif* lurks.' Baldric shuddered, and crossed himself. He was one who believed in the malign presence as firmly as a child. 'Many a time they 'as been told not to go there, but lads will be bold where wiser folk would be cautious.' He said this with a shake of the head and a sigh. 'Seems they came to a clearin' and saw a body and she flew down, laughin', and pecked its eyes out, and they ran away. As they ran away they looked back and saw a black figure among the trees, watchin', so she 'ad changed shape again. Our lord says 'tis all foolishness, the *Hrafn Wif*, and shows no fear to go up there, but this proves she kills, and for pleasure.'

Catchpoll glanced at Bradecote, and then Walkelin, who were clearly as taken aback as he was. They had expected a few basic details and a denial of anyone knowing the identity of the man, and here was a tale of a shape-changing woman, a spectral figure clearly feared in Ribbesford, who had reputedly killed a man and gouged out his eyes. Bradecote recovered the fastest.

'But this Raven Woman has not been taken up for the killing?'

'No, my lord, but what chance would there be to capture 'er,

when she changes shape from woman to bird in an eye's blink?'
Baldric looked surprised.

Bradecote did not pursue the question further. Superstition was a weed that sent down deep roots.

'You say you set off this afternoon from Ribbesford. Was the body discovered yesterday in the afternoon or this morning?'

'Oh, well afore noontide, my lord, but then Herluin the Steward rode to Rock, our lord's other manor, to tell 'im of the deed, that 'e might decide what to do. But our lord were not there, so 'e came back, and 'e and Father Laurentius said I must come to Worcester and report the death.'

It was apparent that Baldric was the sort of man who did exactly as he was told, and never took a step beyond the order. Catchpoll gave silent thanks that the steward and priest were able to make decisions.

'How long will it take to reach Ribbesford, do you think, Catchpoll?' Bradecote looked to the serjeant.

'To the northern shire border upriver would be a long forenoon, this time o' year and settin' off at dawn, so mayhap a little less, my lord, at our pace.'

'As I expected. I will escort my lady back to Bradecote, collect my bedroll, and be back before deep dark. Make your own arrangements, and we will leave here tomorrow at sunrise. You, Baldric' – the undersheriff regarded the man-at-arms once more – 'will eat and sleep in the barracks here and accompany us, as long as you can keep up.' Bradecote thought it worth adding that caveat.

'Yes, my lord.' Baldric took this as his dismissal, and withdrew gratefully, leaving the trio to speak openly.

'Could it be *drycræft*?' Walkelin felt the question needed to be asked, but tried to make it sound as if he felt it fanciful.

'I possess more'n twice your years, Young Walkelin, and in all that time I never saw a spirit, nor a witch. Been warned about 'em often enough, but that were either to keep me from nosin' about where some did not wish, or just plain malice, accusin' old women as 'ad cared for their neighbours long years and grown bold enough to tell folk not to be fools, or became a mite forgetful in their potions. 'Tis also easier for a man to blame a twist-'anded old woman when the pig dies, than say 'twere *wyrd*, and thus meant to be, or bad 'usbandry. And as for shape-shiftin', I does not believe in it. Mind you, if it could be done I would shift my knees to be those of a lad again.'

'Why stop at the knees, Catchpoll?' Bradecote was mildly curious.

'Well, my lord, the rest 'as matured nicely, like a good wine, and 'tis just the knees as give me grief. Besides, when the rest of me lacked even a score of years but the knees was right good, I made more mistakes than I would care to recall.'

'So whoever killed the knight were not a woman-bird, or bird-woman, but it might 'ave been an act of madness. Such a person would not be lookin' for a message.' Walkelin, accepting his superior's calm dismissal of the occult, focused upon the real.

'That is possible, and if so, puts Ribbesford at risk, but we were told the man was found in a clearing, not beside the trackway, so my first question would be how he came to be there.' Bradecote, concerned more that superstition and fear would influence what they learnt, also set pointless worry aside.

'My lord, until the morrow, we possess but answerless questions. Once we is there, things will clear.' Catchpoll was unconcerned, and he was right to be so, Bradecote acknowledged.

'Then we part, and meet on the morrow in the bailey at sunrise. I am not going to come back early this evening to listen to Simon Furnaux's bleating, but intend to arrive just after dusk and get straight to bed.'

Bradecote met Christina as she passed through the castle gate, and she smiled at him.

'My dear lord, I have not dithered. In fact, I am sure Roger the Healer thinks I was in a strange haste, but that was only so that I could also call briefly upon Walkelin's wife. You see, I bought a little extra cloth, so that I might give her a length to make a gown for the baby, as a gift. She looks very well, but, when Walkelin's mother left us for a moment, she confessed that she is feeling too cared for, as if she might break just from doing tasks about the house, and that Walkelin's mother is determined that it will be a boy and be called Hubert, after her late husband, and Walkelin's wife is keen that a son bear her own sire's name, Rhodri.'

'Just imagine what Catchpoll would say to that.' Bradecote laughed.

'It would not be fit for my ears, I know. Let us hope, for Walkelin's peace in his own home, that the babe is a girl!'

They rode home with their horses on a loose rein, side by side, and Christina, well used to her husband deserting her for the duties of the Law, did not fuss over him as he packed the few essentials he needed, and he spent a half hour with his son before they ate. As the sun dipped behind the Malvern Hills to the west, he kissed her goodbye, and rode out. She stood in the little bailey with baby Edeva on her hip and gave a sigh, then told herself off for foolishness, and went back to the solar to begin her sewing.

It was not full dawn when Bradecote stepped out into the castle bailey. There was no hint of autumn in the air, but it was early enough to feel cool and fresh. A groom, kicked early from his blanket by Catchpoll, who had ordered him to wait upon the lord Undersheriff, came out of the stables leading Bradecote's distinctive steel-grey horse, and was followed by Catchpoll and Walkelin, bringing their own mounts. Walkelin was stifling a yawn.

'Where is our Ribbesford man?' enquired Bradecote, frowning. Having risen at such an hour he did not appreciate the man-at-arms not being likewise up and ready.

'Er, prayin', my lord, in the stable.' Walkelin could not keep a straight face. 'I told 'im that we is not goin' to gallop all the way, but . . .' He shrugged. Once upon a time Walkelin had been uncertain on horseback, but without noticing it, he had become perfectly at ease. 'I did offer Snægl, my lord, since they would suit each other, wantin' to go slow, but then Snægl tried to nip 'is arm and 'e said no.'

'If he is not swift I may bite him also.' Bradecote rubbed his gauntleted hands together. At this point Baldric did appear, looking like a man about to undergo a trial. 'Ah, there you are. Good. We mount up and head north. We take the road to Bridgnorth, yes?'

'Aye, my lord, but cuts off at 'artlebury, where the lord

Bishop lives sometimes. Ribbesford lies upon the western bank, across the ford. I went to 'artlebury, where I got directions on the road to Worcester. Never been this far, nor seen a place as big. My father went to Bridgnorth as a lad, after King 'enry took the castle from the lord of Bellême, but Worcester must be much bigger.'

Catchpoll pursed his lips. Who would even be fool enough to compare Bridgnorth with Worcester? The serjeant was very proud of the place of his birth. He said nothing, however, other than to recommend Baldric to mount up and not fall off. The latter instruction was not followed, since as soon as Bradecote urged his horse into a gentle canter beyond the Worcester boundary, Baldric and the mule parted company. After a second fall and consequent stoppage, Bradecote, exasperated, told the man to make his way home at his own pace, for they could not afford to delay.

Once he had been left behind, progress was quicker, although little was said until the horses were brought to a walk for a while to rest them.

'What chance do we have of getting sound sense from the folk of Ribbesford if they are convinced this Raven Woman is to blame, Catchpoll?'

'Not much, my lord, leastways not until we 'as proved it all shadows on the wall, used to frighten children. These things tend to start small, and over time they grows like tares in the pease field.'

'Says the man who has never laboured in a pease field.'

'As you says, my lord, and glad of it I am. No doubt I would not think that way if born to it, but each unto their own. What we needs to do is pull the tare out by the roots, not just trim off the top, else it will keep growin'.'

'And how do we do that, Serjeant?' Walkelin saw the sense of it, but did not see how it was to be effected.

'My guess is that once upon a time some woman lived apart in the woods, for what reason we no longer know, and so folk made up reasons and they became stories, and then there came belief in it all. I would like to say we finds this woman and shows she be but flesh and blood, but most like she became bleached bones long afore even I came into the world. Provin' somethin' not to be is 'arder than the other way about, but we must show from the start we looks only for a real killer and a real reason for the death.'

'I wonder what the lord of Ribbesford makes of it.' Bradecote was thoughtful. 'Baldric said he did not believe in the Raven Woman, and I hope he really is above such superstition, not just trying to sound it.' Before he had sought his bed the previous evening he had called back the clerk, and asked if it was written who held Ribbesford and Rock, and of whom, for he knew little of the northernmost part of the shire. It turned out that it was held by one William, and he held it of Hugh de Mortemer, the lord of Wigmore, and the man to whom the vellum message had been written. It had occurred to him that William de Ribbesford's absence might actually have a connection to the killing, and that even if it did not, they would have to be cautious what they revealed before him. Might he already know that his lord, supposed staunch supporter of King Stephen, was ready to change his allegiance, and if he did, had he accepted it? Bradecote shared his thoughts with his companions.

'You thinks right to be wary of the lord of Ribbesford, my lord. If the dead man be unknown in the manor, and we discounts the *Hrafn Wif*, the most likely reason can only be to do with King and Empress, dislike it as I does. Knots within knots within knots may lie ahead of us.'

Chapter Three

It was a thoughtful trio that splashed across the ford and rode into Ribbesford a little after the sun reached its zenith, though it was being coy, occasionally peeping out from behind thin bands of wispy cloud. The harvested fields were silent but for the alarm call of a yellowhammer as they passed by and a multitude of gossiping rooks, and were otherwise populated only by sheep now grazing upon them and fertilising the ground for the following year. Looking upon the manor from a lord's standpoint, Bradecote thought it a good place to hold, and it looked well kept. There was a church with some of its pinkish-red sandstone still unblemished by the passage of years, so there was recent money to give to the glory of God, beyond the yield that kept everyone fed. The manor building itself was close by, and had a well-ordered air. A few chickens scattered as they came to a halt and dismounted. The only source of voices emanated from what was obviously the threshing barn, but as Walkelin took the grey's reins a sparrow-boned priest, his habit looking a little loose upon him and his tonsure ringed by whitening hair that looked as delicate as the seeds on a dandelion, emerged from the church. He might look weak of body, but he came forward briskly and greeted the trio politely.

'You are sent from the lord Sheriff in Worcester, my lord?' The tone was curious more than deferential, and he might as easily have said 'my son'.

'We are, Father.'

'The lord of Ribbesford is not here, I am afraid, but his steward, Herluin, is a good man. The body of the poor soul who was killed lies within our church. I have kept his garb, but laid his surcoat over the shroud, since it bears the cross of Our Lord upon it. I am hopeful that he lived a life worthy of that cross.' The priest sighed, but then turned to practical matters. 'Your horses, I am sure, would be welcome in the lord's stable, so I will fetch Herluin, and he will arrange for their care.'

'Thank you, Father. We would also wish to view the body – on our own.'

'Ah. I understand, my lord. Er, you should remove the binding about the jaw that Estrith the Healer put in place to hold it shut. I know you will show no disrespect to the body, and the soul is beyond the touch of any man.' With which he smiled, and turned to enter the threshing barn.

Bradecote thought about leaving Walkelin with the horses to see what he might learn, casually, from the steward, but it would be better both that he should be present for all the viewing of the corpse, and introducing themselves to the steward would be needful at some point, so the three sheriff's men waited, Bradecote's horse lipping gently at his sleeve.

Herluin was a bear of a man with a mane of dark hair that seemed to want to encompass him entirely. His voice was a rumble, but there was nothing slow about him. His obeisance was a little stiff, but then, as Walkelin later commented when he and the priest had taken their mounts and they went into the church, huge tree trunks did not bend well either.

'Our lord would invite you into his hall, but he is from home these last few days, and there is, alas, no lady to greet you. On his behalf I welcome you, and will have preparations made within so that you may eat and sleep in comfort.'

'Thank you. I am Hugh Bradecote, Undersheriff of Worcester, and I am here, with Serjeant Catchpoll, and Underserjeant Walkelin, to try and discover who the man found dead might be, and who killed him.'

'None of us within the manor knows the name of 'im, my lord, I swears oath, but from what 'e wore alone we know the murdrum fine will be upon the 'undred, for assuredly he were not one o' us – I means not English. Not that you does not count as . . .' Herluin's face, where not covered with hair, assumed a beetroot hue of embarrassment and no small degree of concern.

'I understand your meaning, and I will report back to the lord Sheriff that there is no proof of Englishry for the dead man. We are going to look upon the body, and then we would speak with the boys who found it, and those who went to bring it to the church.'

'As you command, my lord. None are difficult to bring to you, for the children are kept close today, and none seek to stray.' He looked very serious. 'They will be 'ere when you are ready.'

'Thank you.' Bradecote nodded dismissal and handed Herluin the reins of his horse. Father Laurentius took the bridle of Snægl, and Catchpoll also gave his horse to Herluin with a grunt of thanks, then the sheriff's men went in to view the body in the cool of the church. Hugh Bradecote noted the freshness and quality of the fine carving as he passed beneath the arch of the north door. Having become more cynical since taking up the office of undersheriff, he wondered whether the lords of Ribbesford were particularly devout, or felt a great need to do penance for misdeeds.

It was not as dark as they had expected inside, for the walls were whitened. It was not a large building, but well built, and care had been taken with the decoration of the chancel arch. Before the altar, feet to the eastwards, a shrouded body lay upon boarded trestles, and over it had been placed the white surcoat, sullied a little with blood stains and with a bold scarlet cross emblazoned upon the left breast, and the knight's sword laid over all. They genuflected and crossed themselves before the altar, and then Walkelin bent and removed, with a care bordering on reverence, the weapon and the surcoat, and laid them gently aside. Catchpoll, meanwhile, unfolded the shrouding linen at the head, and loosened the binding about the jaw.

The face, pale and waxy in death, was not of an old man, but one perhaps of an age with Bradecote, or a little older. His near black hair showed no grey, even at the temples, and covered cheek and jaw in a short beard that had been well kept, though the ravens' attentions meant it was now a ragged mess with glimpses of pale bone visible. Where the eyes would be were ravaged voids, and the healing woman had not bothered to try and draw down the damaged lids, since they would only sag into the hollows. It was a sight that would be unnerving to one not used to gruesome death. Bradecote's expression was one of distaste but not horror. Walkelin, who had been very squeamish when he first became a serjeanting apprentice, looked without his gorge rising, and began turning back the shrouding cloth from the rest of the body. Catchpoll was simply focused upon gleaning as much as he could from the cadaver. There was no obvious sign of injury upon the cleaned corpse at first glance, only an old, pale scar, about an inch long, running into the hairline on the forehead, and it was when Catchpoll did as the priest had suggested, and fully removed the bandage that kept the jaw from falling slack, that the small wound among the beard hairs under the chin was discovered.

'So that were the way you died, friend.' Catchpoll peered closely. 'My lord, 'twas a thin blade, either a crafty dagger or mayhap even just an eating knife, but someone thrust it up under the chin, right up inside the skull. It would account for the blood seeping down the neck and betwixt the aketon and 'is chest to stain the message. Now then . . .' Catchpoll opened the mouth wider and peered within. 'Yes, up through the roof of the mouth at the back and at a slight angle. That would do for 'im.'

'So it might have been done when he was already unconscious, or at least knocked to the ground and unable to resist?' Bradecote frowned.

'Might 'ave been, my lord, but easier if a man stood right in front of 'im, up quite close, or even from behind, though more common it would be to slit a man's throat from that way, and the angle would be more a chance.'

'Yes, that is true. I would not suppose there to be any other mark of violence upon the body, since the man would be dead in a moment, which accounts for the small amount of blood other than where the ravens treated him as carrion.'

'Aye, my lord, 'ere and then gone.' Catchpoll made a life departing at the behest of another sound matter-of-fact.

'So did he know the man who killed him, or was he taken by surprise and killed by a total stranger? That sits ill with me.' Bradecote's frown had not lessened.

'And a knight would 'ave a squire or attendant, and a good 'orse and most likely a pack animal, so where did they go? A beast runnin' away would surely find the track and sooner or later be found, unless whoever attended 'im led them away.' Walkelin was puzzled. 'Yet if they did, why did they not take the knight's sword, for it be a good 'un.'

''Acos they wanted it in 'is grasp to make it seem 'e defended hisself against robbers. It might fool some.' Catchpoll said this in a tone that made it clear any sheriff's man worth his salt would not be deceived for an instant.

'But an attendant might be the one person to know that he carried an important message that had to remain hidden, and yet they left it. It is perplexing.' Bradecote shook his head.

'The scarlet cross, my lord. What manner of knight wears such?' Walkelin had moved on to the next question in his filing-system mind.

'I have not seen it before. The Templars wear white surcoats, I think, for I recall one took shelter where I was myself a squire, when a storm broke, but I would think it must be some order linked to the Holy Land, though it is not the Hospitaller knights.'

'I 'as seen it, my lord, when one of the Templar Order came

through Worcester about Ascensiontide, and met with the lord Sheriff. Some distant kinsman, as I 'eard after. Must 'ave been added to make their callin' stand out the more.' Catchpoll was still staring at the body. 'The knights upon crusade would be fightin' fit, just to survive battle. This man 'as been fit for battle, leastways in the past, but the palms is softer, and though the firmness of the muscles seems to melt when the soul departs, the arms does not look those of a man as wielded a sword as a warrior in the last months.'

'If he caught a fever or the flux in Outremer he would lose fighting condition, Catchpoll, and if he felt too weak to continue he might have decided to return to England, and offered his services as a messenger to his former overlord. It has struck me that he might well have been a vassal of William fitzAlan. Until Shrewsbury the man was the most powerful in the northern part of the Marches, and many would have owed him fealty. Remnants of that fealty might remain even after becoming a warrior monk.'

'Is that what they are, my lord?' Walkelin was surprised.

'Yes, they give up much of their holdings, to relatives, or to the Order, dress simply according to the Rule, and keep from all women, even their own mothers and sisters. The one I met when I was a youth, he said they had just been given land outside of Bristow, by Earl Robert of Gloucester, where they were building a – now it was not a monastery, but I cannot remember what he called it. However, it would serve that purpose.'

'But monks do not just leave their brethren and go and do things in the outside world, so why would this knight go back to 'is old lord, William fitzAlan?' Catchpoll was dubious.

'I know, but it is a possibility we need to consider. And I hate to say this, Catchpoll, but I suppose a woman, and please note, not a raven, could have done this? It is not a matter of great strength.'

'Oh yes, my lord, for it just takes the willingness to look a man right in the eye up close as you takes 'is life.'

'So our Raven Woman, a real flesh-and-blood woman, might have been responsible, though yes, I know it does not account for the companion, Walkelin. Hmm. We need to see everything found with the knight, speak with those who saw him in the clearing, and visit the place for ourselves. We have a busy afternoon ahead of us.'

When they emerged into the sunlight they blinked in its brightness, and it was a moment before the gathering at the churchyard gate resolved into distinct individuals. Father Laurentius was there, and Herluin the Steward, with half a dozen nervous-looking men and two small boys who were patently very frightened. There was a collective obeisance as Bradecote approached, and Father Laurentius made the introductions.

'These are the men who went with Herluin to carry the body to the church on a hurdle, and these are the brothers Edric and Agar, who found him.'

'We seek from you only what your eyes saw. None of you' – Bradecote looked primarily at the boys – 'is in any trouble with the Law or with me. Father, we would speak first with the boys, so shall we all draw into the shadow of the barn, where it is not so hot, and the tale can be told without haste?' It was not really a question, more a very gently put command.

The priest guided his small charges into the shade, and the adults, after some indecision over whether they were part of the 'all' or not, followed but stood apart. Only Herluin and the priest remained close to the children.

'Now, which of you is Edric, and which is Agar?' Bradecote tried to sound approachable and less 'lordly'. For several moments there was a nervous silence.

'I be Agar,' piped up the smaller of the two children, a boy with very blond hair that stuck out at all angles, and a nose that turned up at the tip, 'and my big brother be Edric.' Edric nodded in corroboration. His hair was pale straw in colour and his ears very flat to his head.

'I see. We hear that you went up into the woods to seek cobnuts. Is that so?'

'Yes . . .' Agar received a bellowing whisper in his ear to show respect to the lord Undersheriff of the shire, and added hastily, 'lord,' in a trembling voice. Then his face crumpled, and a trickle of warm urine ran down his thin legs. Agar had never spoken directly to William de Ribbesford, his own lord, and this unknown one must be even more mighty and important, and thus dangerous.

Bradecote, after a moment of stunned surprise, just repeated, 'You went to seek cobnuts. Tell us what you saw.' He thought 'us' less frightening than 'me' if the child was so afraid of him.

Agar gulped, sniffed, and it was his older brother who took up the tale.

'My lord, we thought we would find the best nuts up in the woods yonder.' He jerked his head towards a low promontory around which the Severn had been forced to bend. 'We does

51

not go right off the track from the ford, not usual-wise, but we sort of made each other brave because no other boys would 'ave gone there and only the squirrels would be takin' the nuts there. And so it were, my lord. Cobnuts the size o' my thumb's end we found.' He stuck up a grubby thumb in vindication of the decision. 'We stepped off the track to the right side and picked mostly off the ground, 'cos the others was still a day or so short o' bein' ripe, and they was not quite enough. We 'ad seen nothin' but squirrels, and we is not afraid o' those, so we went on aways and then saw the clearin' with the dead tree lyin' in it, and on the far side a real good tree for the cobnuts.' Edric's voice had grown stronger and more confident, but now it faltered. 'We 'eard bees, 'cept it were flies, and then a *hrafn* swooped down, a great black bird like this.' He spread his arms out wide, and shuddered. 'Fair scared us, it did, and it hopped to start peckin' at what was on the ground beyond the tree, and then I saw it was not a dead animal but a man, and right then She flew in, the *Hrafn Wif*, laughin' like a devil from 'ell, and the two was eatin' 'im and Agar cried out. She came and stared at us and – we ran away.' Edric was breathing fast now, remembering. 'I tripped a little and stumbled, and dared to look back and then She was a woman again, full size, *hrafn* black all over and the face veiled too. I thought She would get us. We both did.'

There was no doubting that the boy, who could be, thought Bradecote, no more than eight or nine years old, was telling what he believed to be true. It was no tale made large to sound exciting or gain attention.

'You have told what you saw well, Edric. Now, think hard. Did you see anything, or anyone, other than the big black birds and the woman, even as you went up the track?'

Edric frowned, and looked at Agar, who bit his lip and shook his head.

'No my lord. We saw nobody and 'eard no more'n the squirrels.'

'And a robin,' added Agar, in case this omission counted as lying to the Law. 'I saw one.'

'Then thank you. You may return to your mother.' Bradecote glanced at the priest, who smiled, and ushered the little boys away, and then looked at the huddle, for it could be described no other way, of worried men.

'So the boys came back and told what they had seen. What happened next?'

'I picked these men and we took a new-mended 'urdle to carry the body on, and went to where they said they found it, my lord.' This was Herluin, and the other men nodded in support.

'And what more, if anything, did you all see?' Bradecote tried to make the question to all of them so as not to just get the spokesman's answer, and looked straight at each in turn.

'There was three birds when we got there,' offered one man, 'and they took off when we drew close.'

'And the lord lay in the grass, still grippin' 'is sword, though it 'ad aided 'im none,' added Odda, shaking his head. 'Poor man.'

'At his side?'

'No, my lord, like this.' Odda stretched out his right arm to full extension. 'Starin' up 'e would 'ave been, but the birds took the eyes so – bad it looked, 'orrible bad with blood on the face and garb.' There was a murmur of agreement, and shaking of heads.

'Did you see any sign the dead man 'ad stopped there? Signs of a fire, mayhap?' Walkelin, gathering all the details in his head, asked the question that had formed there.

'We looked only at the corpse and gettin' it safe back.'

'And if it cannot be seen from the trackway, be the clearin' known to all in Ribbesford and about?' Catchpoll was also putting things in place.

'That struck me as odd, after.' Herluin frowned. 'Locals know of it, but you cannot see the clearin' from the track, so why did the lordly man leave the track at all? If 'e needed but a branch to squat over, why there's undergrowth aplenty within three strides of it.'

'Could 'ave been meetin' someone.' A man who had so far been silent spoke up. 'An old stump lies on that side o' the track close to where we left it, and if'n you kept below the little ridge you would be bound to reach the clearin' with the dead tree.'

'Or the *Hrafn Wif* seduced 'im to go there.'

'What madness would make a man follow 'er?'

'The madness that *drycræft* can put on a man,' muttered another, softly.

Herluin, who believed in the Raven Woman far less than the rest of the inhabitants, other than his lord and the priest, could not help but think the answer made some sense, and he could not dismiss it out of hand. He looked at the lord Sheriff's men to see how they took the idea, but their expressions told him nothing.

'Well, it means we will have no trouble finding the clearing either, but I would ask you to accompany us, Herluin, up the track to show where your party left it.' Bradecote did not think any more could be learnt from the men of Ribbesford, and he saw them visibly relax. Their ordeal, and they saw it as such, was over.

Herluin led the way up the track from Ribbesford, and what occurred to all three of the lord Sheriff's men was that if the dead man had crossed the ford and come along it, he must have passed right through the settlement. A rider, even alone, dressed as he had been, would be noted as worthy of comment and remarked upon. Catchpoll asked Herluin about it, and the steward shook his head.

'If the rider came through the mornin' the lads found 'im, we was all in the barn threshin' and baggin' the grain for the granary.'

'But not the children, since Agar and Edric were out gathering,' Bradecote reminded him.

'No, not the children, my lord, but none said a word about 'im when we brought the body to the church.'

'But did they see the body?' This was Walkelin.

'What sort o' sight be that for little 'uns! No, we kept that from all but Edric and Agar, and told 'em not to speak of it.' Herluin was slightly shocked, and then realised what it meant. 'Ah, I sees now. Well, I did not ask if any saw a stranger with a red cross upon 'is chest, but all everyone spoke of yesterday were the death and the body, so you would think any child would 'ave spoken up as they sat about their own pottage pot, at the least.'

'Most like, but best we ask anyways. Sometimes the young

keep things secret unless asked direct.' Catchpoll had come across that often enough over the years.

'Need I come with you further, my lord?' Herluin had no great wish to revisit the clearing just yet, and he did not want his lord to return and find that Ribbesford had abandoned the threshing. He pointed to the right of the trackway, where broken twigs and a degree of trampling indicated where the party of men had passed.

'No, we will find the clearing easily enough from here. Thank you.' Bradecote nodded a dismissal, but then asked a final question. 'Do you believe in the *Hrafn Wif?*'

'Yes, and also no, my lord. There be someone in these woods, but I does not think it a spirit that can turn into a bird. Might they be evil? I could not say. Sometimes I gets the feelin' we is watched, a bit like when a wild animal watches to keep out the path. But no more'n that can I say true, my lord.' He frowned, his thick brows drawing together as if colluding to give him a thought. 'Course it could be a leper knows a place that gives shelter on the way down from Wenlock or the monks at Shrewsbury.'

'It is a fair answer and a reasonable idea. Thank you.'

Taking this as his dismissal, Herluin gave a small bow, then turned back and ambled down the track.

'I reckons any beast would keep out the way o' a man that big,' murmured Walkelin, thoughtfully.

'But it is interesting that he believes someone exists.' Bradecote watched the steward until the track turned and he was lost from view. 'Now, let us see what the clearing gives us.'

'Does we go the way the boys did, my lord?' Walkelin had

already noted a hazel that was in clear view and only just off the track. 'That looks the first tree, right there.' He pointed at it.

'Well, I am assuming that they did not follow where a horse had been and were just nut hunting, but you go that way, and see if you can find their path to the clearing. Catchpoll and I will take the more obvious one made by the party carrying the body, in case that had already been made easier by a horse's passing.'

'Though I doubts we would see much sign o' that, with all the tramplin' thereafter.' Catchpoll was realistic rather than pessimistic.

'True, but I wonder also whether there was any sign of a path before. I will ask Herluin when we return to the manor. If there was none, then why did our dead man strike off the track and go to the place where he was killed? That is the thing that puzzles me.'

'My lord, mayhap the knight 'eard a noise, a noise that was not like an animal, and thought there might be robbers or outlaws in the wood and, bein' a knight not a merchant, drew 'is sword to be the attacker not the attacked?' Walkelin's suggestion was tentative. 'And if 'e killed or injured one of 'em, well others pulled 'im from the saddle and then did for 'im.' It was the last part that did not ring true to Walkelin, since the death wound seemed deliberate rather than part of a scuffle, and he could see that it did not sit easily with his superiors either, though Bradecote acknowledged it as a possibility.

'We shall see,' was Catchpoll's only comment, and the trio split up.

* * *

As they followed the obvious trail to the clearing, Catchpoll was scouring the ground and foliage with narrowed eyes, in case any sign remained of a horse or horses passing the same way. If it had been a path before the events of the last few days, it must have been very faint, and Catchpoll remarked that all he could see was broken twigs, slightly crushed woodland floor and the signs of men passing through without care. He took a pulled thread of wool from a twig at about his own head height as proof.

'From a cap, and most like on one of the body bearers.' He cast it away as useless. 'The clearin' itself might prove better.'

Within about fifty paces they reached it, and found Walkelin already studying the ground to their left.

'The boys took a shorter path, and I could see the tree they was makin' for easy enough only a short way from the first. The dead ash would 'ave made the body 'arder to see if you was only a little lad.'

'You tread careful there, Walkelin,' warned Catchpoll, coming forward.

'Oh, never fear, Serjeant, I steps careful enough, and I can see there were a fire made further away from the dead tree, so looks like the dead man, alone or not, chose this spot for the night. I wonders when threshin' began, for it would be odd to make camp mid-afternoon, when they might 'ave pushed on to Bridgnorth afore dark.' He frowned. 'Or would it be too far away, my lord?'

'I have never been to Bridgnorth, so I am not sure, Walkelin. I agree it seems strange, but it does show that whoever he was, he did not want to attract attention to his journey, which fits with the nature of the message he carried.'

'But wearin' a surcoat with a scarlet cross would make 'im stick in the mind of any who saw 'im, my lord, which runs 'gainst that idea.' Catchpoll sniffed, and made a 'thinking' face. 'Unless 'e wore a cloak over all 'cept when out the way of folk.'

'And if he was some religious knight, there would be no choice but to wear the garb of his Order.' Bradecote nodded. 'I think you are right, Catchpoll, and he might have concealed it. The days have not been so warm this last week that it would look strange for a man to be cloaked. It does mean we need to ask about any mounted knight.'

'And the 'orse were tethered to the fallen tree, for there be dung, part dried, length of a beast from it.' Catchpoll pointed.

'And over 'ere also, Serjeant,' Walkelin declared, 'though this 'un were tethered to a branch, and it grazed on the grass it could reach.'

'He might have travelled with a pack animal as well, but I doubt it. A messenger travels light, but might have a companion if there was a risk they might be intercepted. This makes the whole Raven Woman idea even less likely, even as a real woman.' Bradecote wanted to dismiss a phantom female.

'But she were seen, my lord, if Edric did not just imagine 'er in 'is fear. And that means another witness, at least after the killin'. She might even 'ave seen the other man, or avoided the clearin', knowin' folk was sleepin' there.' Walkelin saw the opportunity for more information.

At that moment there was a rustle above their heads and they looked up and saw a raven alight upon a branch, settle its wings and cock its head to one side to stare at them. Without thinking, Walkelin crossed himself.

'Just remember, ravens be clever and curious, so do not go thinkin' fool's thoughts,' admonished Catchpoll. 'If the bird found carrion 'ere, it will 'ave returned to see what goes on now, no more.'

'Oh, I knows, Serjeant, just – well, took me by surprise it did.' Walkelin coloured, embarrassed.

'If there is a woman living in these woods, the ravens and other creatures will know and have accepted her presence as they do not ou—' Bradecote was interrupted by croaking laughter. 'Holy Virgin, that was the bird!' He sounded taken aback. Catchpoll, who had also been surprised, but hid it better, found an explanation.

'When I were a lad, a friend found a jackdaw, not quite ready to fly, and fed it, and kept the cats from it, and it used to stay close, even sit on 'is shoulder, when 'e clicked 'is fingers to call it, and it learnt to make the click sound. I reckon as that raven learnt the laugh from someone. I think we can say there be someone livin' "wild".'

'Who would be useful to meet, but who is not our killer, and in truth, was never so, for what would they do with two horses? A person who keeps out of the sight of others, for whatever reason, would not take them to sell, not have need of them in a woodland life. Is there anything where the knight was found, Catchpoll?' Bradecote felt he was being distracted by the Raven Woman.

'Well, my lord.' Catchpoll knelt, with a wince, where he could still see some sign of the grass being crushed. 'Give another day and there would be no sign at all, and dew 'as washed away any traces of blood after two morns, but since we knows the 'eight of the man and a thrust up into the throat would kill so fast 'e would fall back, not stagger around, we should look about . . .' He paused for effect. 'About 'ere.' He pointed to the ground. 'See there, a little dig in the ground? Spur made that. Whoever faced 'im, and that must be the way of it, wore spurs, and most servants does not possess 'em. I reckons another knight came with 'im, whether to make sure 'e delivered the message as ordered, or to protect the messenger.'

'But if the dead man's courage failed, and he spoke of turning back, the killer, still determined to finish the task and knowing he had the message with him, would have searched diligently, and taken it, bloodstained or not, Catchpoll.'

'True, my lord, but that might be where our laughin' raven or the *Hrafn Wif* 'ad a part in the tale. If they disturbed the killer, and 'e could not find them to silence them . . .'

'No, Catchpoll, if the man killed for the message, he would not have left without it, and if they travelled some way together, chances were he knew where it was hidden. Something makes this wrong, and I am not sure what. If there is nothing more here, I think we return to the hall at Ribbesford, ask if any riders were seen the day before the death, study the knight's garb, and then eat and rest. A night's sleep might order our thoughts the better.'

This was something upon which all three men could agree, and so they retraced their steps, though not before Walkelin had shaken a bough of the hazel and filled his cap with nuts.

'I likes a cobnut, and if the pottage be late, well, my lord, we needs not complain with rumblin' stomachs.' He smiled.

Chapter Four

Ribbesford seemed empty until they were close enough to hear the noise from the threshing barn. Walkelin was sent to fetch Herluin from within, and the steward emerged, coughing to clear the dust of the threshing from his throat.

'We would see whatever was found upon the dead man, clothing or personal items, for only the surcoat was laid upon the corpse and we did not see anything else in the church. We can view them before we eat, if the preparations are made for us in your lord's hall.' Bradecote did not quite like taking over another man's hall, but until such time as the lord of Ribbesford returned, there was no help for it.

'Indeed, my lord. My wife's sister cooks for the lord, and 'as a good pottage bubblin', and there be fresh bread and cheese and a good ale, if you would care for it.'

'Thank you. And can you tell me when your harvest was completed and threshing began?'

'Why, we got all in safe day afore yesterday, by the middle o' the afternoon, my lord, and then our lord, William de Ribbesford, left for Rock. Did not want to leave earlier, see, though I promised 'im it would be all away by eventide latest. We made ready later in the afternoon, since a day 'ad been lost with the Holy Day this week, and then commenced threshin' yestermorn.'

'And why did he go to Rock?'

'Could not say, my lord, nor be it my business to know. I can say that I 'ad no idea of it in the forenoon, but then, mayhap it were mentioned and I forgot.'

'I want to know if anyone saw either one or two riders come this way, across the ford, that afternoon.'

'I will ask, my lord, and the lord's groom 'ad a care to your mounts and saw 'em fed and watered.' Herluin made a small bow, and Bradecote and Walkelin carried on to the hall. Herluin disappeared back into the threshing barn, thinking none would follow him, but Catchpoll, with no more than a glance and nod at his superior, was quick to step in behind him. The presence of Serjeant Catchpoll tended to make memories sharper, without him saying a word.

Herluin put the question simply, though he glanced at Catchpoll as he did so. It was met with blank looks from those nearest, but Catchpoll sensed rather than saw some agitation towards the rear.

'Any information will be good information, and keepin' it back means the King's Peace suffers. A reckonin' there will be for any as says nought but knows.' Catchpoll judged these 'sheep' would react to the baring of the 'sheepdog's' teeth rather than gentle encouragement. He heard a cough and a shuffling of feet, but nobody stepped forward.

'And none even 'eard one, mayhap two, mounted men pass through when the labour ended?' Catchpoll looked over the assembly and saw heads shake. 'We knows at least the dead man did so.'

'We was all tired, and knew threshin' would begin next day. We just ate and went to our rest,' a voice offered in explanation.

It rang true, and nobody had cause to lie.

'Fair enough.' Catchpoll did not give any thanks, but nodded to signify he had all he needed, and left the barn. He heard the chatter that began once the door shut behind him, but though he put his ear to the oak, it was evident that there was much exclamation, but nothing more. Deep down he did not believe that nobody in Ribbesford would have seen or heard the horsemen if they had come through, but clearly they were worried that any connection to the death of a lord was a dangerous thing, and more frightening than Serjeant Catchpoll's gimlet stare.

Ribbesford's hall was like the manor, small but tidy and well-kept, though it did not feel a hall that was a home. There was a dry ditch about it on the side towards the Severn and then curving up the north and south sides, with a low bank on the outer face, no doubt to give some protection if the Severn flooded up through the great field and to the base of the high ground. The palisade enclosed the hall, stable and two other buildings, probably one for the men-at-arms and a kitchen. The hall itself was of wooden construction, with a swept hearth showing a newly laid fire and a door at the far end that would lead to the lord's solar. Bradecote had no intention of taking that for his sleeping quarters. There were benches and a long trestle table set against the far wall, and a smaller table at the solar end. It looked as if the lord lived in solitary state, and even if he had not been told, Bradecote would have guessed that it lacked a woman's presence.

Walkelin lit the fire, and as the kindling crackled into life, a motherly looking woman entered, bearing the dead man's effects, though she struggled a little, for the mailcoat was heavy. She made an obeisance to Bradecote and offered up her name.

'I bring these from Father Laurentius, my lord. My name be Estrith the Healer, and I washed the poor body in the church, as were fittin', the man bein' without kin in Ribbesford.'

'And you saw the knife wound. Was there any blood on the hands that showed he had put his hands to his throat as he died?' Bradecote did not think it important, but more a way to ease into finding out other things.

'None, my lord. The man would 'ave died in a moment as I reckons, and were thus spared a sufferin' death, for which God be thanked. There were some blood on the neck, and not from them birds a-peckin', you can be sure, which be the reason I even looked in the beard. Blood must come from somewheres.' The healer handed the pile of clothes, with a small scrip and a knife laid on the top, to Walkelin, who looked eager to take them. 'And nothin' did I find on the body, other than that vellum, that I would not find on any man. In the scrip, with the coin, I put the ring that came from the middle finger on the right 'and, lest it fall and be lost and me thought to 'ave taken it, which I never would.'

'Thank you. That has been very useful.' Bradecote made it gentle dismissal, and the woman bobbed and then departed. Walkelin laid out all the clothing upon the long trestle table and handed the scrip to Bradecote, who opened it.

'A ring of gold, not very heavy, but with a shell engraved on it. A pilgrim's ring from Santiago de Compostela, I assume. I suppose a Templar knight would be allowed to keep such a thing, if that is what he was. There are also ten silver pennies, which is not much for a journey, but then he might have expected to be given food and shelter without cost, as the member of a holy order.'

'And nothin' you would not expect among the clothes, my lord, but we did think there would be a cloak and there be none.' Catchpoll, who had entered as Estrith left, surveyed the outspread garments.

'And an eatin' knife but no dagger, so if one were used upon 'im, it might be 'is own, my lord.' Walkelin had been checking in case something else was secreted within the layers.

'Does not really aid us much, though any coin in a scrip would have been taken by a man who possessed little. I cannot see how we can hope to name him, other than by giving his description to the Templars in the hope that they recognise him.' Bradecote rubbed the back of his neck and was about to mention food when there came a knock, and another woman, whom he took to be Herluin's sister-in-law, entered, followed by a girl of about twelve and a small boy bearing a loaf and a cheese. The woman carried a short plank on which were set three bowls and spoons, with an enticing aroma rising from the contents, and the girl carried three beakers and a jug. The woman smiled a little nervously, voiced the hope that they liked the pottage, and offered the information that there was more should they want it. Since the bowls were large, Bradecote thanked her and declined more, knowing that any spare would find its way into the stomachs of her family.

The three sheriff's men ate in companionable silence, and Catchpoll told them of the silent barn. After they had finished they began to lay out their bedrolls near the hearth. It was then that the door opened without a knock, and a man entered, demanding to know the identity of his guests.

'I am William de Ribbesford. Who are you, besides being the undersheriff? My steward is not good at remembering names.' That was not necessarily true, but the man was asserting that this was his hall, his manor.

'Hugh Bradecote, Undersheriff of Worcestershire, and this is the lord Sheriff's Serjeant, Catchpoll, and Underserjeant Walkelin, here to look into the killing of a man within this manor, possibly a Templar knight.' Bradecote made the introductions, beating Catchpoll to it, since he felt he was in some way trespassing, being about to bed down in a hall uninvited by its owner.

'Herluin said a body had been found and it would mean the murdrum fine upon the Hundred. Never had a killing in Ribbesford, not since my father first took seisin of it, not even one without intent. I wonder why it happened here?'

'We cannot give any answer to that, but before you go to your bed, I would ask you to come with me and view the body, in case it is someone you recall seeing in another place at another time. Lords see other lords when upon their service.' Bradecote thought it unlikely, but it would be thorough to check.

'If you must, though I have had a long day, mostly in the saddle.' William de Ribbesford sounded slightly reluctant, but then he did look tired. He was a man perhaps a little over two score years in age, with an aquiline nose that was rather pinched at the bridge, a faint cleft to his chin and a smattering of grey at his temples.

'It will not take long, and I am as eager for my own bed.'

Bradecote wanted to sound companionable rather than confrontational. He abandoned his preparations and went to the door, with William de Ribbesford in his wake.

'It is a pity that you were elsewhere when this was discovered, and not only because it means we "invaded" your hall. Time was wasted trying to reach you.'

'Yes, no sooner had I reached Rock than I received a command from my overlord to meet with him. I am just glad that the messenger thought to seek me there before coming on to Ribbesford, and I was able to see that the harvest is gathered in there as I had hoped.'

'Is your steward at Rock more reliant upon direct command?'

'Ah no. You see my son Walter is nearing his twentieth year and I want him to gain experience. I have left him in charge of my manor there, making the decisions, and the steward is sound enough to support him. I did not want to interfere, but the harvest is so important. You understand, of course.'

'Yes.' Bradecote actually thought the answer a little odd. If he trusted his son and steward to run the manor, rushing there even as the last wagonload of stooks was being brought in at the most important of his honours seemed precipitate. Perhaps it was just that his confidence had wavered at such a vital time.

They crossed the bailey, and de Ribbesford called out one of his men to ensure nobody barred the gate before they returned. The air was still and held a fading warmth that seemed to match the gloaming. As they walked to the church a barn owl, a pale phantom-bird, glided silently past them en route to hunt mouse and vole among the stubble stalks. The church door opened with only the faintest sigh of a hinge easing. It was nearly dark within, although candles burnt upon the altar ready for when Father Laurentius came to say Compline. They genuflected and crossed themselves and then Bradecote intentionally placed himself on the opposite side of the body to de Ribbesford. He slowly uncovered the face, watching the other man's expression closely. There was initial grimace of distaste, and de Ribbesford swallowed rather obviously. Then he frowned, very slightly, which Bradecote thought indicated that the deceased at least reminded him of someone.

'Is he known to you?' It was a simple question, to which a simple answer, given immediately, might be expected, but there was a very slight pause, a hesitation of barely a breath.

'No, he is not, though in such a state that is no surprise.'

'But there is something about him that stirs a memory. Might you have seen him in the past, a younger version of him?' Bradecote pressed.

'No. I thought for a moment he reminded me of someone, but it was only for a moment, and a foolish thought. This man I have not seen before and do not know.'

The denial was firm, but Bradecote thought de Ribbesford was trying too hard, and there had been more than just 'a reminder' in his eyes, even by the light of candles. It might be that what William de Ribbesford said was true, but the man had doubts he would not share.

'Then he will go to a grave unmourned by kindred and known only to God.' Bradecote's response was merely an acceptance that he would get no further by the questions, and he was surprised to see that the other man's expression hardened, fleetingly, at it.

'If we are known to God, it is enough, in the end,' William de Ribbesford murmured, and there was an old grief in his tone.

'True enough.' Bradecote nodded, and made to leave, changing the subject. 'Did you have this church built? The stone looks fresh enough.'

'My father had it begun, and I managed to get the carvers employed by Olivier de Merlimond, erstwhile steward to my lord, Hugh de Mortemer of Wigmore. I thought him a good man until he turned traitor to both lord and King and gave his support to King Henry's daughter.' William de Ribbesford shook his head. 'A man should stay true, whatever befalls.'

Bradecote wondered how this man would react to hearing that his overlord had probably broken faith with King Stephen. He was not going to tell him of it, in part because he just wanted to get to his bed, and also because of the nebulous thought that the betrayal was not actually proven. He yawned.

It was a sleepy Baldric who barred the gate behind them, and de Ribbesford went first into his hall, as was his right. He bade Bradecote a civil good night and headed to his solar and a far more comfortable bed than the undersheriff. Catchpoll was not asleep, and when the solar door had shut, asked the obvious question.

'Never seen 'im afore then?'

'Possibly, Catchpoll, but there is a little doubt and I would sleep on it and come fresh to the problem on the morrow.'

'Fair enough, my lord. Sleep well.'

It was a clear night, and the moon, though beginning to wane, had risen before the sun had slipped below the western horizon and was high in the sky only a little after darkness had encompassed the landscape. Among the dark shadows one moved with purpose, though without haste and silently. It came to the trackway and followed it down into slumbering Ribbesford. Only a cat, a flaccid rat held triumphantly in its jaws, saw it and slipped down the side of a dwelling and out of its way. The church was set a little apart, the sacred kept from the secular, though the priest's house sat so close by the churchyard that it was laughingly said that he might conduct a burial from his own bed if needs must. The shadow waited in the depths of a yew tree's looming blackness, at ease with the night, and untroubled by the closeness of the dead, for the dead did not judge.

After a little while the church door opened, and Father Laurentius emerged, pulling his cowl over his tonsure and making his way home without recourse to any guiding light, for his feet knew their way from the habit of years. The shadow did not move until his door closed behind him, and then drifted more than walked to step inside the building. Only when the door was open did they hesitate, for being within walls created by man rather than nature had become alien.

The nave was in deep darkness, but the sanctuary light in the chancel gave a hint of illumination. The shadow cast back the hood that covered face and head, and walked, hands clasped together before them, to where the shrouded knight lay with the white of his surcoat upon him like a coverlet. Had any been there to see, they might have correctly deduced the figure to be female, for the shape was delicate and the pale hands that emerged from the folds of the encompassing cloak were small, with tapering fingers ending in poorly trimmed nails, and with the nail rims engrained with grime. They shook slightly as they uncovered the face, and the woman went to bring the sanctuary light to make the features more clear. There came a wet, hissing intake of breath, though it was not from shock or disgust. A finger traced a gouge.

'So blind you were, and blind you go to whatever fate your life's deeds condemn you.' The voice was low and the words indistinct, as though spoken with a mouth full of pebbles, but there was no doubt that they were uttered without sorrow or sympathy. 'I am glad fate brought you here to die. I will spare you one prayer, and that is more than ever you offered up for me.' There was a pause. 'I am glad also my companions made good use of you, though such a visage makes no difference to the dead.' She laughed, though it was a rasping laugh curtailed by a sucking noise, and then she covered the face again, replaced the sanctuary lamp and knelt before the altar, where she remained for some time, though only the one prayer was for the dead man. Then she rose, left the church and retraced her soundless steps the way she had come, to fade into the night.

Hugh Bradecote had learnt to sleep anywhere, but it did not mean he slept as well as in his own bed with his wife curled up against him, soft and warm. In the middle of the night he surfaced, his feet cold and sticking out the end of his blanket, and lay half-awake for some time, his brain trying to work out what was niggling him about the vellum message, why William de Ribbesford might lie about the dead knight, and whether it was possible that he could have killed him and taken his horse, whether to Rock or even simply to abandon it somewhere. The thoughts twisted and combined so that no real sense could be made of them, and he felt even more confused. When he dozed off again it was to muddled dreams, and, unusually, he was not awake before Serjeant Catchpoll, who shook him by the shoulder, not quite gently.

'Mmm? Ah, Catchpoll, you look more rested than I feel.' Bradecote rubbed his eyes.

'Sleep o' the righteous, I gets, my lord.' Catchpoll kept a straight face, though it made his superior smile and then yawn.

'As opposed to the muddled head of the ungodly? That makes me wonder where I have erred. I have—' He stopped, as the solar door creaked and opened, and William de Ribbesford entered, bidding the three men a civil good morrow, and offering to have bread and small beer brought for them.

'I suppose you will be returning to Worcester to report upon the body,' he remarked, striving to sound casual.

'Then you supposes wrong, my lord.' Catchpoll frowned. It sounded as though de Ribbesford thought all they would do would be shrug at the killing being unsolvable, and leave the body for the priest to say prayers over.

'But how could you find out anything more when the dead man is an unknown stranger here, none saw him killed, for none have come forward, and whoever did the deed must be long gone?' The lord of Ribbesford sounded genuinely perplexed, and Bradecote thought even slightly disappointed. Why was that?

'It may not be that we find the killer, but we do not give up just because there is no obvious culprit. The killings where it is easy to work out who did it are those where Serjeant Catchpoll, or Underserjeant Walkelin here, simply goes and brings in the person taken up by the local hue and cry. We look into the deaths that are not simple.' There was a touch of pride in the undersheriff's voice, but he was careful to keep out any challenge from his tone that might alert the lord of Ribbesford to the fact that he was under suspicion.

'Yes, I see.' William de Ribbesford nodded, and sounded emollient. 'Of course, you must deal with matters most never even need to consider.'

'We would ask your view upon something.' Bradecote thought it would be interesting, at the least, to hear de Ribbesford's view of the Raven Woman. 'What do you think of the local belief in the Raven Woman, the *Hrafn Wif* as they call her? When we arrived it seemed that blame for the killing was put upon a shape-changing woman-raven.' The undersheriff raised an eyebrow and looked suitably above such fancies.

'My lord Undersheriff, the folk of Ribbesford are simple souls, good people, but few have ever travelled more than a day's walk from the place they were born, and the Raven Woman is a way to keep children from straying in the woods and being lost. There was a recluse in the woods a score years past, or thereabouts, and no doubt that gave the start of the story, which just grew.'

''Tis certainly very much alive, even if the real person be long dead, my lord,' commented Catchpoll, 'and makes things more difficult for us, and we does not want folk scourin' the woods for a ghost of their own imaginin'. Clouds things.'

'I will be very firm with them that no such search is needed or will take place.' De Ribbesford looked very serious. 'And ask

Father Laurentius to make it clear that belief in her is not godly. Besides, they will be occupied with the threshing for some time to come, and that will keep them from getting in your way. Now, I will set a servant to bring food.' He went out, and Bradecote watched him, thoughtfully.

'Ribbesford really does not want us to believe there is anyone in the woods, and when he looked at the body last night I would swear that he thought that he might recall him, even if just for a moment, yet he denied it absolutely.'

'And he did not seem much pleased that we remain, my lord,' added Walkelin.

'No, he did not. I tried to make sense of it in the night and failed. He was away from Ribbesford when the body was found, but left the day the killing took place. Is it possible that he encountered the knight by chance and was a sworn enemy, and killed him? He could have taken the horse with him if he went to Rock at all, and left it there or set it loose.'

'Would 'e wear spurs, if all 'e planned were ridin' to a manor a few miles away?' Walkelin focused on details.

'If his horse was like yours, he might.' Bradecote managed a small smile. 'William de Ribbesford does not look the sort of man used to fighting and able to kill one man and defeat another, if we assume the dead man was not riding alone. Yet that being so, why would he lie to me?'

'How sure are you, my lord, that 'e did lie?' Walkelin did not doubt his superior, but wanted to know just how likely it was to be true.

'I could not swear an oath to it, but something changed when he saw the body – a wariness perhaps, a doubt. Until that point I felt he was prepared to aid us, and afterwards, well, you saw how he hoped we might go away quickly.'

'If'n the dead man knew the lie o' the land, mayhap from years back, it could be that the lord de Ribbesford did recognise the face, changed by time, and did not want to say 'e knew 'im, just in case we linked them and thought 'im guilty.' Catchpoll thought the lord might be like the rest of Ribbesford. 'And if you sends a messenger, it can be useful if they does not need to ask directions upon the way, my lord.' Catchpoll was very reasonable.

'You are right, Catchpoll. I may well be trying to make too many things join together. I do think it worth pressing de Ribbesford, with us all there, on a possible identity, even if he is otherwise unconnected to the death. If we had a name we could then inform the Templars and the lord Sheriff might even be able to find out whether he was in the service of William fitzAlan, which looks likely, and who travelled with him. If anyone can have some contact with those who support the Empress Maud it is William de Beauchamp, and I doubt the lord of Oswestry would be pleased to discover one of his men had murdered another, and bearing such an important message. Also, I do not like the thought of returning to Worcester saying that not only could we not discover the killer but could not give a name to the victim. It sits badly with me.'

'My lord, mayhap only the ravens saw the actual killin', but it still might be that the *Hrafn Wif* saw more than the victim and could be a witness. Should we look further within the woods?' Walkelin was torn between rather wishing they need not do so, and his eagerness to collect every possible piece of the puzzle.

'True, Walkelin, and if we believe someone lives there, I wonder why de Ribbesford does not, or pretends he does not. Before we seek our possible witness we could see if de Ribbesford will give us anything more, because I feel he does know things he has not told us.'

The girl from the previous evening came in at that point, bearing a platter of bread and a flagon and beakers. She dipped in a curtsey only once she had set this down, and said there was also cheese, though the lord had only mentioned bread and small beer.

Catchpoll, who believed it was always better to eat when it was offered lest the next meal be missed, made it clear that cheese would be very welcome. Bradecote wondered what had delayed their host's return to break his fast.

William de Ribbesford looked down into the face of the dead knight with the morning light flooding through the east window of the little church, and making certain what had been more of a feeling the previous night, when candlelight alone illuminated the features. He looked grim. It was not a face he had seen in two decades, and had altered even without the attention of the ravens, but the hair, shape of the head and, most of all, the old scar, were enough for him to feel it was almost certainly Ivo de Mitton, and his mind went back to the last time they had met, and the animosity between them. He did not hear the church door open and Father Laurentius enter, and looked a little surprised when he heard his footfall upon the flagstones of the nave, for it was not yet the time of the Office. The priest saw William de Ribbesford's troubled expression.

'You knew this man, my son?'

'I think so, Father, but long years ago, so I cannot be oath-sure.'

'Nevertheless you can name him in your prayers.' The priest paused. 'There is something I think you should know, my lord.' The change of appellation was meaningful. 'He carried a message, which had not been delivered and has been sent to the lord Sheriff in Worcester, since it may have led to his death. It is many years since I learnt the Offices and prayers, and many secular words would be unknown to me in Latin, but you should know that it was sent to your lord, the lord Hugh de Mortemer of Wigmore, was to do with "our lady" and I do not think it meant the Queen of Heaven, and came from William fitzAlan, lord of Oswestry.'

'FitzAlan? No, that must be a mistake, Father.' William de Ribbesford was vehement. 'He and my lord have been at odds since the moment fitzAlan broke his oath of fealty to the lord King, and I do not think they were on friendly terms even before that. He would not send a message to him, not for any reason.'

'In these difficult times, have not many noble lords changed allegiances?'

'Hugh de Mortemer would never abandon King Stephen. Why, he has been shown great favour by him, not least by being given Bridgnorth to hold, and King Henry spent much upon it so that it has a fine keep that rivals any in the Marches. Besides, he is a man of honour, and when others turned to the Empress Maud when the lord King was taken after Lincoln, he did not rush to bend the knee to her.'

'Might the lord of Oswestry simply be sending to ask if

he might consider supporting the lady?' Father Laurentius enquired, tentatively.

'If he did he was wasting ink and vellum, and, it seems, the life of Ivo de Mitton.' De Ribbesford was dismissive, but looked worried. 'What worries me is how it comes that Ivo de Mitton, who left family and manor more than twenty years ago and has not been seen since, should end up dying here, when he might have been anywhere, not only in England but the world. The surcoat tells us he was a Christian knight, so he might have been in Outremer as atonement.'

'Atonement? For what?'

'I am sorry, Father, I forgot you came here a couple of years afterwards. His father had recently died whilst on pilgrimage to St David's, and his older brother, Olivier, was fulfilling his father's dying wish to see the vow completed by the lord of Mitton. Ivo was left in charge, but committed an act of family betrayal, and when Olivier returned, Ivo was disowned and cast out. The very same night the hall burnt down and brother, mother and sister died within. Suspicion always fell upon him, since the two things happened so close in time.'

'So who is the man who is lord of Mitton now?'

'The youngest brother, Simon, who had just gone to the lord Sheriff, Walter de Beauchamp it was then, as a squire. The manor is held of the lord King and de Beauchamp, as his representative, passed on all dues and took their vassal service. Simon de Mitton only took his place ten years later, when he was old enough to take seisin without need of a guiding hand, and he built a new hall, not where the old one stood.'

'Ah yes, I recall the young lord building the hall, but did not know what had happened before. It is a sad tale, and his family will be in my prayers at the Offices today.'

'Thank you, Father.' William de Ribbesford sounded very solemn, even sad.

Father Laurentius was slightly surprised to be thanked, but it must be that William de Ribbesford had known those lost in the fire quite well. He was probably the same age as Olivier de Mitton.

'Blessed are those that mourn, my son, even when the wound of grief is old and almost a memory of grief. Our love for others is a pale shadow of the love that Almighty God bestows upon us.'

'But we cannot love evil, Father.' It was a caveat.

'No, but we should seek the good in those who appear to lack it, for we are all in God's image as the Sons of Adam.'

William de Ribbesford said nothing, and covered the dead face. He joined the priest in a prayer for the dead, and then stood and turned to leave. It was then that he saw the shrieval trio standing silently just within the nave and in front of the door.

'So you lied to me last night, de Ribbesford. I would have to ask why?' Hugh Bradecote spoke softly, as was seemly in a church, but his tone was steely.

'I was not sure in the candlelight, my lord Undersheriff,' William de Ribbesford answered carefully, 'and even now could not swear my oath upon his name. The scar upon the forehead is very like one he came by in childhood, and the age and colour of hair would fit, but that is all. To give you mistaken information would be worse than giving none.' It sounded reasonable enough, but the man's expression told them he was making an excuse for the lie.

'A name, even with doubt attached, would be of use, and you must know that. What is more, the lord of Mitton should be told his brother might be lying before the altar in Ribbesford.'

'I doubt he would wish to pay his respects.' De Ribbesford shook his head.

'But he would be able to give us his own thoughts upon the identity, and that would make our hunt for the killer easier. Whatever this man did in the past, he was killed for something to do with the present.' Bradecote did not think this necessarily true, but wanted to see if de Ribbesford grasped the reason to distance himself from suspicion. He was surprised that the man's face clouded, and his mouth became a grim line. 'You do not agree with me?'

'I think some things only God can forgive, for His mercy is infinite.' It was a guarded response, and yet none of those watching him doubted he believed it.

'Good Father, we would ask that your "guest" remain before the altar until we have spoken with the lord of Mitton.' Bradecote decided he would get no more at the moment from the lord of Ribbesford,

'He is welcome in God's House, even if he proves to be one for whom prayers are most needed.' Father Laurentius nodded his assent, and Bradecote stood aside to let de Ribbesford leave. After a few moments, the sheriff's men also left the church, but halted in the peace of the churchyard, where only the dead might overhear them.

Chapter Five

Bradecote was already wondering how this younger brother who had buried the rest of his family would react to the news that his banished sibling might lie dead so close to home. Might he already know of the death? Had chance meant that someone had recognised the Templar, despite the passing of time, and told Simon de Mitton, who had then followed and confronted him, and killed him with no knowledge or interest in a message, but simply to avenge a wrong so great that time could not diminish it? It made sense. He turned to Catchpoll and Walkelin.

'Well, that gives us a new path. We will go and speak with this Simon de Mitton, and have him come and view the body. If he confirms it is his brother I want you, Walkelin, to return to Worcester, or Elmley, if the lord Sheriff is not there, and inform him. Not only can he then send to the Templars with a name, but if he knows Simon de Mitton well it would be wise to inform him he is, at the very least, a connection in this death. Do you recall a squire of that name, Catchpoll?'

'I might see a likeness and remember when I sees the man, my lord, but squires was just lordlings in the way, much of the time, little more'n servants in finer wool, and the lord Undersheriff of the time liked to be the one who spoke with the lord Sheriff, and then pass on 'is words to the serjeant as needful, not to mention I were but the underserjeant at the time. In the early years the lord Sheriffs did not know who really did the work.' Catchpoll paused. 'And that, my lord, be different now. No undersheriff ever worked as you does, and though I did not like it at the first, we does better for it.' This was not said grudgingly, but as a truth, and Bradecote accepted it as such.

'Then let us go and do better this day. Time to cross the Severn, and find out whether our dead man is Ivo de Mitton and whether his brother already knows of his death.'

The manor of Mitton lay on the eastern bank of the River Severn, a couple of miles south of Ribbesford and was traversed by the trackway that led to the Ribbesford ford. The land was low and fertile, though part was so low that it existed only as marshland, the haunt of heron, bittern and moorhen among the reeds, and overall it was devoid of the trees that formed part of the King's Forest. The wooden hall was set above the level of the river's winter torrent, and was a simple single-storey building, within a palisade that enclosed a bailey that would have served a rather larger hall, and made it seem even smaller, though knowledge of its recent history made sense of it. Some thirty paces from the hall, in a slightly more pre-eminent position for a lord's hall, a small wooden chapel, surmounted by a cross, stood within a hurdle-fenced area the size and shape of a medium-sized rectangular hall. Simon de Mitton had spent some of the silver that would have made his new hall in building a memorial to his lost family and giving them an eternal resting place where they had lived and breathed.

The other buildings, kitchen, stable and stores, showed this was a modest holding, though it was tidy and those at their tasks within did not look sluggardly. The gates were open, and none challenged the three men as they rode in. In fact, when Bradecote dismounted, Walkelin felt the need to call a youth to come and take the lord Undersheriff's horse. Catchpoll noted that this caused several people to cease their activity and stare at them, and a woman went into the hall. By the time all three horses were being led away, a man who looked a few years short of thirty came out. He was dressed well, but without great ostentation, and shared the same colour hair as the dead Templar, though any greater resemblance was too subtle to strike Bradecote at a distance. He did not look guarded or suspicious, merely curious. Bradecote was sure he had never encountered him while on his vassal service, but then William de Beauchamp had many manorial lords who did service directly to him, like Bradecote, or with him as their service to the King.

'Simon de Mitton?' Bradecote took the initiative.

'Yes.' Now a little caution entered the voice, and Bradecote saw the man glance at Catchpoll and narrow his eyes a fraction as he placed him in his memory.

'I am Hugh Bradecote, Undersheriff of Worcestershire, and this is Serjeant Catchpoll and Underserjeant Walkelin. We are looking into the killing of a Templar knight at Ribbesford. Did anyone of this manor see such a man, alone or with a companion, three days past?' Bradecote wanted to see if there was an initial change in the man's demeanour.

'I did not, and my steward will confirm that everyone was

about the business of threshing that day.' It was given as an unforced answer.

'There are also things that would be better spoken of in private, my lord de Mitton.'

'Then come within. Does my lord de Beauchamp have some private message for me? Is he in good health?' There was a hint of eagerness in the tone, as though Simon de Mitton felt he had been forgotten by the de Beauchamp family and hoped somehow that he had come back into William de Beauchamp's thoughts.

'When last I saw him, yes.' Bradecote did not want to get into a conversation purely designed to show that de Mitton had a long association with the lord Sheriff. He followed Simon de Mitton into his hall, with Catchpoll and Walkelin in his wake. It was neat, clean and yet showed no sign of having a châtelaine.

De Mitton spoke to a servant to bring wine for the lord Undersheriff.

'What I have to say does not come from William de Beauchamp, but concerns your family.' Bradecote inwardly chastised himself for the choice of words, for a muscle moved in the cheek of Simon de Mitton.

'I have no family, my lord Bradecote.' It was a bald statement, and there, beneath the mask of hospitality, lay an old wound that had never quite healed.

'I am sorry. The word was badly chosen, but is the most true. We know that you suffered great loss when you were young, and that you had a brother who—'

'I deny him that title. No brother could have done what he did.' The rejection was vehement. Whatever Simon de Mitton might feel if he identified the dead man, it would not contain even a hint of grief.

'Then what I have to say may not give you any pain. The man found dead in Ribbesford has been named by the lord of Ribbesford, though he is not oath-sure, as Ivo de Mitton, who left these parts many years ago. I would have you look upon him and say whether you agree with him.' It occurred to all three sheriff's men that Simon de Mitton would likely deny the corpse a name if he had committed the murder, but that could not be avoided without asking him to come and view a body without reasonable cause.

'I have no wish to see him, if it be him, and wherever he shall be buried it will not be here.' Simon de Mitton spoke through near-gritted teeth.

'Your "wish" is not relevant at this point. The dead knight was bearing a secret message, and knowing his name may aid us in discovering who killed him.' Revealing this was a calculated risk upon the part of Hugh Bradecote. It increased the chance that de Mitton might make the identification, and gave another reason that the killing had taken place, other than a blood debt. Bradecote felt optimistic that if de Mitton had killed his long-banished brother, and denied it, they would be able to prove otherwise.

'I will send to my overlord and comp—'

'If you think the lord Sheriff will consider your feelings above discovering who killed a Templar, you do not know William de Beauchamp as well as you think you do.' Bradecote could not be certain of this, but unless de Beauchamp had come to treat de Mitton better than his own kin, it seemed very unlikely. In the final analysis, if your name was not de Beauchamp, you were dispensable, and even if you were of the family, having heard of antagonisms within the wider kindred, support was not absolutely guaranteed.

Simon de Mitton looked less sure of himself. Bradecote's initial impression of the man was that he was the sort who found security in being popular, hoping those about him with sharper tongues, if not sharper swords, would defend him at need. He was not a natural aggressor, but when he had spoken of his banished brother he had gone beyond his own nature and assumed the mantle of a whole family's need for retribution. Dead brother, dead mother and dead sister gave him strength. Such an avenger might do what Simon de Mitton, simply a man, could not.

'I will have you come with us back to Ribbesford, which will not take much from your day, so do not tell me you have not the time, and you will speak truthfully whether the body is that of Ivo de Mitton, whether you call him brother or not.' Bradecote was firm, and de Mitton buckled.

'As you command, my lord Undersheriff.'

'And on the way you will, however much it pains you to do so, tell us what happened that gave rise to the rift between you that is unreconcilable, even with his possible death by violence.'

At this de Mitton looked mulish, and then emotional, but neither weighed with Hugh Bradecote.

Having instructed his steward to ask if any had seen a knight with a scarlet cross upon his breast in the last few days, Simon de Mitton called for his horse, and when it was brought to him, mounted slowly, like a man who had ridden all day and suddenly had to travel further. He looked older than when he had greeted them, as though the burden of the past, when recalled, added years to him. He fidgeted with his reins so that his horse mouthed the bit moving in its mouth, and looked at Bradecote with mild resentment. Once they had left the manor enclosure, the undersheriff began his questions.

'You were a squire of Walter de Beauchamp, we know that, and were not here when tragedy occurred, but you can tell us what happened as was told to you, and why you believe that your older brother was responsible.' Bradecote did not want preamble or prevarication, for the ride would not take long.

'Yes, I was sent to our overlord when I was seven years old, and had been there less than one year when – they all died. My sire died before I left Mitton, and it was my oldest brother, Olivier, who asked Walter de Beauchamp to take me as a squire, out of respect for our father, who had served him faithfully. It felt like an exile, but' – Simon de Mitton shrugged – 'it is the way of things. Olivier was fourteen years older than me, but though young, had a serious head upon his shoulders. He saw to it that the manor continued as before, but some months later had a dream. Our father died while on pilgrimage to St David's. He fell sick and died among the monks at Neath Abbey. In this dream, our father appeared to Olivier and begged him, for the good of his soul, to complete the pilgrimage for him. So my brother went upon the pilgrimage and fulfilled the request. It was while he was away that evil fell upon our family.'

Bradecote thought it a strange choice of words, but said nothing, only raising an eyebrow.

'In Olivier's absence, Ivo, three years the younger, was in charge of the day-to-day running of the manor, with our mother's "guidance", as was told to me. But Ivo did not look to her, but to a kinsman of ours, the bastard son of our mother's sister. Eustace fitzRobert lies at the core of our family's ruination, and, kin or not, should never have been allowed across our threshold. He was the age of Olivier, but the opposite in character. He was full of spite and anger and cruelty. I saw that even as a small child, but Ivo idolised him, wanted to copy him and be his greatest friend. Our father tried to keep him from us, but our mother could not, or would not, have a chasm grow between her and her sister.'

'This Eustace lived close enough to Mitton?'

'Yes, at Sudwale, the neighbouring bailiwick of Kidderminster, and we cross the river-most edge of it as we come to the ford. When first given, it was even more bleak and poor than this one. My family made what is here, for when the Conqueror had the great book written of all holdings, Kidderminster, and everything that combined to make it, was still wasteland after the King's own harrying, and earlier attacks by the Danes. It is a royal manor, and controlled by the lord Sheriff on the King's behalf. My mother's sire held Sudwale, though it barely gave enough for a lord to live upon. Then Robert de Bellême seduced my mother's sister a few years before he was deprived of all his honours and exiled in 1102. He gave the manor he held at Eardington, a little south of Bridgnorth, to my grandsire, so that there would be something for the child, but after de Bellême's exile, King Henry decreed Eardington would revert to the Crown upon my grandsire's death, which left only the family manor at Sudwale for my aunt and then Eustace. Eustace blamed my grandsire, though it was not his fault, and was filled with bitterness. He used the name fitzRobert proudly, rather than my grandsire's, and even I can recall he was always saying his sire was a far greater man who was so powerful that the King dare not let him remain in England. Eustace would say that Bridgnorth, and the rest of his paternal inheritance, had been stolen. Since he was a bastard, and this is not Wales, I cannot see how that has merit, but he believed it. It twisted him, or perhaps it was his inheritance from the Devil's line.'

Simon de Mitton did not have to explain this, for the tale of the family of Bellême was one told around noble hearths throughout England and across the Channel also, since it combined the sinister with the ghoulish, and the bloodline was, to many, considered tainted, going back to feuds in Normandy before Duke William even landed in England. These tales grew in the telling, but stemmed from a cruel streak that was undeniable. Robert's mother, Mabel de Bellême, was reputed to have committed crimes, including murder, whilst it was said that her father had her mother strangled, and had broken all rules of hospitality by imprisoning, torturing and mutilating a rival lord he had invited to a wedding feast. Robert de Bellême had inherited his mother's character as well as her lands. When he also inherited lands in England, he swiftly bolstered his power in the Welsh Marches, including building a tower keep castle at Bridgnorth, but rebelled against Henry I only four years later and was exiled. Thereafter he campaigned against Henry in Normandy until captured and imprisoned for life.

That the Bellême story had developed to say their ancestry included Satan was not a surprise.

'And this is the man Ivo chose to follow.'

'Chose, or was bewitched by. Some say Mabel de Bellême was a sorceress, and who knows, that might also have been in Eustace's blood. He liked to torment things, people and animals. I remember, as a small boy, seeing him cut the ears off a coney while it still lived, and laughing as he did it.' Simon de Mitton shuddered. 'Then, while Olivier was away, my sister Rohese was attacked and left for dead in the Severn. Nobody ever told me exactly what happened, and, although she survived, soon after Ivo told everyone she had leprosy, and had her declared "dead" and cast out. When Olivier returned she was gone, and Olivier found out enough to say that she blamed Eustace for the attack and he had told Ivo to get rid of her. I do not know how he achieved it, but the priest was immediately replaced, so I think he was involved in the plot. Olivier disowned Ivo and said he would send to the lord Sheriff, making it clear that Eustace would be arraigned for the attack on my sister. Ivo left that very day, and that night our hall burnt to the ground. Ivo was nowhere to be found.'

'That could have been an accident.' Bradecote tried to avoid jumping to conclusions, though it was pretty damning.

'Wait, now I remembers,' Catchpoll interrupted, his face grim. ''Twas still in the old lord Sheriff's time when I were learnin' the serjeantin' craft. We was not sent to seek the truth, so I never came up, but I recalls a fire at a northern manor and the steward came to report that the remains of the lord were discovered with 'is 'ands behind as though the wrists 'ad been tied, and the girl and lady—' Catchpoll suddenly seemed to realise he was revealing this in front of son and brother, and paused. When he began again, Bradecote thought he was omitting something. '—also. The man as did it 'ad fled the country, as were told to us, so I assumes the lord Sheriff knew all about it.'

'Holy Virgin!' Simon de Mitton paled so fast Bradecote thought he would faint, and then turned slightly green. Some things, it seemed, had never been divulged to him, but then who would tell a small boy such details.

'A man would not do that to his mother and sister.' Bradecote shook his head.

'A man who would see his sister declared a leper would, if in thrall to the Devil.' The words seemed wrung from de Mitton.

The man, thought Bradecote, could apportion blame to his estranged sibling, but had not considered that if Eustace fitzRobert was as evil as he claimed, then he might be an even better candidate as the killer, for no better reason than it was cruel. Bradecote thought back to hunting down Reynald de Roules, a man who had been as keen upon torture and malice as enjoyment. Such men were very rare, thank God in Heaven, but they did exist.

The riders splashed across the ford, watched only by an aggrieved heron, disturbed from his fishing on the far bank, and who flapped in a laborious manner to the opposite side a little upstream. Bradecote thought it best they leave their mounts at the hall, and so they walked to the church, which was cool and empty of the living. Simon de Mitton looked tense, though that might have a variety of causes. Having paid their respects before the altar, Bradecote nodded to Catchpoll to uncover the face of the corpse. There was silence, and Simon de Mitton looked away after a single glance, his face a little green-tinged.

'Is this Ivo de Mitton?' Bradecote did not say 'your brother' to avoid a denial of the relationship being confused with recognition.

There was a pause as Simon de Mitton composed himself and took a second glance.

'It might be.' Simon de Mitton sounded like a sulky child, perhaps even the small boy whose mental image of his older brother was clouded both by time and the creation of him into a monster.

'We know it is many years since you saw him, but if William de Ribbesford feels it is him—'

'He is older. He was Olivier's best friend and was often at the manor. Olivier even encouraged his betrothal to Rohese.'

'Rohese? Was that your sister's name? William de Ribbesford was betrothed to your sister?' Bradecote could not disguise the surprise in his voice.

'Yes, though of course it came to nothing after—' De Mitton sighed. 'A year later he wed the daughter of another of the lord of Wigmore's vassals, and she bore him a son and daughter, but was dead before I returned to Mitton.'

'But you were in the same hall with your brothers all your life until you went to the household of Walter de Beauchamp. You would have a sense of whether this man was once your brother Ivo.' Bradecote was persistent. 'And the scar upon the forehead – de Ribbesford said your brother gained such a scar in childhood. You would recognise that.'

'I cannot be sure, I tell you. Another might bear such a scar.'

'Then look upon the face longer, my lord,' Catchpoll growled, and in obedience to that growl, de Mitton looked again. The eyes narrowed a little, perhaps as he imagined the metamorphosis from beardless youth to the time-weathered man upon the trestle.

'Yes, the scar means it might well be him, though, like de Ribbesford, I would not swear my oath upon it.'

'And do you recognise this, my lord?' Walkelin had been a silent observer, but now drew from his scrip the pilgrim ring that had been among the dead knight's effects. He had thought it unlikely it had come to him before he left England, but had brought out it to be thorough. Simon de Mitton stared at it, and then held out a hand trembling with shock, and shock not from the ghastliness of the dead face.

'Yes,' he whispered, hoarsely. 'It belonged to my mother's grandsire, who completed the pilgrimage before he married, and she wore it after he died. She always said it was to be Ivo's, but she wore it about her neck and said he could have it when he wed. It is mine now.' He held out his hand.

With a glance at Bradecote for his agreement, Walkelin dropped the gold ring into Simon de Mitton's palm, and they watched the fingers close over it slowly.

'Then the identity is proven well enough. This man was Ivo de Mitton.'

'And he will not lie in Ribbesford's earth.' The voice was William de Ribbesford's, who was now standing at the far end of the nave. 'You can take him all the way to Worcester if you wish, but he will not be buried here.'

'You were not so adamant before, de Ribbesford.' Bradecote wondered at the change.

'Then it was not certain. If the Law needs no more proof, then nor do I. However charitable Father Laurentius might be, and though this is God's House, it is upon my land. Take him elsewhere.' He sounded angry.

Bradecote made a decision. He could not force either man to accept the body, and he had no great wish to take it all the way to Worcester.

'Whatever sort of man he was when you knew him, he became a Templar knight, and I am sure that Bishop Simon, or at least his priest at Hartlebury, will give him earth to lie in and say prayers over him. Once the body has been delivered there, we will return, for there is more to discover. Neither of you' – Bradecote looked at both lords in turn – 'has been open with us. I suggest you think hard before continuing with less than the full truth, since it gives us reason to wonder whether yours was the knife that killed him and you have both made it clear how you regarded him. Walkelin, go and find Father Laurentius, and tell him what will now happen, and you, de Ribbesford, arrange for a cart for the body. A Templar knight will not be taken for burial slung across a horse's back like goods across a pack pony.'

William de Ribbesford did not look willing, but gave a short nod and left, telling himself that at least it got rid of Ivo de Mitton once and for all.

'And me, my lord Undersheriff?' Simon de Mitton was unsure whether he too would be given a command.

'You may return to your manor, but we may yet visit you

again, to hear if your steward has found any who saw the Templar knight, and with further questions for you.'

'And *if* I can answer them, I will do so.' De Mitton tried to sound gracious, but it emerged as petulant, and he shrugged a shoulder as he turned away.

Once they were left alone with the body, Bradecote looked at Catchpoll.

'So we have two men who loathe Ivo de Mitton even in death, and had cause, strong cause, to wish him dead, though it would mean they were sure of who he was. A man would not kill another because he "looked like" someone not seen in over twenty years'.

'And do we think that Ivo de Mitton felt safe to pass through their land, if they would want 'im dead, my lord?' Catchpoll wondered.

'Either that, or his message was so important that it was worth the small risk. After all, the chances of either lord coming face to face with him was small.'

'Which means if either did it, 'twas *wyrd*, which might be so, but then again we cannot say the reason were not the message to the lord of Wigmore. There be few lords to rival the lord Sheriff along the Severn, but the de Mortemers grew strong under King 'enry, and power makes enemies easily.' The serjeant sighed.

'Holy Mary, you do not think that the lord Sheriff found out about the plot and had de Mitton killed?' For a moment Bradecote's brain reeled.

'Ah, no, my lord. You mistakes me, there. If'n the lord Sheriff knew what 'e carried, 'e would see to it that the man were taken and brought before 'im, alive from choice, and would for sure 'ave demanded the message be found. That way 'e could send it on to King Stephen as a fresh proof of 'is loyalty to the Crown.'

'But if the killer's aim was to prevent the message reaching Hugh de Mortemer, it means the killer would have to know Ivo de Mitton was carrying it, trail him close enough to pick his time for the killing, and be one who wanted the mission to fail, so a supporter of King Stephen but with links to the supporters of the Empress Maud. That still fits with our overlord.' Bradecote looked deeply unhappy.

'Or the man who rode with him. There were the signs of two 'orses in the clearin'.'

'Which might have belonged to Simon de Mitton or William de Ribbesford, Catchpoll.'

'"Might", my lord, but can you see de Mitton lettin' either a stranger, or, even less likely, a man 'e knew considered 'im a murderer, get up close? Much more likely to 'ave belonged to Ivo de Mitton's companion. As you says, deliverin' this message meant a lot, so it would be wise to send another for defence or in case the messenger simply fell sick on the way.'

'But if neither of them recognised the body, de Mitton may not have recognised them either.' Bradecote wanted to consider every possibility. 'Though if the message were that secret, would he let anyone unknown get close to him? The thing is that part of me still wonders how it came to be that the killing, if about the message and treachery among lords, took place in Ribbesford, not miles away and in another shire. It seems too – connected.'

'You never can tell with *wyrd*, my lord. And there be another thing. The lady de Mitton and the daughter – well, 'twas not quite as I said, for their throats 'ad been cut.'

'Even more reason to think it was not Ivo de Mitton who killed them, then.' Bradecote's expression was one of distaste.

'But not likely either 'e knew nought of it, my lord. Mayhap 'e told fitzRobert the best way in, or persuaded someone in the manor to let them in, and were so under the bastard's control 'e could face 'is womenfolk dyin' too. May never 'ave known the details.' Catchpoll scratched his ear and looked thoughtful, and his expression was still pensive when Walkelin returned with Father Laurentius and the news that a cart, with an ox to pull it and a driver, were being made ready.

A short time afterwards the three sheriff's men were riding behind the lumbering cart back across the Severn, heading for Hartlebury. Catchpoll told Walkelin what had been discussed in his absence, and the young underserjeant nodded.

'A tangle for sure, and several ways it could be, my lord. There be one thing that 'as me wonderin'.'

'Which is, Walkelin?'

'I wonders what 'appened to Eustace fitzRobert when 'e left, and whether Ivo de Mitton followed 'im. Like as not 'e be dead by now, but 'tis not tidy and I likes things tidy in my mind.'

'You think the bond might be so strong they were travelling together still?' Bradecote frowned. 'Unless Eustace fitzRobert underwent a change of heart as great as Saul on the road to Damascus, I cannot see him taking up the life of a warrior monk. There is too much about others and humility, and – the Bellême bloodline is a tainted one.'

'No, my lord, I could not go that far. I just wonders about the untidiness, 'tis all.'

'Well, if neither local lord is involved we have neither name nor description of the unseen companion, so it leads us no further.'

'Unless the *Hrafn Wif* saw them. Someone were in the clearin' when the boys left, and might 'ave known what lay there already from seein' the killer in the act. Until we knows if they saw anythin', our path cannot be closed, my lord.'

'Very true, Walkelin.'

Chapter Six

The lord Bishop of Worcester was not in residence at Hartlebury, but this was not a problem. No cleric was going to refuse to bury a Templar knight, however great the probable sins of his youth. Bishop Simon's chaplain was respectful towards the secular authority, but seemed almost eager to give the fallen knight full honours at his interment, despite the fact, which was revealed honestly, that Ivo de Mitton's own brother, and the man who had been betrothed to his sister, wanted nothing to do with him, even in death. Perhaps, thought Bradecote, the chaplain hoped that the news might filter back to the Order, since it was growing in numbers and influence. The bishop's steward was able to say, categorically, that no Templar had sought a night's rest in recent weeks, or indeed months, though if Ivo de Mitton had wanted to make his way north without attracting attention, he would have been right to sleep beneath the stars rather than beneath a roof in a hall. Having sent the ox cart back straight away, since its progress was slow, and accepted refreshment for himself and his companions, it was well after noon when Bradecote, Catchpoll and Walkelin called for their mounts, and as they awaited them being brought from the stables a clattering of hooves announced the arrival of a body of mounted men. That they were led by William de Beauchamp took them all aback.

'My lord, I was about to send Underserjeant Walkelin to tell you of the advances we have made.' Bradecote tried to disguise his surprise.

'Well, you need not think I have ridden here to save him a journey,' William de Beauchamp responded tersely. He had come from Elmley without even halting in Worcester. Not a naturally happy man, the lord Sheriff's unhappiness had been increased upon the reading of the missive from his undersheriff. His brow had clouded so much that the clerk, not normally put off by his lord's ill humour, had been hesitant when asking if there was a reply, and was told in pithy terms that there was not and that he was no longer needed. De Beauchamp had needed to think. He liked to keep abreast of the politics of the realm, not least from self-preservation, and had wondered if Robert of Gloucester's power was fading after his castle at Faringdon had fallen after a four-day siege, and his son had deserted to King Stephen. Earl Robert of Gloucester was the Empress's half-brother and her most powerful and loyal supporter, without whom she would have long ago failed, and de Beauchamp always needed to keep a close eye upon the southern border of his shire. If the Earl was declining in power, it was vital he knew about it, and who was taking his place with the Empress. It looked like it might be William fitzAlan. There was also the question of Hugh de Mortemer. If William de Beauchamp had been asked to name the staunchest of King Stephen's supporters, then Hugh de Mortemer would be almost at the top of his list. No whisper of any rift between lord and King was circulating, and de Mortemer had cast off his own trusted steward for deserting to the Empress. It made no sense for him to abandon the King who had given the prize of Bridgnorth to him, but if – no, surely it could not be true. Something was stirring, and de Beauchamp was uncomfortably aware that he did not know what it might be. The answer might be to confront Hugh de Mortemer and see his reaction to the accusation of treachery. He was as powerful a lord as de Beauchamp, but as lord Sheriff of Worcestershire, de Beauchamp had the superior rank when it came to any holdings in the shire, and could thus demand to see him. There was a chance the man might refuse, which would be damaging to the shrievalty, but de Beauchamp guessed that if phrased the right way, de Mortemer would be so keen to discover the nature of the accusation he would present himself swiftly. William de Beauchamp had called back the clerk, and made immediate preparations to head to the north of his shire.

Hartlebury, the lord Bishop of Worcester's comfortable residence, seemed the ideal place to demand hospitality, but the thought of good food and a decent bed had not improved his temper. He now glowered at Bradecote as if the whole thing were his fault and the undersheriff was very relieved that he could at least make a positive report.

'We have a name to the dead knight, for he was Ivo de Mitton.'

It was Bradecote's turn to see astonishment.

'Ivo de Mitton?' For a brief moment they could see William de Beauchamp linking the name to a memory, and then the surprise. 'But he . . . is it certain?'

'Yes, my lord, for he wore a ring that had belonged to his

mother's family, and although changed in visage, both William de Ribbesford and the lord of Mitton, Ivo's youngest brother, thought it very likely him.'

'But why would he ever return to England, let alone the very place where he committed murder, even after a score years and more?' William de Beauchamp still struggled to believe the news. He dismounted, waving away the ingratiating welcome of the lord Bishop's steward and walking towards the hall as though he owned it. Bradecote got into step beside him, with Catchpoll and Walkelin in their wake.

'It may not be that he wished to come so close, my lord, but if he had cause to be in England, and was selected for a task particularly because he knew the lie of the land in northern Worcestershire and the Marches, that would be a reason.' Bradecote had thought of this.

'I suppose that is true.'

'My lord, Simon de Mitton was a squire of your father. Did you know him?'

'Knew him, yes, by sight, and a little by character. He was only a child when he came to my father upon the death of his own. Oswald de Mitton had been a loyal vassal, and I know my father saw it as an honour to his memory to take the lad. He remained almost until my father died, and then took control of his manor, though he was not of the stamp of his father, and when I have seen him since, which has been rarely, I still thought him weak and lacking in command.'

This tallied with Bradecote's own reading of the man.

'I can say, my lord, that however weak, he was adamant that his older brother would not be buried in Mitton earth, and the corpse has been brought here for burial.'

'It is understandable why. I assume you were told the tale?'

'I was, my lord, though some of it seems . . .' Bradecote did not want to say he thought that presumption of Ivo de Mitton's guilt seemed a little hasty.

'What, Bradecote?' De Beauchamp's eyes narrowed. He eyed the lord Bishop's own chair and paused, but then thought better of it and took the one adjacent to it upon the dais.

'Well, my lord, it might seem likely that Ivo de Mitton set fire to his brother's hall, especially since it has been discovered he wore the ring his mother had inherited, and which was ultimately to go to him. But if the report that Serjeant Catchpoll recalls is true, the mutilation of both mother and sister seem so great a foul deed as to put in a doubt, when there was also the option of Eustace fitzRobert, known even then for his cruel attitude.'

'Devil's spawn, you mean? He could, but then why would he go to so much trouble when, by all accounts, he thought of none but himself?'

'For that very reason, my lord. Because he could. Perhaps he even did it so that de Mitton would be such an outcast as to need him more, and one day, if and when he chose, he could see the man's face when he told him the truth?'

'Possible, but it was all so long ago, and Eustace fitzRobert was the sort to go too far and be bleached bones long before age would take him, and my father knew the family well enough to make his judgement of Ivo, which I doubt would be wrong.' This was clearly William de Beauchamp's last word on the subject, and Bradecote was not foolish enough to persist out loud, whatever he might think. He moved on from his answer to his question.

'Is it the contents of the message de Mitton carried that brings you north in person, my lord?'

'Yes. I have sent my own messenger on a fleet horse to Wigmore, and called upon de Mortemer, as one who holds in this shire, to meet me here. I want to see his face when I tell him he is a traitor to his king, On the occasions we have met I would not say he was one who concealed his thoughts well.'

'You mean if it is news to him, and he had no plans to change his allegiance, you will see it.'

'Indeed. Either way, I will enjoy watching his discomfort. He has too much self-assurance after his victories over the Welsh.' De Beauchamp looked thoughtful, then changed the subject. 'You are not, I take it, staying here?'

'No, my lord. We are in Ribbesford itself, and that suits us well.'

'And do you have any idea who killed Ivo de Mitton?'

'Possibilities, my lord, rather than ideas, and we hope to find a possible witness that may advance us.' Bradecote was watching his superior carefully, but not by even the tremor of a single muscle did William de Beauchamp show concern, which meant that Bradecote relaxed a little. He might be berated, in a vague way, if they got no further, but at least he was not going to blunder into his own lord's involvement.

'Well, off with you, then. I want to know what the lord Bishop's cook can find for me. Never met a bishop yet who did not eat like a prince.' De Beauchamp gave a crack of laughter, and Bradecote made his bow.

As they rode out of Hartlebury, Walkelin asked a question.

'Does the lord Sheriff bein' 'ere make our task easier or more difficult, my lord?'

'I wish I knew, Walkelin, truly I do.'

The man upon the mule was wondering whether he would reach his home in time for the evening pottage. He was the representative of Shrewsbury Abbey in Wich, overseeing their salt houses, and was returning from his annual visit to the abbot to make his report. He was thinking how fortunate he had been to do so in good weather, which had made travelling an enjoyable change from the everyday, and the mule was a good-tempered beast with an even pace. The track made a detour about a sandstone outcrop as it climbed from the riverside to the ridge that lay to the north of Ribbesford, and it was there he encountered only the third person he had seen since leaving Bridgnorth that morning. The man's horse was of good quality, and his garb, though worn, marked him as of rank. Weirdly, he looked almost relieved to see him. The abbey's man gave the lordly man a respectful nod, and bade him safe travels as he passed him.

He never did get to eat his pottage.

William de Ribbesford had not been idle in the absence of the law officers. He had sent a man-at-arms, the one now returned from visiting his dying relative rather than Baldric, at best speed to his overlord, with a very exact message. He then saw that Herluin had everyone set upon the threshing, and, when he was alone, set off up the trackway, away from the river. He stepped

106

from the path with confidence, even though he had to push twigs away from his face, and he followed the higher ground as it turned northward to curve with the course of the river. Below the ridge line, and partway along, the red sandstone erupted through the woodland in a less obvious manner than the outcrop on the eastern bank, which had a very prominent cave that overlooked the river. Here, the dark hollow nestled behind a shield of ash, beech and oak. As he drew near, a raven filled the woodland silence with its sharp alarm call. He advanced slowly, and at the cave mouth called a name, softly, as though it might be overheard.

'Rohese.'

Upon their return to Ribbesford, the lord Sheriff's men were greeted by William de Ribbesford, who seemed to be almost too pleased to see them, as though making up for his previous, more surly, behaviour.

'I have not been a good host, nor have I been as open with you as I should, Bradecote. I confess, the memory of Ivo de Mitton put me out of humour with everything and everyone, and now he is gone from here at last, I feel the better for it.'

'You had not told us you were betrothed to Ivo's sister.' Bradecote made the omission sound a disappointment rather than a mistake.

'It was a long time ago.'

'And was it simply the union of two neighbouring families or did you like her?' The undersheriff avoided 'love'.

'I was fond of her, for we had known each other growing up and as she changed from girl to woman.'

'"Fond" enough that you hate her brother even in death.'

'You wouldn't have had to be fond of her to feel that way, not the way he treated her.' The welcoming look had been replaced by one that was grim. 'After what happened to her, for all it made a marriage impossible, there should have been a care for her. She was noticed, by a passing boat, half in the shallows and near-naked, with her head bludgeoned so that she was barely recognisable. It was a miracle, they said, that she had not drowned. I did not see her, but I was told her looks were ruined and her life was in the balance for several weeks, so she could not even speak. Then, as she seemed to be recovering, it became clear she had been violated also, for she lost what had been foisted upon her, very early. The cry of leprosy came from Ivo, who put pressure upon the healing woman to confirm it, and upon the priest to go through with the service that "buried" her to the world and cast her out. I saw her brother Olivier, the very day he died, and he said the healing woman had come to him in tears, and said it was just a little rash on the back of her hand such as she had suffered as a baby and little girl. She also said it was when she had eventually been able to speak and claimed that it had been Eustace fitzRobert who had attacked her that her brother decided to get rid of her.'

'Did not her mother speak up for her?'

'I do not know, but Ivo was the sort who wore people down with complaint and petulance. Or perhaps he just told her that her view did not count. The only person he ever cared about was his cousin, Eustace fitzRobert, and that was not so much friendship as master and hound. Whatever fitzRobert said, Ivo would agree with it, and all Ivo wanted to do was bask in the bastard's approval. My father and his both regarded the man as not just tainted, for he carried the blood of Bellême, but plain evil, yet Ivo would not hear a single word against him. I do not know whether he was a fool or under an enchantment. So Olivier disowned his brother, and sent to the lord Sheriff that his sister had identified Eustace fitzRobert as her attacker. That night the hall burnt down and none within survived.' William de Ribbesford crossed himself. 'The steward sent word to me, being near and having been Olivier's friend, and I went to Mitton. I saw what was left.' De Ribbesford's voice shook a little even after so many years had passed. 'There was no sign anyone had tried to escape, and Olivier was facing his mother and sister in the solar. The body had curled up, as a leaf shrivels in heat, but his arms were not before his face as you would think, but behind him, and the blackened flesh of mother and sister still showed a jagged edge at the throat. I was the one who had the steward send to Worcester with the news that Ivo de Mitton had murdered his own family, and for that he will, assuredly, burn in the fires of Hell for eternity. You understand now why I would not give him Ribbesford earth to lie in?'

'Yes, but why did you think it Ivo, and not Eustace fitzRobert?'

'Because the steward told me that when Ivo was cast out, he had yelled that he would be back.'

'Such a defiant claim would be easy words, without having substance. It could have been just flung in anger.' Bradecote did not think it a proof, and a glance at Catchpoll's face showed that he felt the same.

'I suppose that is so.' De Ribbesford was grudging. 'But a

man who would have his sister condemned to the life of a leper, to protect his friend, was a man who cared nothing for his family.'

This was true enough, and Bradecote acknowledged it.

'But all this just means you would 'ave been glad to be the one to end the man's life if'n you came face to face, my lord, and none can say they saw you about the time of the death.' Catchpoll was not accusing, but sounding reasonable.

'Which means it would be very helpful, for you, if you were to tell us why it was that the lord of Wigmore called you from Rock, and whether you actually met with him.'

'He sent for me and so I went to him.' De Ribbesford scowled. 'What my overlord demands of me is not part of this, and no matter for any but him and me. It should be enough that I tell you it had nothing to do with Ivo de Mitton in any way.'

'When killin' be involved, my lord, everythin' becomes part of it, and if I 'ad been given a silver penny for every 'onest man as told me a lie when faced with a death, I would 'ave more silver than the lord King's treasury in Winchester.' Catchpoll shook his head regretfully.

'Can you at least tell us if anyone might have seen you who could swear to it?' Bradecote could see that de Ribbesford was beginning to look resentful, and at this he shook his head. 'Then you must understand that you are yet to be cleared from our list of those who might have committed murder.'

'I did not kill Ivo de Mitton, but whoever did, I do not see it as murder. More than one life was owing.'

'And the Law alone is there to see the penalty paid. Surely

you can see, de Ribbesford, that murder cannot be declared only where the victim has lived some blameless life. Should a robber be allowed to carry on robbing because his last victim was a "bad" person? Only the killing of those who have been declared outside the Law, by the Law, avoids consequences.' Bradecote knew he sounded as repressive as one of the Justices in Eyre, but he felt it was important.

'But can you say the Law, good as it is, finds all those it should punish? You cannot, my lord, which leaves justice to others when the Law has failed.' De Ribbesford was not cowed, and in fact gave a small, weary smile. 'You have turned me from a good host yet again, my lord Undersheriff. I have no wish to argue with you.'

It was, Bradecote thought, pointless to pursue what was a philosophical argument at this point.

'It would make for a very strained evening meal.' He smiled too, and wondered if de Ribbesford's had been as half-genuine.

'And I can at least please you with the news that there is a roasted fowl for us this evening.' De Ribbesford was looking at Bradecote, and Walkelin, quite correctly, did not think that much, if any, of the bird would reach him.

'You have a good cook and—' Whatever Bradecote was going to say remained unsaid, because they all turned at the sound of hoofbeats, and more than one horse. In fact eight men arrived, led by a tall, well-dressed lord on a fine horse that looked as proud as its rider.

'My lord.' De Ribbesford bowed. 'I did not—' He suddenly abandoned the planned pleasantry and blurted out, 'This is the lord Undersheriff of Worcestershire, and his men.' There was a warning in the words, which the sheriff's trio all picked up.

'Has de Beauchamp slighted me by sending his minion?' The lord, who could only be de Ribbesford's overlord, Hugh de Mortemer, lord of Wigmore, glared at Bradecote.

'My lord of Wigmore, the lord Sheriff awaits you at Hartlebury. We are here to continue the hunt for the killer of Ivo de Mitton, and I am not sent in his place.'

'Well, he can keep waiting for me at Hartlebury until the morrow. I shall stay here tonight, de Ribbesford.' Hugh de Mortemer spared his vassal a swift glance.

'I shall be honoured, my lord.' It was de Ribbesford's turn to realise that there would be little chicken for him to savour.

It was clear that the lord of Wigmore wished to speak privately with his vassal, but Bradecote knew he could not demand to be present, and he also wished to have speech with Catchpoll and Walkelin in private. He had been focused upon de Mortemer, and frowned when he realised that Walkelin had disappeared. However, the underserjeant returned in a few minutes, bearing a smile that was worthy of Catchpoll.

'My lord, I wondered why the lord de Mortemer came with seven men. Most times, lords who 'as plenty of men bring 'em out in pairs. Mayhap it looks tidier or more powerful. I went to the stable to "look at Snægl's fetlock", and it were clear that one of those who rode in be the lord of Ribbesford's man, for 'e and the lad groomin' your grey was talkin' of Ribbesford matters, and the other men ignored 'em. So the lord of Ribbesford sent to his overlord about the death of Ivo de Mitton, or about the message, as well as the lord Sheriff demandin' 'e come.' Walkelin could not keep the pride from his voice.

'Well done, Walkelin. It did occur to me that he might have done so, but you have enabled us to know it. Now, was it so that his overlord could assure us he did indeed call de Ribbesford to him, or was it to alert him to the accusation of betraying his king?'

'You can be sure the lord of Wigmore would not 'ave ridden 'ere just to say "Yes, William de Ribbesford answered my command and came to me", my lord.' Catchpoll thought few overlords would have done so, and certainly none of the stamp of Hugh de Mortemer.

'Agreed, but there is the small chance that the messenger from here and from the lord Sheriff arrived at about the same time, and so de Mortemer could both consult with de Ribbesford and show that he did not rush to fulfil the lord Sheriff's command to go to Hartlebury. He might claim to de Beauchamp's face that he had ridden far enough for one day, but both will know that it says he is as powerful as de Beauchamp.'

'And be that true, my lord?' Walkelin knew little of powerful lords, but had gradually come to the conclusion that ignorance of them might put a serjeant at a disadvantage.

'Yes, I think so. There is Josce de Dinan at Ludlow, which is a commanding stronghold on the March, but with fitzAlan absent from Shropshire, de Mortemer must be the greatest lord between here and the Earl of Chester, and he has proved himself in battle with the Welsh. For a man who inherited his lands and title less than ten years ago, and cannot have yet reached thirty, he has done much.'

'And knows it. Proud as a dunghill cock, the lord of Wigmore.

I doubts 'e would bend the knee much even to King Stephen.'
Catchpoll sniffed.

'Oh, he might be sensible enough to do so, just not mean it, Catchpoll. Now, whatever we discover this evening, which may be little, I want you, Walkelin, to ride to Rock tomorrow, and discover all you can about William de Ribbesford's arrival at the manor and the messenger from his overlord. Someone there, unaware how significant or private it might be, might let slip useful information that can make the uncertain certain.'

'I will find out all I can, my lord.' Walkelin nodded in both agreement with the plan and acceptance.

'And we, Catchpoll, will look for ravens, and our possible witness.'

'One will be far easier than the other, my lord.'

'Yet I am hopeful of success. Now, let us see whether Hugh de Mortemer is going to eat a whole fowl in front of us just to prove his superiority.'

As it turned out, Hugh de Mortemer did not eat all the bird, quite. He very ostentatiously removed the legs and proffered one to his vassal host and the other to the undersheriff, in that order. It was not a convivial meal, more because Hugh de Mortemer chose to eat in silence and clearly did not want conversation. The man Bradecote observed exuded authority and power in his bearing, and a self-confidence that accounted for William de Beauchamp's accusation of arrogance. Hugh Bradecote would have liked to be an observer of the two of them when they met, for it would be like two rival stags in the rut, locking antlers.

When de Mortemer had wiped his fingers clean of the

grease from the chicken and was savouring the best wine that William de Ribbesford possessed, Bradecote waited until he relaxed a little, and then asked his question in a casual manner.

'What was it, my lord, that needed our host here to come to you a few days past?'

De Mortemer stiffened, and he looked at Bradecote coldly. 'Private matters between overlord and vassal are just that – private. And what right do you, some minor vassal of de Beauchamp's, have to even seek answers from me?' His lip curled derisively. He wanted to put the Undersheriff of Worcestershire firmly in his place, far below him.

'As lord of Bradecote and as William de Beauchamp's vassal I have no such right, my lord, but as Undersheriff of Worcestershire, I have every right, for I ask in the name of the Law, the King's Law, and no lord, however puissant, is superior to that.'

'Would you demand answers even of the lord King himself?' De Mortemer gave a tight smile, attempting to disguise his annoyance that Bradecote was not set down.

'Ah, now since they are his own laws, that might be interesting, my lord, but I can say that I would not "demand" and I would be *very* polite in the asking.'

Catchpoll, seated with Walkelin at a trestle table set towards the back of the hall, and far from the dais, could not understand more than the barest gist of the interchange when de Mortemer raised his voice in annoyance, but could tell a lot from the tone of his superior's own voice, and smiled into his beaker of ale.

De Mortemer did not smile. 'You think this a cause for jest, my lord Undersheriff?'

'No. I think I asked a reasonable question that deserves a reasonable answer.'

'And I tell you that it has nothing to do with any death.' De Mortemer set his wine upon the table so suddenly a little was spilt.

'My lord Bradecote, the matter was personal, and—' William de Ribbesford looked uncomfortable.

'You have no reason to give any answer.' De Mortemer cut him off.

'Other than it would make clear whether or not you killed Ivo de Mitton.' Bradecote spoke softly, in contrast to the lord of Wigmore, and looked de Ribbesford in the eye. The man dropped his own gaze and stared at the wine stain on the elm board.

'William de Ribbesford is an honourable man who would not commit murder. I vouch for him, and that is enough.' De Mortemer genuinely thought that his word counted for so much more than another's.

'But he himself admitted' – and Bradecote used the word with intent – 'that he did not see the killing of Ivo de Mitton as murder.'

'It was self-defence? Then why are you here?' De Mortemer's air of haughty arrogance slipped, and he looked slightly confused.

'The manner of the death means self-defence was not the reason, my lord.' Bradecote was sure that Catchpoll would agree with that. 'And de Ribbesford's reason was that Ivo de Mitton's life was already owing this last twenty years and more.'

'Oh, so he was outlawed, I see.'

'No, my lord, he was suspected, but having already been disowned and sent from his family's manor, he was never taken and arraigned. His guilt, whilst possible, was never declared by the Justices and no sentence of outlawry passed upon him.'

Hugh de Mortemer sniffed, downed the last of his wine and stood up.

'I have had enough of talking in circles. I am for my bed' – by which he meant William de Ribbesford's bed – 'and I sleep lightly, so do not lumber about like bears in the night.'

De Ribbesford and Bradecote both rose also, out of courtesy.

'Then I wish you a good night, my lord de Mortemer, that you will be fresh for the morning and the lord Sheriff's own questions.' Bradecote thought that a good parting shot, especially when de Mortemer threw him a look that undoubtedly hoped that his own slumbers would be fitful and incomplete.

De Ribbesford followed his lord into the solar, ostensibly to make a formal offer of his private chamber, though he remained a little longer than necessary and when he came out, bearing blankets and a bolster, he looked reproachfully at Bradecote.

'My lord de Mortemer is a good overlord, whom I trust with my life. He is a proud man, with just reason, and he is also not one who would betray the trust of the King who has shown him favour. As he has vouched for me, I vouch for him. I cannot explain whatever was in the message de Mitton carried, though I know little of what it said, but I can say I would swear my oath that the lord de Mortemer had no knowledge of it, and no connection to whoever sent it.' William de Ribbesford was solemn and very serious. Bradecote had no doubt he spoke the truth as he saw it.

'I bear that in mind, de Ribbesford, but in this my view is not important. It is up to the lord Sheriff to decide.'

'I will wish you good night, my lord Undersheriff.' De Ribbesford laid himself down upon the dais, further from the hearth but at least showing it was still his hall, even if his solar belonged, temporarily, to another.

Chapter Seven

The morning dawned a little colder than in previous days, though it boded well to improve as the morning passed. Bradecote had slept far better than during his previous night in the hall, and woke in a positive frame of mind. Yesterday they had given a name to the dead man, and seen his body delivered for burial. Today offered the possibility of discounting de Ribbesford as a suspect, and might even give them something more solid if they found the Raven Woman and she had seen someone other than Ivo de Mitton in the clearing. They had not yet run out of paths to follow.

Walkelin was already up and tidying his bedroll away, and Catchpoll was absent, though de Ribbesford was still snoring gently upon the dais. Bradecote pointed to the hall door, and Walkelin nodded. They made their way to the end of the hall and exited quietly.

'I thought to get off afore the lord de Ribbesford wakes and wonders, my lord.'

'A good thought, Walkelin. I do not think it will take you long to reach Rock or to discover all that can be gleaned, so I would hope you are returned well before noontide.'

'That is my hope also, my lord.'

'Rock has not only a steward, but William de Ribbesford's son, one Walter, in command of it. De Ribbesford wants him to gain experience of running a manor. I doubt very much he even knows there is anything he should keep hidden, and, in normal times, I would say de Ribbesford was a straightforward man, so the son ought to be similar. He might not even have heard the name of Ivo de Mitton, since I doubt his father would want to ever think of the man.'

'So a young lord.' Once, not that long ago, speaking with anyone of rank would have worried Walkelin, but now he was more confident.

'Yes.'

'Then I will smile in the bakehouse, grab a fresh crust if I can, and be away, my lord.' Walkelin sounded as bright as Bradecote felt this morning. Catchpoll, groaning gently as he eased his back, and drying water from his face with his sleeve, appeared from the direction of the well. He looked resigned to another day of prising truth from folk as closed as oysters, but his grunt of greeting was affable enough, and he too wished Walkelin luck as the underserjeant made to leave.

'Will we be a-goin' to see the lord Sheriff after 'is meetin' with the lord of Wigmore, my lord?' It was a question that might also have been a hint, though Catchpoll's eyes were upon Walkelin climbing into the saddle whilst a hunk of bread was still clamped in his jaws.

'Yes, Catchpoll, though I would prefer it to be with news of our own and not just to find out what the lord Sheriff makes of the message and de Mortemer. We will break our fast before we go up into the woods and seek the black-feathered and black-garbed.'

* * *

When those in the hall at Ribbesford had eaten, and seen Hugh de Mortemer and his men ride out towards the ford, which meant no further collusion between lord and vassal, Bradecote was quite open with de Ribbesford about his plan for the morning, and, indeed, where he had sent Walkelin. The latter drew a frown and a muttering that a lord's word should be good enough for anyone, but it was the former that most interested the undersheriff, as he afterwards said to Catchpoll as they walked up the trackway, with de Ribbesford's baleful gaze following them.

'He was so very keen that we were wasting our time, Catchpoll.'

'Indeed, my lord. Whenever a body tells me I need not look somewhere, that helpfully, I knows it will be just the place I will find answers. What we cannot know would be whether the lord de Ribbesford spent the time we was away yesterday, in seekin' out this *Hrafn Wif* and warnin' 'er.'

'Indeed. I am thinking Walkelin will bring us news that means de Ribbesford is no longer suspect of the killing, so he would not be warning, or threatening her, not to come to us. Are we being too suspicious and he did not go at all?'

'We will discover that when we finds 'er, my lord. Now, does we try bein' silent and 'unters, or does we shout out and declare ourselves?'

'We try the quiet way first, but I think we have to hope she answers to the second.'

In the end they actually discovered where the Raven Woman must live quite easily, and realised that her remaining concealed to those in Ribbesford was more down to them not daring to wander in her part of the woods than anything clever or mystical. They found a small cave, within which, set back from the opening, was a thickly woven hedge of branches, almost as tall as a man, keeping out both the curious and the cold. One small part was made like a narrow hurdle on its end, and could be moved aside as a door. Catchpoll set it aside cautiously. The gloom was foetid although not damp, and made both turn up their noses and grimace.

'Cold air I expected, not foul air. It is as if something – died here.'

'I was dead before I ever came here.' The words, followed by a deep sucking noise, came from the furthest and darkest recess of the cave, and they were in a low, mangled whisper, as though uttered by someone unused to speech and how to form the sounds. 'Keep back.' It was a warning more than a plea.

Bradecote's heart had missed a beat, for the voice out of the darkness came as a shock, and now he recoiled. What if this was the retreat of a leper?

'I am Hugh Bradecote, Undersheriff of Worcestershire, and with the lord Sheriff's Serjeant. Who are you?'

'Nobody, unless you too think I will turn into a bird and peck at your eyes.'

'We doesn't believe in shape-changing folk.' This was Catchpoll, and his voice was calm, even reassuring. 'And we doesn't seek to disturb them as lives quiet. But a man met a violent death in this 'ere wood a few days past and we would find out when it were done and who did the deed. Since you lives 'ere, and sees without bein' seen, we would know if you saw aught that might point our way, mistress.' For all the strangeness of the voice, Catchpoll knew it came from a woman.

'I did not see a killing.'

'But did you see the knight with the scarlet cross upon his surcoat, and was he alone? Did you see his horse and its markings?' Bradecote, setting his disinclination to converse in any closeness with a leper aside, caught the particular nature of the answer.

'Two mounted knights.' The answer came slowly, and was interspersed with the strange sucking noise. 'Late afternoon not that long before the evening falls. They halted to make camp. I avoided them. One horse was bay and a little lame. The other, the taller man's, chestnut with a star upon its forehead. He was tethering it. I did not see faces or hear clear voices. It was a horse's whinny and some sound of argument that alerted me. I came close enough to see they were not outlaws and then kept away.'

'But you saw the dead man, after the ravens found him? Two small boys ran away when they saw them pecking the corpse.'

'Yes. My friends must eat. Carrion is carrion.'

'But this was a man.' Bradecote was shocked.

'It was a man no longer, and at the resurrection those destined for Heaven shall be raised whole and clean. What happens to an earthly body does not matter.' This was said vehemently. 'And God created the raven, as surely as he created man.'

Bradecote was pleased with the information so far, but surprised that the woman called the ravens her 'friends'.

'And you did not hear the horses leave?'

'No. I hid here.'

'Thank you. What you say aids us. We may yet find the killer, and we do at least know the name of the man who was killed. He was from just across the river, once.'

'I know.' The sucking sound was drawn out even more.

'You knows?' Catchpoll did not hide his surprise.

'Even after all these years, yes.'

'You recognised Ivo de Mitton?' Bradecote wanted to be sure.

'Yes. I recognised my brother.' There was no emotion in the strange voice.

There was silence as the two sheriff's men assimilated this information.

'But his sister died in the fire.' Bradecote sounded confused.

'Little Iveta died. My mother died. Olivier died.'

'Then – Holy Virgin, you are the sister, Rohese—' Bradecote stopped himself just in time from saying 'who was raped and left for dead in the river', and ended, after a small pause, with 'who he cast out.' What he could not disguise was the pity in his voice. This woman, now more a creature of the woods, and friend only of the ravens, had been of good birth, on the verge of a marriage that would have made her the lady of Ribbesford, and had survived over twenty years with – Bradecote's eyes had become a little more accustomed to the gloom by now, and he could see there was a hearth, though no hearthstone was needed upon the bare rock floor, a cooking pot and bowls, a small quern stone, a horn beaker, a pitcher, and a bed of branches and leaves with a thick, coarse blanket folded at one end and several sheepskins with various degrees of wear at the other. The only other things in the cave were a flour crock and another large vessel that might contain oats or dried peas, two willow baskets and a fish trap. It was not nothing, but very nearly so.

'You came here? To your betrothed?'

'I could not stay the other side. I was hunted. William – helped me. Helps still, God be merciful to him and his children.' The voice was croaking now. 'Have not spoken to any man but him, since however long ago it was. My voice is tired.'

'I am sorry. Is there anything we can do for you?'

'Nothing. I give thanks God let me see how Ivo ended this life. Need no more. Go now.'

'We will go, yes, but if we find out who killed him, we will return and tell you, lady.' Bradecote gave her the courtesy, though the sound she made at it was more like a raven's croak.

It was only when they were outside that Bradecote realised that they had become slightly used to the smell in the cave. The air of the September woodland was sweet and fragrant, and he took a great lungful of it before he said anything.

'Did not expect that, my lord, though I suppose it might 'ave been a thought.' Catchpoll shook his head.

'Could she have lied? If she did recognise her brother, she had greater reason to wish him dead than anyone, and by asking if he rode alone I gave her the chance to invent another man. Could it have been her, or de Ribbesford even? She said he helped her still. Did she mean in this?' Only now did Bradecote consider the idea.

'Could be so, my lord, but – I thinks she be a woman with nothin' to lose, not even life. She considers 'erself as dead. She said it clear and true enough. If she killed 'im, 'erself, I thinks she would 'ave said so, and I for one would not 'ave wanted to drag 'er to Worcester for judgement over it, whatever we said to the lord of Ribbesford about the Law.'

'I know. I feel it, but would prefer to be sure. William de Ribbesford may still be our man but it would be better if he were not. Oh well, let us assume she spoke true in all things. We can ask after two horses, one bay and perhaps still lame, and another Templar, upon a chestnut with a white star. We might get his direction if we asked in several different places.'

Bridgnorth had grown, or at least it seemed more secure, almost contented with itself. At least that was what the erstwhile Templar felt as he rode up the winding track that ascended and then turned almost back upon itself to skirt about the imposing outer palisade to the castle bailey, which occupied the high ground and was augmented with ditches as well as the natural scarp. He felt watched, not by any man-at-arms upon his duty, but by the edifice itself. As he made his way northwards along the western side, his only small doubt was that the town, which had essentially grown up within the huge outer bailey, might not possess a horse dealer. It looked prosperous enough to do so, but fate had not smiled upon him in the last couple of days. He had been confident that a suitable victim would present themselves after he spent his night under the forest canopy, but much to his chagrin, the only people who had passed by that day and until the afternoon of the next

126

had been undersized peasants, youths or women. When he had seen the man upon the mule he had come close to offering up a prayer of thanks to Heaven for him, and he had proved all too easy to kill, though less easy to manhandle into the mail. It had been a great pity to lose that mail, for it was valuable, but he had kept coif and helm, and of course his sword, and the sale of the mule and spare horse would provide some recompense. The loss of the boots was not so great a thing, for they were almost worn out, but the victim's feet were a little smaller than his own, and the shoes pinched, reminding him at every step of the dead man who had worn them, although that in itself did not perturb him. The first thing he would do with his silver would be get a corviser to make him a new pair, and swiftly. It would mean a night in Bridgnorth, which was not ideal, for acting less than lordly and authoritative went against his nature. He had been happy enough to 'demand' lodging the previous night at Eardington, but there was no lord there, only a steward, as he had remembered. He had been thinking how he would explain that he was selling both a mule and a horse, and having found no easy solution would brazen it out and trust to the horse dealer being like many of his trade, none too inquisitive about the origins of the stock they purchased, though he might get less for each animal.

He was fortunate in that Bridgnorth was busy, and most folk were too focused upon their own affairs to pay much attention to the newcomer on the chestnut horse. He threaded his way between vendors and purchasers, looking nonchalant whilst in reality being very aware of every glance in his direction, and, having asked directions for the horse trader from a woman with a cockerel under each arm, he reached his objective and dismounted.

Selling the chestnut had not been an easy decision, for it was a good animal, with very even paces and good looks, and had proved fleet of foot in the past. It was almost a wrench to part with him, but the bay would not fetch nearly such a good price, since it still showed a hint of lameness that would be pounced upon by anyone who knew horses. It would get him as far as he needed, and, if given several days' complete rest, would be serviceable, if not exciting. There would be time to buy a better horse in the future. The second saddle, minus one stirrup leather, was worth something, since replacing that one part would not be difficult, and the horse dealer would be able to sell a good saddle once it had been given a little care and attention.

Thurstan Horsweard, the horse dealer, had already mentally priced the animals as he saw the bearded man coming towards him. He was not a man to pry into how a vendor had come by the animals he wished to sell, and was looking forward to dealing with the man with whom he would be haggling. The lordly sort needed more polite words, but were generally easier to bring down to an advantageous price. The mule was a decent enough beast, and the chestnut had a real quality to him and would fetch a tidy sum.

It was only when the negotiations had been completed and Thurstan Horsweard was alone with his purchases that he admitted to himself that the lordly man had proved difficult to beat down to a good price after all.

Seeking out a corviser was not difficult, for there were

two in Bridgnorth these days, and, having made a single-glance assessment of the size of the buyer's feet, one told his prospective client that he was in luck. When they had been measured accurately, the corviser felt very pleased with himself, for the size was almost exactly as he had guessed, that of a pair of boots he had nearly completed. What was more, the man who had commissioned them was not due to return to Bridgnorth to collect them for another five days, not that he told all that to the lordly-looking man who jangled more than the normal number of silver coins in his hand as payment. Making much of both his speed and dexterity with a needle, the corviser promised the boots by the end of the day, which drew a gracious thanks from the man. Fickle fate had now clearly decided, in its perversity, to smile upon him, since this meant he could leave Bridgnorth, and being inconspicuous, by the evening, and seek lodging over the river at the college of secular canons in Quatford, without the need to return. It was this feeling that things were now going his way that made him go back to the vicinity of the horse trader's yard, having first bought himself a hat that could be used to shade his face a little. He loitered and watched, just in case such a fine horse as the chestnut should find a quick buyer. He certainly thought the horse trader might be quite keen to sell the animal on if he was suspicious of its origins.

He was, by nature, observant, but did not watch people for pleasure. After a few hours he was bored. There were not even enough pretty women to keep his attention, and he gave short shrift to the one who approached him and offered 'a good hour'. The September day became hot, and he felt sweat trickle down the back of his neck, so that the hat was no longer merely a mild disguise. His abstemiousness and patience were rewarded just after noon, when a man of lordly class stopped at the horse dealer's yard. He was riding upon an unexciting brown horse that exuded an air of weary boredom. There was something about the rider that was familiar, and yet that should not be so, since the loitering lord had not been within a hundred miles of Bridgnorth for over twenty years. It made him frown, and wonder if someone seen elsewhere had come this far north and west. If they recognised him it would not be helpful. Before any answer had come to mind, the rider of the brown horse emerged from the yard, and the loiterer could not help but grin, for he was now leading the chestnut with the white star, who looked as though he would rather not have him upon his back. Knowing the horse's propensity for liveliness made his former owner grin and wonder if he had already unseated his purchaser, and the man was avoiding further public embarrassment. Then the smile became fixed as a thought struck him. If the buyer was known in Bridgnorth it might be possible to find out where he would be going, and it might be possible to regain the animal after all, without paying a single silver penny. Following the horse was easy, for its coat alone advertised it. His concern was that it might be led to the town gate and then be ridden away without the rider interacting with anyone, but again fate favoured him. A large man with a squirrel-fur collar to his cloak, and who must have set off from home before the day had warmed, hailed the lordly man and spoke with him for some minutes. The loiterer thought that this was as much to be seen with him as actually exchange any news, and put the cloaked man down as an aspiring merchant. Once horse and man passed on, the loiterer followed the cloaked merchant, and 'accidentally' knocked into him. He turned and made as though he would be dismissive in his most arrogant manner, but then thawed as if he knew the merchant of old, and exclaimed that he had had not seen him for so long, but he was clearly prospering. He asked how he did, ignored the loquacious answer, and then pounced with the vital question.

'I thought I saw you a short while past with – oh, my memory so often betrays me! I can recognise a face but not a name. A fellow a little younger than I am, and with a very good-looking chestnut.'

'Ah, you mean the lord of Mitton. Not so often he comes to Bridgnorth these days, but I sold him a nice little casket of Spanish origin, very decorated, two years past, and a few things since. I had thought they would be for a bride, mayhap, but it seems that was not the case. It was him you meant, yes?'

'Indeed it was. De Mitton. Of course it was. Thank you.'

The merchant, still not at all sure he had ever met the curious lord before, shook his head as he watched him walk away.

William de Ribbesford had reclaimed his lord's seat, at least while de Mortemer was not present. He sat, hands steepled before him in something between an attitude of prayer and resignation. When he looked Bradecote in the eye, the undersheriff saw guilt.

'So the Raven Woman was just a foolish legend to scare

children. For an honest man you do seem to tell us a lot of lies.'

'She deserves to be left in peace. That is all she has, Bradecote.' William de Ribbesford made it an assertion, not a plea. 'If I had to lie to allow her that, it was worth it.' His shoulders sagged.

'Well, we found her anyway, and she has given us useful information, which would have been better discovered earlier.' Bradecote did not reveal that, if believed, it exonerated the man before him.

'I think it ordained by Heaven that Ivo de Mitton died where she could know of it. When you think how far he must have wandered in the years since he left the Severn's banks, that he should be here to die, where she is, is a miracle.' It was said with sincerity, and de Ribbesford clearly did not see that he was actually giving weight to the possibility that she was somehow involved, though she could have had no forewarning that he would appear. Just for a moment, Bradecote wondered whether this man, who seemed so ordinary and honest, despite his lies to them, was playing a deeper game, and wanted to counter any suspicion that Rohese de Mitton might have cast upon him. 'Rohese de Mitton' – it felt strange giving a name to a woman who existed yet said herself was dead, a hidden figure of the woods. Perhaps she would even prefer 'the Raven Woman' if her only companions were the birds who sought the dead. Then he gave himself a mental shake. He was making too much of this. He was about to ask about whether she had come to him when she had fled the eastern side of the river all those years ago, or whether he had simply come across her and taken pity on her, but there came the sound of a woman's voice, haranguing, and then a firm knock upon the oaken door of the hall. Catchpoll, who was the nearer, went to admit whoever was clearly keen to enter. He was slightly surprised to see an old woman, her face as line-etched as the bark of an aged oak, bent of back and with a stout ash stick in her gnarled grasp, holding a lad of near tithing age by the arm, not leaning upon him for support, but very much propelling him.

'We needs to speak with the lord.' The old woman's voice was the loud sort that belonged to those whose hearing had faded. Catchpoll nearly asked which lord she meant, but then thought that if it was only a manorial matter, they, the lord Sheriff's men, could ignore it and wait. He stood aside, though the old woman's expression made him think if he had not done so she would have prodded him with her stick. He followed them into the hall, where the old woman made a token obeisance to lord and Law, commanded the boy to do so also, but more deeply, and then addressed William de Ribbesford.

'Lord, this good-for-little *nefa* o' mine 'as kept quiet when 'e should 'ave spoken up as 'e' – here she pointed a bony finger at Serjeant Catchpoll – 'demanded. I only found out this morn, and so I brings 'im now. Just like 'is father were afore 'im, God rest 'is soul. Never could do as 'e were told.' She shook her head, crossed herself and then pushed the lad forward with the end of her stick.

He was a surly-looking boy with a mop of nut-brown hair, who kept his eyes on the rush-strewn floor and looked both worried and also embarrassed at being berated before his lord by his oldmother.

'Go on, tell 'im, Wulfric,' she hissed, 'or the Law will take you.'

There was silence, so much that the sound of a scurrying mouse could be heard, then the boy spoke, in a reluctant monotone.

'I saw two men on good beasts cross the ford just after the wagon took the last load o' stooks.' There was a short pause, a grumbling reminder from the old woman and an added, 'My lord – lords.'

'Did you see the faces, or were it from a distance?' Catchpoll had glanced at his superior, received a small nod and took the lead. His long experience kept him from sounding too urgent.

'I were down by the river and they crossed the ford.'

'When 'e should still 'ave been 'elpin' and leavin' less work for 'is oldmother,' added the old woman behind him. 'My eyes be not so good and this idle-'ands went to cool 'is feet. What about my poor old feet?' The old woman was clearly incensed by the desertion, but Catchpoll raised a hand to silence her.

'And what did you see, Wulfric? Tell me every detail.' Catchpoll was old enough to be the lad's oldfather, but not the sort who sat idly by the hearth and muttered about days long gone. There was compulsion in the tone.

'Two riders, lords both. One on a bay, and cloaked, but I saw a white, long tunic showin' from beneath it, and t'other also wore a cloak, tight-clasped and with the 'ood up, and rode a chestnut with a white star. They splashed across and the bay stumbled badly so that the lord nearly fell off. The other one, upon the chestnut, shouted at me for laughin' and for not bendin' the knee, when it would 'ave made me wet, and pulled 'is 'orse over and kicked me so I fell into the water.' The monotone had been replaced by resentment at the injustice.

'Describe the two lords.'

'The both of 'em 'ad a short beard, brown colour, and the one on the chestnut, the one as kicked me, 'is eyes was like stone, grey and – soulless.' Wulfric was not a youth who often showed fear, but he shuddered at the memory. 'They must 'ave passed the church and gone up the track, but I were all wet and did not watch.' He sounded even more sulky now.

''Tis true enough, for 'e came 'ome wet and said as 'e went into the water 'cos 'e thought 'e 'eard a little 'un, and fell in – tripped over a stone. No mention did 'e make of lords.' The oldmother corroborated the story. 'Them as tells lies comes to a bad end, so I 'as told 'im, for lies be the words the Devil puts in our mouths and will choke us, sure enough.' The oldmother spoke with pious certainty.

'Is there anything more you can tell us about the lord who kicked you? Any small thing.' Bradecote thought it worth teasing every detail from Wulfric.

''Is boots was old, all creased, though the kickin' 'urt, and the leather as 'eld the stirrup on were worn so much it might 'ave dropped off in the river. If 'e kicked 'is 'orse as 'e kicked me the beast would be glad if it fell off and 'im with it.'

'Did he wear a ring?'

'Wore gauntlets, lord, so I cannot say.'

'Thank you. Your oldmother is right. You should pay more attention to her, for age brings wisdom.' Bradecote felt that this was suitable gratitude for the old woman bringing her grandson forward, and saw the slight surprise, followed by pleasure, in her rheumy eyes. Rightly hearing this also as a dismissal, she bent a little forward respectfully, said there was work to be done, and took the lad's arm in a more 'I am an old lady in need of support' manner, which clearly came as a shock to him. He bowed, and began to walk backwards, though his oldmother tutted and guided him to walk out normally, whispering in a loud undertone that she did not want to fall upon her arse in front of lords. All the men present watched her with varying degrees of respect.

'So you see, my lord Undersheriff, the killer of Ivo de Mitton was his companion.' De Ribbesford sounded both relieved and a little jubilant.

'It seems that way indeed.' Bradecote was sure, or very nearly so.

'And there is something in what Wulfric said, about that man having "soulless" grey eyes.' William de Ribbesford paused for a moment, and then said, 'Eustace fitzRobert was brown-haired and had grey eyes as hard as flint. You could never see what he was thinking, nor any sign of – humanity in him.'

'Yet the chances of him being still in company with Ivo de Mitton after more than a score years must be small, and would he not have found the man's hound-like devotion, as you and Simon de Mitton described it, wearied him after a while?'

'I tell you because it is the truth to be spoken, and – sometimes an oldmother's wisdom is indeed worth listening to.' De Ribbesford gave a small, wry smile.

'We will bear it in mind. Is there anything more you can tell us about the way Eustace fitzRobert looked that might linger as he aged? Then if we learn more about our unknown knight it may be that it is proved to be him.'

De Ribbesford frowned, in concentration rather than annoyance. 'He was not much more than a year past twenty. We are all a lot older but – those eyes would not change, and his lips were thin so that when he smiled they became a straight line so thin it was almost as though he had no mouth at all.' De Ribbesford actually shuddered at the memory. 'How can I say the man looked evil personified, when Ivo de Mitton, and others as well, saw only power and charm?'

'Because you is talkin' of character, my lord, not just looks, and the way we sees others depends upon our own minds. Men as thinks much the same way, sees much the same way. I reckons you and Ivo de Mitton saw the world mightily different.' Catchpoll understood William de Ribbesford's doubt. 'If 'twas easy to see wrong 'uns, our life would be very simple, and too often folk think someone bad 'acos of a scar or a droopin' eye, and is judgin' with the eyes, not the mind at all.'

Bradecote looked at Catchpoll. The serjeant was right, and Bradecote realised that over the time he had been undersheriff and dealing with those who broke the law, he had come to make judgements based upon an instinct, not of guilt, but the likelihood of guilt, and although he had kept William de Ribbesford in mind as the killer of Ivo de Mitton for logical reasons, he knew that his inner voice, seeing the character of the man, thought him an unlikely suspect. It was good that he had not dismissed him without due cause, but just as good that he had felt uneasy about it.

'We await the return of Underserjeant Walkelin from Rock, and then we will go to the lord Sheriff at Hartlebury and tell him what we now know.' It struck Bradecote that if, by chance, the other knight was indeed Eustace fitzRobert, a man who had always felt a de Bellême inheritance stolen from him would have good reason to wish to make the lord who had been given control of Bridgnorth by King Stephen seem a turncoat. That none of the lands that once formed the holdings of Roger de Montgomery's son would devolve upon a bastard was not important as long as fitzRobert believed they should. It was a possibility the undersheriff wanted to discuss with Catchpoll and with Walkelin before they reached Hartlebury. He paused, and then returned to the question he had been going to ask de Ribbesford before Wulfric's 'confession'.

'Did you find Rohese de Mitton, or did she come to you, all those years ago?'

'She came to me. All I knew at the time was what had drifted up river like mist of a morning. I knew she had been found in the Severn, injured. That was the first that came to me, and when I went to see how she fared, I was not permitted to see her, for she was too ill. Some while later Ivo de Mitton came and said, very solemnly, that the betrothal was declared void, because her injuries made it impossible for her marry. When I pressed him, he at first said only that as a neighbour and "friend", though I was none to Ivo himself, he would not ask me to wed his sister when she was not a maid. He did not say how that came to be. He was clearly shamed by it and I asked no more details. Even then I offered to wed her anyway, but he said it was her own wish to release me. Some weeks after that I heard that she had been declared a leper, given the "burial" and left Mitton. It felt so sudden, but nobody, so I thought, would go through with such a final act without having another choice. That was shortly before Olivier returned from pilgrimage to St David's.' De Ribbesford sighed. 'I am at least glad that he died having fulfilled his father's wish and with a soul cleansed by pilgrimage.'

'So why did Rohese not go to her brother Olivier?' Bradecote frowned.

'Because by the time he returned she knew she was being hunted, by Eustace fitzRobert. He clearly thought she might yet make known his vile act, and did not think the healing woman would dare reveal anything, not least because she had, under threat, been involved in the casting out. She came over the river one night, and knew it was my custom to attend Compline when I could. She waited in the churchyard, and I did not come that night, so she hid in the woods and returned the next. When I left the church it was alone, and she came to me, a black spirit more than my betrothed, and told her tale, haltingly. At the first I did not believe it was her, for it was not like her voice, but she told me something only she and Olivier knew, of a foolish act that nearly cost us, Olivier and me, our lives as boys. Then I knew it was her.' He paused again. 'I have never seen her, you know, not as she is. She has always been just a dark, face-covered spirit. I told her Olivier would come home and she could return to Mitton, but she said it was too late, for she was "dead" and should remain so for the happiness of her family. She said she was no leper, but her disfigurement would make all recoil even worse than facing one so afflicted. She said she was condemned to exist upon the earth until God freed her with death, and she could not seek that end, or God would judge her harshly. Yet by that time, though it was summer, she was without shelter or food. The cave upon the far bank was too well known, and poor travellers had been known to use it, so she came to the only man she dared – me. I have accounted it a gift that she did so.' De Ribbesford's voice was shaking a little now with emotion.

'I promised to aid her, as long as I lived, for I had made her a promise before, one that could not be kept. I went to Bridgnorth, far enough away for me to buy a cooking pot, a quern stone and a few other things without much interest being shown. I take her a little wheat and oats for pottage sometimes, and, with her permission, I sent our old healing woman, then very aged and not long for this world, to teach her the autumn mushrooms that were safe, and the plants of the forest. God's own truth, I do not know how she has survived so long. Three times have I had to take her black cloth where her garments had become too damaged to be even rags. I encouraged the fear of the *Hrafn Wif*, as the folk call her, carefully, but with each generation of children, who would be the ones to wander and play in the woods, the story has grown. Thankfully, the woods are part of the King's Forest, and I have right of pannage for the pigs, and the gathering of firewood, but have told all here it is only up above the church and southwest along the ridge, so the adults do not forage where Rohese lives. After – what happened – I did not marry for a year, feeling still in part bound, but Rohese urged me to wed, and I was very happy with my dear wife, God keep her soul. I never loved Rohese as a man loves a wife, but we are bound, she and I, by our secret.'

'Which we will not reveal, de Ribbesford.'

'Thank you. I have been – afraid for her.'

'No harm will come to her through us, I swear it.' Bradecote was solemn.

There was silence again, and for some time, as the three men contemplated the existence of a woman who had been so betrayed, and forced into a life that was not a life. It was sobering.

Chapter Eight

The arrival of Walkelin, who came in the knowledge that he could provide answers his superiors needed, brought them fully into the present, though he was unwilling to speak of all that he knew before William de Ribbesford and looked suddenly awkward. De Ribbesford, who needed time alone to fully compose himself, and to wrestle with a difficult decision, thankfully announced that he would be in his solar if needed, and withdrew. Walkelin, who looked bursting with news, let out a huge breath.

'So you discovered somethin', then?' Catchpoll was deadpan.

'I did, and more'n I expected. My lord, the young lord Walter 'as not the years to realise when to keep 'is own counsel.' This, from Walkelin, made Catchpoll choke.

'So what did he reveal by accident, Walkelin?' Only Bradecote's dancing eyes declared he found it equally humorous.

'Not by accident, my lord, for 'e were eager to tell me.' Walkelin was incredulous. He had never encountered anyone less guarded. 'Seems 'is father "worries" over 'im and keeps ridin' to Rock to make sure all is well, which Messire Walter is starting to find a burden. 'E wants to make 'is own mistakes.'

'Not 'avin' discovered it to be better learnin' by the mistakes of others,' interjected Catchpoll.

'Aye, Serjeant. Messire Walter said, proudly, as 'is father came towards the end o' the afternoon, the day gatherin' ended in Ribbesford, and found that the folk in Rock was threshin' already. A messenger came from the lord of Wigmore, and called both father and son to meet with 'im in Brimfield, so they went. Seems the overlord proposed a betrothal for Messire Walter that would ally the de Ribbesfords with a Shropshire family, and the marriage would keep the lady's father from waverin' in 'is support of the lord King, and of the lord of Wigmore. Messire Walter sees it as proof that their overlord trusts son as 'e does father.'

'Which was why both de Mortemer and de Ribbesford were loud in their declarations that it had no connection to the death of Ivo de Mitton and was no business of the Law. It seems both spoke true in that. Well done, Walkelin.' Bradecote was approving. 'And proposing such an alliance would be odd if de Mortemer plans to desert King Stephen.' He frowned.

'I learnt more, my lord, but from within the stables, not the young lord. I suggested, bein' careful like, that the lord de Ribbesford must 'ave put spur to 'is 'orse's flank to reach Rock that afternoon, and the groom said the lord never uses a spur, 'is animal bein' fleet of foot anyways. Since we saw the marks of spurs from whoever killed de Mitton, it could not be the lord of Ribbesford.'

'That is definitely the final proof, though Serjeant Catchpoll and I had come to the conclusion that it was very unlikely that he was involved. Good work.'

'Aye, done like a serjeant should.' Catchpoll actually clapped Walkelin on the shoulder, and the underserjeant blushed.

'We will tell you what has come to light here on the way to Hartlebury, where we will present what we know so far to the lord Sheriff and see whether the lord of Wigmore is still thought to have been about to change his allegiance.'

'Did you find the *Hrafn Wif*, then?' Walkelin was curious.

'We did, and her real identity is – interesting.'

The trio took the track to Hartlebury at a steady trot. Walkelin was an attentive listener, though he asked for a few things to be repeated as he filed them in his memory.

'So by my reckonin', my lord, since we knows the lord de Ribbesford did not kill Ivo de Mitton, he would not have warned the *Hrafn Wif* – Rohese de Mitton – to lie for 'im. That means we can take what she said as true, or true as she knows it, and it fits with what the lad Wulfric said, which also could not be from 'is lord tellin' 'im to come forward with information on the second knight.' Walkelin spoke slowly, working it out as he said it.

'Exactly.'

'And since the second knight did exist, it must 'ave been 'im as killed Ivo de Mitton, and being the man's companion, could 'ave come up close to do the deed without de Mitton seekin' to defend 'isself.'

'Trouble is, in four days, the killer, and it *could* be Eustace fitzRobert, but the description could apply to many men, has most likely left the shire and may already be returned to William fitzAlan and the Empress's supporters.' Bradecote felt frustrated.

'And would 'e be reportin' success or failure in the mission, my lord?' Catchpoll had been dealing with something that niggled in his mind. 'What would 'ave 'appened if the message 'ad been delivered to the lord of Wigmore? The message did not ask for the lord's support, but took it as promised, which would mean other messages must 'ave gone to and fro. If'n they used the same messengers, well, pickin' two Templar knights would be noticed far too easily, so why stand out? Strikes me it looks more like they wanted to be remembered. We do not even know they was Templars, only looked like 'em.'

'A good point, Catchpoll. William de Ribbesford, as De Mortemer's loyal vassal, was loud in his protestations of his lord's own loyalty to the King. If that is true, and the message false, de Mortemer would have not only seen to it that the contents were destroyed, but the messengers would be treated as his enemies, so it may have been intended all along that the message did not reach de Mortemer at all, but fall into the hands of the lord Sheriff and the information passed on to King Stephen. Hugh de Mortemer would not hold Bridgnorth for long after that, and might even be stripped of his ancestral holdings.'

'And Eustace fitzRobert felt Bridgnorth should be 'is, my lord,' Walkelin reminded them.

'Indeed, though it would never have come to him as a bastard son, and he would know it. No, the person who would gain the most from his fall would be William fitzAlan, who sent the message, and has been at the Empress's side. If he thinks she may still prevail and he will regain his lost lands, it would be an advantage to lose a powerful adversary on his southern border.'

'So that makes Ivo de Mitton a sacrifice, my lord, intended from the start, and the death very much in cold blood.'

Catchpoll looked grim. 'The lord fitzAlan must 'ave selected the weaker of the pair to "cull", like an October pig.'

'Or fitzRobert offered up de Mitton to improve the plan.' Bradecote had a feeling Eustace fitzRobert was the sort of man who could do such a thing.

'And would a man kill 'is companion of over twenty years in cold blood?' Walkelin sounded almost shocked. 'I knows friends as falls out might become mortal enemies, but if this were planned . . . ?'

'It should make fitzRobert less likely, I know, and yet . . . If it was a plot to remove de Mortemer from his power in the Marches, killing the messenger would work anywhere in the shire, or even another where the sheriff keeps the Law tightly, but Ivo de Mitton was killed within a couple of miles of his family's holding, and where his "dead" sister lives on. And yes, I know that it is beyond belief that Eustace fitzRobert knew she was there but . . .' Bradecote paused and only after several moments continued. 'Could it have been to put William de Ribbesford under suspicion? Did Eustace fitzRobert recall him with as much loathing as de Ribbesford retains for him? He might assume the man still lived, but could not know it, and what motive would last so long in the memory? Part of me thinks Bellême's bastard is our man, but at the same time I cannot see how we could prove it, and see no chance of us finding him this long after the murder.' He sighed. 'I suppose we just tell the lord Sheriff we have witnesses who have proved there was a second knight, and that he killed Ivo de Mitton, which means the murdrum fine should not be imposed. He seemed dismissive of the idea that it might be Eustace fitzRobert before, and may still do so.'

It was with this less than positive thought that they came into Hartlebury.

William de Ribbesford dithered, caught between the desire to maintain the secret he had kept without even whispering a hint of it for over two decades, and the realisation that now the lord Sheriff's men knew of it, the integrity of the silence had been lost, and that it might be time to tell Simon de Mitton that his older sister was not dead, assuming that Bradecote was not going to delay briefly on his way to Hartlebury to do just that himself. De Ribbesford felt no huge liking for Simon de Mitton, whom he remembered mostly as a small boy and minor annoyance to those a decade and more his senior, and now regarded as a somewhat ineffectual lord. At the same time he knew he lived under the burden of being kinless, and his attitude of neither needing nor wanting anyone's counsel was the barrier he had raised about himself. Some wondered why he had not wed and created a family of his own, but de Ribbesford had a suspicion that the man felt the de Mittons were cursed, and would give no more victims to a cruel and unfair fate. Perhaps the man was right. He would ride over and speak with him, though telling him the truth might as easily cause an outburst of anger at the long silence as – delight? Pity? Horror? And would Rohese approve? De Ribbesford doubted very much she would wish to be seen as she was, the ragged creature of the woods, the companion of ravens. He sighed. No decision seemed fair to both brother and sister.

He waited until he could be certain that the lord Sheriff's men would be well upon their way to Hartlebury, and then called for his horse. The groom that saw him ride away remarked to the stable boy that he looked so solemn that it was as if he were going to tell someone of a death. He could not know that the opposite was the case.

There was an atmosphere at Hartlebury that Bishop Simon would not recognise, for it was full of tension. Hugh de Mortemer's men kept away from those of William de Beauchamp as though they carried contagion, and the daily life of the lord Bishop's favoured residence was upset. The clerics looked worried and the servants nervous. The steward, used to at least the appearance of goodwill, wondered if he ought to send a messenger to his master and request that he come and mediate before blood was shed. There had been loud words in the bishop's solar, to which the two puissant lords had withdrawn, and then an angry call from the lord Sheriff for wine. The steward prayed most fervently that this was to seal some agreement between the two, but the servant who delivered it reported that both men still looked choleric. The steward had spent a restless night, and the arrival of the lord Undersheriff and his subordinates did not appear helpful, unless they might provide a distraction. When he ushered them to the solar and did not warn them of what had gone on, he felt slightly guilty.

That William de Beauchamp and Hugh de Mortemer were pacing the floor, and bore thunderous expressions, did not surprise Bradecote in the least. In fact it was what he had expected, and he greeted them with respect but no sign of agitation. He made a small bow to the lord of Wigmore and a slightly deeper one to his overlord, and it was he whom he addressed.

'My lord Sheriff, from what we have discovered today, we can now be sure that Ivo de Mitton was killed by whoever accompanied him upon his mission, and not someone seeking revenge for his past actions.'

'See,' declared the lord of Wigmore, pouncing upon the words triumphantly and pointing at de Beauchamp accusingly, 'it has nothing to do with me. I could not have known of the man's presence and did not set my vassal to kill him.'

'My lord de Mortemer, that may not be entirely true, in that we believe you may be unknowingly involved.' Bradecote chose his words carefully. 'If it happens that you have had no contact with anyone on the side of the Empress Maud, then there are those who would happily see you fall from favour with the lord King. You are a powerful lord in the Marches, and have enemies.'

'"If"? You dare doubt my honour and loyalty? How dare you.'

'My lord, I have no proof either way and so must—'

'I swore fealty to one man, and to no woman.'

'Then, it could be, as I say, the work of an enemy.'

'You think de Dinan planned this?' The words came swiftly. De Mortemer and Josce de Dinan, lord of Ludlow, were almost enemies sworn.

'It might be possible, but your relations with William fitzAlan, whose name is upon the message, were never cordial, and the connection seems more likely linked to this area, and to Bridgnorth rather than Ludlow and the lord de Dinan.'

'Yes, true enough. The traitorous bastard would like to think Shropshire will be his for retaking, and it is not. Besmirching my good name would be just the sort of thing he would do.' De Mortemer sounded suitably outraged, though in truth, he would have had little compunction about tarnishing that of his enemies. A successful lord needed a hard head, a hard heart and a sharp sword. Then he turned again on de Beauchamp. 'You call me here by shrieval right and accuse me of betraying my lord and King when I have ever been his true man, even after Lincoln, when he languished in chains. I was not among those, like you, de Beauchamp, who grovelled at the feet of That Woman' – he almost spat the words – 'and while she held sway. What a disappointment it must have been when the crown slipped from her grasp. I always wondered how you managed to persuade the King to keep you as sheriff, and if any deserve to have their loyalty doubted it is you, not me. Sweet Lady of Heaven, it might well have been you who set all this in motion. Was Ivo de Mitton doing your bidding?'

William de Beauchamp's eyes narrowed and his hands clenched. A muscle worked in his cheek. For a moment Bradecote even wondered whether he might launch himself at the lord of Wigmore. His response came in a low growl.

'I hold this shire as my sire and grandsire did before me, and by right of blood. I see the lord King's laws upheld and collect his taxes.'

'With no doubt more than he knows staying in your own coffers,' sneered de Mortemer. His own holdings were spread wide over three shires and now part of Wales, and the office of sheriff entailed some tiresome responsibilities, but had a lucrative shrievalty been offered to him, he would have accepted in a heartbeat.

It looked to Bradecote that it would be difficult to present their findings to William de Beauchamp while de Mortemer remained, but he could think of no way to get him to withdraw. However, a knock upon the solar door, followed by the entry of the steward, accompanied by a monk in a slightly dusty habit, achieved what he could not.

'What now?' de Beauchamp snarled at the steward.

'My lord, I am sorry, but there is an important message come for you from the prior of Astley.' The steward indicated the cowled figure beside him.

'I will hear it then.' De Beauchamp considered dismissing de Mortemer, but if the man refused to leave it would be an embarrassment, so he simply turned from him and pointedly ignored him.

Seeing this, de Mortemer, in his turn, declared that he had no time to listen to the complaints made to the shrieval authority, and stalked out so that de Beauchamp could not say that he had dismissed him. It was all about perceptions of power.

The Benedictine came forward, his hands clasped together before him beneath his scapular. He inclined his head slightly to both lords, and when he spoke, he addressed William de Beauchamp in fluent Norman-French, which was his mother tongue.

'*Mon seigneur*, I am Brother Martin, from the priory at Astley, a few miles to the south and across the river, though today I have ridden first to Worcester to find you, and was told you were here.' He gave a small sigh. 'I am not used to riding as once I was before I took the cowl, though Father Prior selected me as the most able upon a horse. My aching muscles are penance for the sin of pride in that accomplishment.'

'And you have a message for me, from the prior.' De Beauchamp had no interest in the man's aches and pains.

'A message, yes, but not exactly from Father Prior, though he bade me bring the document.'

This sounded somewhat cryptic, and de Beauchamp frowned. He did not appreciate the word games of monks, and they always seemed, to him, to use words with craftiness.

'Do not speak in riddles, Brother. I am not in the humour for them.'

'My apologies, *mon seigneur*. The document is a confession, one to evil deeds committed many years past, and made but a few days ago, and brought to you at the wish of he who made it. Indeed he demanded a promise that it would come to your hand.' Brother Martin was now aware he had the interest of his auditors, even the two men who were clearly not of lordly class and who stood a little back in the hall.

'Then read me this "confession" and tell us how it came to be made within your walls.' The lord Sheriff saw no need to call another clerk.

'As you wish, *mon seigneur*.' The monk inclined his head again, and Bradecote thought it likely that the man had begun life as the younger son of a noble Norman family, for he retained a degree of deference to authority that not all the cloistered possessed. He withdrew a roll of vellum from beneath his scapular, and unrolled it with a hint of a flourish, clearing his throat before he began.

'"This is the confession of me, Ivo de Mitton, son of Oswald de Mitton who held that manor of the King in the shire of

Worcestershire. Being sick of body and soul, and feeling death to be close, and having tried to atone for these sins by my life since they were committed, I wish the truth to be known, lest others who cannot defend themselves be blamed for my misdeeds. In the two and twentieth year of the reign of the late King Henry, God grant him rest, I was disowned by my brother, Olivier de Mitton, for casting out our sister, Rohese de Mitton, as a leper, when there was doubt that she was so afflicted. While that was the reason given out, I told him that I believed her to have consorted with the Devil, for she had brought forth a tiny creature that looked unlike any man, and the priest agreed it was not of human form. She had denied it and made a false claim against our dear kinsman Eustace fitzRobert of Sudwale, her mind being subjugated to Evil. My brother refused to believe me, even when I swore my oath, and even my mother would not support me. I was cast from the family in great agitation, and in that agitation succumbed to the instigation of that same Devil who had consumed my poor sister. Come the night, I returned secretly to my home, knowing the wicket gate was rarely secured, and went to the solar where my brother and mother and sister were keeping, and there I did bind my brother's hands and before his eyes foully kill my mother and sister who had not spoken for me, and then I set a fire, thinking to end my own life with theirs, but could not face the smoke and flames and so escaped before all burnt. I went to my kinsman Eustace fitzRobert, in whom I trusted, and he said such sin could only be atoned for by a life of devotion and piety, and that he, tired of the life he led, would be my companion for the rest of his days if we left England and were guided by God. These words brought me to my senses, and we did as he said, fleeing to Normandy, from whence we went as pilgrims to Santiago de Compostela, where my grandsire had been before me, and from there we took ship from Vigo for the Holy Land and the defence of the Holy Sepulchre, and did good service many years until my dear kinsman was lost to the Saracens and I took vows as a Poor Fellow-Soldier of Christ and the Temple of Solomon. Having grown too weak to bear witness with my sword, I sought permission to return to England to die, and now have come home. I have discovered I have yet a brother living, and I will go to him and prostrate myself before him and tell him what I say now, and beg his forgiveness, but it is important that the lord Sheriff of Worcestershire is told the truth also, so I plead and request that this confession be taken to him.'"

There was silence when Brother Martin stopped speaking. Hugh Bradecote glanced at Catchpoll and Walkelin, wondering how much they might have understood. The names mentioned would at least have made them attend as closely as they might. One question rose as paramount and Bradecote voiced it.

'Good Brother, when was this confession made?'

'Six days past.'

'Yet only now do you come to me?' De Beauchamp scowled.

'*Mon seigneur*,' the monk was swift to respond, 'Ivo de Mitton asked that two days pass from the time he left us before the message should be brought to you, to allow time for him to meet with his brother and not risk being arraigned until he had done so. I am sure you will find him in Mitton now.'

'We will not, for he is already here, in Hartlebury.'

'Here, *mon seigneur*?'

'Yes, or rather beneath it. He was buried yesterday, having been found dead two days before.'

'Then he was indeed sick, though he did not look so close to death.' Brother Martin crossed himself.

'I think, Brother, it was not that he was close to death but that death came close to him. He was killed by intent.' Bradecote spoke up again, and saw the surprise upon the Benedictine's face. 'It is all the more important we hear about his visit to your priory.'

'And I say again, why are you so late coming to me? Since he has been dead these five days past it must have been that day he left Astley, and that means you have exceeded the time delay he requested.' William de Beauchamp threw his undersheriff a look that said his questions took second place to his overlord's.

'Ah, that is because we are a small community, *mon seigneur*, and one of our number went missing. Since the confession was to things many years past, and we were to wait a couple of days anyway, it seemed better that I remain and be part of the search.'

'And did you find him?'

'*Hélas*, we did, yesterday noontide. Brother Albanus, one of our lay brethren, had been due to return from our grange five days ago, but must have been waylaid by outlaws. We found his poor body only a few hundred paces from our gate, concealed deep in the undergrowth, with his throat cut. That even an outlaw would kill a poor brother who possessed nothing is so shocking . . .' Brother Martin shook his head, still disbelieving.

'Was Brother Albanus English?' Catchpoll, who was working out bits of what was being said from the expression and tone of the Benedictine and words he knew in Foreign, such as 'body', thought the monk might understand such a simple question in English if he had lived in England any length of time.

'But yes. We are a daughter house of St Taurinus at Évreux, and the choir monks come from there, but our lay brothers are local men whom God has called to give service with hand rather than voice.'

Catchpoll understood the 'yes' part.

'And where did Brother Albanus come from, Brother?' Bradecote felt his mind was following the same track as Catchpoll's.

'I confess I do not know. I have been in England four years only and he was here when I came. Lives before giving oneself to God are not important or talked of. It will be in the priory records.'

'So that is why you are late in seeking the lord Sheriff. Now, about the visit of Ivo de Mitton. Did he come alone and how long did he stay with you?' Bradecote did not wait for his superior to agree to his continued questioning.

'No, he arrived with the other knight, after Chapter, a week past, and he remained with us two nights, for one of the horses was lame, and departed before Sext the day after having made this confession. He spent that night in vigil in the church, and we saw him there during the night Offices. He said he would not sleep but pray constantly, and he was true to that. He was very humble, and though his sins were of a greatness, he seemed truly penitent. He took a few hours of repose thereafter before continuing their journey.'

'And how did he look and how was he dressed?'

'Why, he was garbed as he had become – a Templar Knight in the service of God. I was not close to him, and he wore his mail coif over any hair. He said it was less comfortable and comfort bordered upon the sinful so he was even sleeping in it. That is devotion, yes? He was bearded, and there was no grey to it. I can say no more.'

'And his horse? He rode, yes?'

'Oh, I know he rode, but I did not myself see the animal.'

Bradecote looked to the lord Sheriff. 'My lord, I think we do not yet abandon our hunt for Ivo de Mitton's killer, for more may be gleaned at Astley Priory.'

'And it ends the idea of Eustace fitzRobert as being guilty of the Mitton killings. Very well, continue.'

Bradecote did not actually say anything about Eustace fitzRobert. He did feel he would like to know more about the Templar's horse and the colour of his eyes before he fully dismissed the idea of a connection.

'Thank you, my lord. Brother, will you accept us as travelling companions back to Astley?' Bradecote indicated both serjeant and underserjeant.

'Gladly, especially if there are murderous outlaws in the woods.'

Bradecote wondered about that.

Newly shod, and none too concerned by the potential unsoundness of his mount, since the next day's journey would not be of any huge distance, the rider of the bay horse entered the enclave at Quatford an hour before Vespers, very much at ease and even with a small smile playing about his thin-lipped mouth.

The college in Quatford had been created by the first Earl of Shrewsbury, the father of Robert de Bellême, to train and maintain a number of clerks for his use, and had come under royal control after de Bellême's rebellion and exile. It was small, with no more than half a dozen canons in residence, and they were always glad of the income from generous guests in their little guest hall, which they ensured provided a good meal and comfortable bed. It was certainly cleaner than hiring a whore and her bed for much of the night in Bridgnorth. There were no individual chambers, but the dormitory contained only eight beds, and only two of them had occupants. The master of the guest hall himself showed him to his allotted bed, which, since he was clearly a man of rank, and certainly far higher up the social scale than the other two travellers, was in the far corner. He professed himself pleased with this arrangement, and requested a bowl of hot water, some soapwort leaves and a cloth. When these were brought to him he proceeded, in a very leisurely manner, to shave off his beard and went to his bed to plan his next move, for the opportunity to recover the chestnut horse coincided with what had been a vague plan he had been formulating to enable him to resume a life left long ago and was now the obvious way forward. Only a few weeks ago it had all been conjectural, dependent upon so many variable things that no clear path could be seen, and it had been like a day in his boyhood, a misty morning, when all was wrapped in a thick white blanket and you could be lost within a hundred paces of the hall. Yet just as those mornings had given way to days of autumnal jewel colours, the sunlight itself almost golden, and the dying leaves a mosaic of ruby, garnet and gold, his way had become clear. He was surprised that those images came into his mind, for not once in all the long years exiled from England had he felt homesick, for life was there to be lived, and regret was a foolish waste of time. He had forgotten the mist and those colours in the shimmering heat of Spain and Outremer, the vine-cloaked hillsides of France, and even in Normandy it had not been quite the same. Yet now that he was back in the places of his youth, it was as though the landscape was nudging him, reminding him what he had missed. He laughed silently at himself. Was he growing old and becoming a dreamer? That would not do.

Chapter Nine

Whilst it was not a long ride to the priory at Astley, it was slightly awkward, in that Bradecote was talking in English with Catchpoll and Walkelin, which left out the Benedictine, and then in Foreign with the monk. He first gave them all that had been divulged in the confession and about the two knights, but then asked some general questions of the monk, which meant his colleagues trying to piece together what might be said, or waiting for a translation. By the time they dismounted and gave their horses to a lay brother, Bradecote's head was almost spinning.

Brother Martin took them immediately to Father Prior, out of courtesy and so they could get permission to ask their questions of all within the enclave. It was, as Brother Martin had said, a small cell of Norman-French monks who were transplanted from the mother-house in Évreux, supported by lay brothers of more local origin. There were a couple of brothers who had been in England several decades and acted as intermediaries if any very complicated exchanges were required. Father Bernard, the prior, was a small, scholarly-looking man with a ring of silvering hair about his tonsure and rather dramatic eyebrows that 'flew' off like the wings of a small white bird above eyes that peered due to his myopia, and a small but beak-like nose, that reminded Walkelin of a little owl. He welcomed them with a sad smile.

'I regret, my sons' – he took in all three of the lord Sheriff's men equally, though his words were comprehended mostly by the undersheriff – 'that such evil has taken place that your presence is needed, and fear that those upon whose heads such sin lies are long gone from here. I appreciate that you have come, however, and will hold your efforts in my prayers.'

'Thank you, Father. The killing of one of your community is a reason for our presence, but I will not conceal that we are also very keen to discover all that we can about the Templar knight who came here to set down his confession for the lord Sheriff.'

'Of course. Ask anything you wish and of any of us. The knight, Ivo de Mitton, was a man whose life weighed upon him, though I hope that burden was lifted a little by the time he left us.'

'It is lifted now, Father, in that he has departed this earthly life entirely, and suddenly, by violence.'

'Ah, do not say he also fell victim to outlaws!' The prior crossed himself. 'I would not think they would dare to attack knights well able to defend themselves, but perhaps they ambushed them elsewhere?'

'There were no signs that he even tried to defend himself, and nor was he robbed, Father. We think he very likely knew the man who killed him, the day he left you, and Brother Martin says he came with a companion to Astley.'

'He did. They were travelling north to Chester at the command of their own prior, and spent two nights within our small guesthouse. I believe one of their horses was lame.'

'Though de Mitton hailed from only a few miles away across the river.'

'Ah, I think the fact that he could unburden his soul in his own tongue rather than Latin made it easier, and meant that perhaps he sought us out. He said he had lived more than half his life away from England, and had even forgotten the little he knew of its language, so an English priest would have been no help. He spoke of Jerusalem itself to me.' The prior sounded almost wistful. 'He made no secret of the sins of his past before he went to the Holy Land and purged them by his service, though he felt they still needed to be known, and he showed deep contrition.'

'Father, could you describe him to us, since you were close enough to have speech with him and see his face.' Bradecote needed to get beyond thoughts of the man's soul.

'He was perhaps of your years, or a little older, his skin slightly weathered by hotter climes, with grey eyes and a neat beard.'

'Grey eyes?'

'Most certainly grey.'

Catchpoll was whispering what he could understand out of the side of his mouth, his lips barely moving, so that Walkelin might glean at least something, and it prompted the young underserjeant to speak up.

'Did he wear a ring, Father?' Walkelin enunciated in slow English, and pointed to his finger, and motioned a ring so that the monk might comprehend him. He feared the question would be forgotten and felt it important enough to raise without asking permission.

'A ring?' Father Bernard frowned, trying to recall. 'No, or at least I do not think so.' His shake of the head gave Walkelin his answer.

'Thank you, Father. Did the other knight give his name?' It seemed too much to hope for, and Bradecote was not surprised by the prior's answer.

'Raoul de Cotigny, but then Ivo de Mitton at first said he was Geoffrey fitzGuimar. A falsehood is a sin, but I think they were trying to conceal their identities because of the dangers of their mission, so I think it forgivable. They arrived describing themselves as mere messengers in the service of their Order and the Lord Christ. It showed humility. The other knight rarely spoke after giving me his name, and I believe then only in whispered tones with de Mitton. I do not know so very much about the Order, but assume that, like us, they do not encourage unnecessary speech that distracts us from our obedience to God's Will.'

'I see. If we could speak with any who had contact with the Templars or their horses, it would be useful, Father. And also, where was it that Brother Albanus came from when he came to you?' Bradecote thought it might be relevant.

'Ah, I will have Brother Gérard look in our record of admissions and come to you with the answer. Is it pertinent?'

'It might yet be so, Father. We will disrupt the work of the priory as little as possible.'

'Do whatever is needful, my son, and may your endeavours be blessed.'

With this gentle dismissal, the lord Sheriff's trio left the prior's parlour and were taken to the warming room, which was empty, with the promise that all who had met with Ivo de Mitton would present themselves. Bradecote made sure his companions knew all he had been told.

'My lord, it might be best if Walkelin and me leaves those that speaks Foreign to you, and just asks questions of the lay brothers. We might be 'ere for days otherwise, and get things wrong.' Catchpoll had spent enough time scrambling to make sense of what information was being given, and his brain almost ached with it all.

'Agreed, Catchpoll, and it was well remembered, Walkelin, to ask about the ring. If nobody else recalls the knight wearing it, then new questions come to mind, and Father Prior said the knight who made confession had grey eyes.'

'My lord, we does not know what colour eyes the dead man possessed, since the ravens took 'em, but if the "confession" were not really made by Ivo de Mitton, the companion must 'ave been Eustace fitzRobert, for it would surely be 'im to know details.'

'And if fitzRobert was giving his name as Geoffrey fitzGuimar but then made confession as Ivo de Mitton, it does make any plot to kill Ivo de Mitton so close to his family holding even more complicated.' Bradecote rubbed this chin. 'Mere malice seems too – convenient. I wonder why they gave those particular false names? Were they thought up at the time or are there connections we will discover?'

'Let us see what the monks say, my lord, and that may begin to make the waters clear for us.' Catchpoll was, as ever, unperturbed.

***

The division of labour proved fruitful. Having passed on all that the prior had said to Walkelin and Catchpoll, Bradecote interviewed three monks who said they had spoken with the Templar, and had clearly come forward because it was their duty rather than because they had anything useful to offer. As the first commented, the conventual life did not make for looking at people to memorise their appearance, though he did say that he thought the knight looked very healthy for one that claimed to be nearing his end of days. He was followed by Brother Gérard, bearing the book listing all those who entered the Order at Astley. He possessed a rather rotund figure, and was one whose natural demeanour appeared friendly and happy, though at present he looked rather deflated and sagging of shoulder. The death of Brother Albanus lay heavily upon him, for it had been he who sent him off to visit the grange and report on the harvest that had been brought in there.

'If I had picked another time . . . or gone myself.' The monk sighed.

'So he was due to return the morning that the Templar knights left?'

'Yes, yes. He was due to be absent for only three days at the grange and might almost have passed them if he returned as he had said he would that day. I suppose the outlaws thought the noble knights too dangerous to confront, but a Benedictine has nothing worth stealing and a knight has so much.'

'It might well be that whoever killed him did so because he had noticed them, Brother.'

'But to what purpose? Even outlaws can look like ordinary men if they choose, and there need have been no reason for

Brother Albanus to give them more than a smile as he passed them. It can only have been simply malice and evil.'

'Hmm. You are the one who can tell me where Brother Albanus came from when he was admitted to this House.' Bradecote avoided giving an affirmation of that theory.

'Indeed. He came to us from the manor of Sudwale, across the river, now let me see . . .' He consulted the book, drawing his finger down the list. 'Yes, fifteen years ago come Michaelmas. His young wife had died, and he said he knew that God wanted him to eschew all women thereafter and devote himself to His service.'

'Thank you, Brother. That has helped us. It may even be that we do discover who killed Brother Albanus after all.'

'I pray that will be the case. One should pray for the most lost of souls, but I have found it so hard to think of whoever took his life with any charity, even though we know the Almighty will have mercy upon so gentle a soul as he was and he will dwell at the last with the saints.'

Bradecote made a vague murmur of agreement, and Brother Gérard departed with a sigh.

Thankfully the priest who had taken down the confession had been long enough with the man for some details to register. When asked if the man wore a ring he was firm in his answer.

'No, my lord, for he made much with his hands during his confession.' The Benedictine wrung his hands and then gripped them tightly before his face, imitating the actions. 'He wore no ring.'

'And did any feature stand out to you?'

'No, *mon seigneur*.' This priest, in the absence of anyone of even higher rank, felt the undersheriff warranted the respectful title, especially since he was probably Bradecote's junior by several years. 'He had grey eyes, no grey in his beard, and' – he paused for a moment – 'perhaps he had said all the things he told me many times in his own head before speaking them, because that was how it felt to me. Every word was said – with a reason. I did not think of it before but now, yes, they were carefully chosen. I am sorry I cannot be of greater aid.' The cleric looked almost guilty.

'No, no, we do better from honest admissions that no more is known than from those who try too hard to remember things and thus their minds invent to fill the gaps.' It was not something Bradecote had consciously thought about, but the reassurance was none the less true. He also felt that everything that 'proved' Ivo de Mitton had made a declaration of his guilt and exculpated Eustace fitzRobert was too good, too neat. He wondered what Catchpoll and Walkelin would make of it.

It was an undersheriff deep in thought who sought out his subordinates, and discovered that they had finished speaking with the lay brothers and were enjoying the offerings of the priory cook, who had taken pity upon Catchpoll's 'poor, dry throat' and had supplied both he and Walkelin with a beaker of small beer warmed and infused with herbs. Catchpoll wiped the back of his hand very obviously across his mouth and made a sound indicative of pleasure.

'Missed a fine beaker, my lord,' he announced cheerfully.

'As long as you also have news, I will not begrudge you.' Bradecote smiled.

'I can ask the cook for another beaker, my lord,' offered Walkelin.

'No, I am content. What news from the lay brothers?'

'The Templar as spent the night upon vigil was the one as rode a bay 'orse, my lord, when 'e arrived, and for all that 'e came for confession, the brother who took the beast said that 'is manner showed pride and 'e treated 'im as of less importance than the animal itself, which does not tally with the way of the man with Father Prior.' Walkelin spoke up first. 'And the animal were just about sound when they left, but the lay brother said 'e felt it would 'ave been better they rested it several more days, and 'e thought it would not stay so.'

'And one of the brethren said that other knight asked, casual like as they were about to leave, if Mitton were still 'eld by Olivier de Mitton.' Catchpoll gave the information slowly, allowing it to sink in.

'And if you knew he was dead, why would you even mention his name? I think we definitely assume one of the knights was Ivo de Mitton and the other Eustace fitzRobert, but have we had them—'

'*Earslings*, my lord? That we might, since just giving the name of Ivo de Mitton does not mean 'twere 'im, and it now looks most like fitzRobert used that name for the confession just to clear 'is name of the murders, but they must 'ave changed 'orses afore they crossed the ford at Ribbesford.' Catchpoll was contemplative.

'No, Serjeant, it might just be that Ivo de Mitton's grey eyes was as "soulless" as fitzRobert's.' Walkelin did not hesitate. 'We always thought de Mitton rode the bay, once Wulfric spoke of the grey eyes that frightened 'im, but for all we knows, that were de Mitton after all, on the chestnut. Even if the ravens 'ad not taken the eyes, and we 'ad seen they was grey ourselves, death robs 'em of any "look".'

'Very true, Walkelin.' Bradecote nodded. 'And even if they did change horses it might have been about weight. If Ivo de Mitton was the lighter of the two and the bay horse was showing signs of being lame again, fitzRobert might have suggested they change mounts for a time.'

'And be to 'is advantage, my lord, since if any was lookin' for "the other knight" they would ask after one on a chestnut, not a bay.' Walkelin was thinking things through.

'Which means we is still left not quite oath-sure which man was which, though I truly believes the penitent were fitzRobert, but that would be all instinct.' Catchpoll shook his head.

'I think we are better placed than that, Catchpoll, because the unfortunate Brother Albanus came to Astley from Sudwale, and at an age when he would clearly have known Eustace fitzRobert. The idea that outlaws would kill a Benedictine just because he passed them on the road seems unlikely, but that Eustace fitzRobert would slit the throat of a man who would otherwise have gone back to his brothers in Christ and said "I almost thought I saw a ghost when I beheld . . ." is all too likely.'

'But, my lord, a man of Sudwale might also recognise Ivo de Mitton, if 'e and Eustace fitzRobert was always in each other's company when young. Granted it might seem less likely Ivo de Mitton would take a knife to 'im, but if there was somethin' else Brother Albanus knew from the past it could just be so.' Walkelin disliked casting out the simple answer too early. 'Could it even be that the man buried as Ivo de Mitton were really Eustace fitzRobert and we was lied to? We now knows one knight asked after Olivier de Mitton, and it would be more likely to be the man's brother. That means 'e did not kill 'im but would 'ave been told 'e died long ago. Such a thing as went on at Mitton would live long in local memory, and the lay brothers at Astley would know of it. So that means Ivo suddenly found out 'is kin was all dead, 'cept mayhap Simon. So did 'e work out it must 'ave been the man 'e 'ad followed all these years as did it and kill 'im, and then go to William de Ribbesford and then Simon de Mitton and tell them all?'

'But for that to be true, not only would William de Ribbesford and Simon de Mitton have had to lie, before knowing the other was asked to identify the body, so would the Raven Woman, and if you had seen Rohese de Mitton – not that we saw her face – you would not say she lied. If it had been the very man who attacked her, she would have been, if not jubilant, then at least relieved of a great weight. And why kill the man right there, in the very wood where Rohese de Mitton is still . . .' Bradecote paused for a moment before saying, 'living, not just somewhere after Astley?'

'Then that makes a difference. I just wanted to ask, my lord, in case we was too eager.' Walkelin moved his mental filing about in his head, and was not in any way disappointed.

'You were right to suggest it, and I do think we need to press Simon de Mitton about whether he did see his brother very recently, but the confession spoke of going to Mitton, and I doubt fitzRobert would have wanted Ivo de Mitton to do that, since he would have found out about his family then. What has happened is that he found out about it without fitzRobert knowing.'

'So if we is workin' on our confession man bein' fitzRobert, we needs to work out why all the pretendin', and whether 'e left the shire as soon as 'e could, or wanted to remain and see what followed.' Catchpoll had a theory forming but it was not yet firm.

'I will tell Father Prior that we think one of the two knights killed Brother Albanus, which he may think impossible, but there. We shall spend the night here, and report back first thing to the lord Sheriff. Then we visit Mitton and also Sudwale, and discover whether Eustace fitzRobert's mother still lives there. I think I need to break the news to the lord Sheriff that his dismissal of Eustace fitzRobert as the possible killer was too swift.' Bradecote was decisive.

'Oh, 'e will like that.' Catchpoll could not help but grin his death's-head smile at the thought.

Hugh de Mortemer was not a man who worried by nature, but nor was he rash. He was also no fool. Whilst he had happily accused William de Beauchamp of the message plot, it had only been because he was angry and wanted to put the man under pressure before his vassal and serjeants. Logic said it had indeed been sent by fitzAlan, in the expectation that de Beauchamp would make much of it and pass it on to King Stephen, but de Beauchamp had not said that he would do so, which slightly surprised the Marcher lord. De Mortemer ground his teeth at the thought of the lord of Oswestry turning King Stephen against him. However, the plan had failed, and it was possible that further instruction had been given to the messenger who had killed Ivo de Mitton. What if he had been told not to return to fitzAlan, but remain to see what came to pass, and if the original plan did not work, to use violence where craft had failed? That there were Welshmen with good cause to want him dead did not concern Hugh de Mortemer overmuch. There seemed very few who could conceal their origins the moment they opened their mouths, and he was careful who he permitted to get close to him. An Anglo-Norman knight could assume any name and reason to present himself, and was thus an unknown danger. Hugh de Mortemer decided that he would not only withdraw to Wigmore, in his own heartland and on the western side of his English holdings, but give instructions to William de Ribbesford.

His vassal had rather hoped that his noble overlord might decide to ride from Hartlebury to Bridgnorth, and not take his bed and solar again, but he hid his disappointment well enough. What he could not hide was his surprise when he was commanded to actively seek a potential assassin.

'But, my lord, I cannot scour my manor and beyond for any stranger. It is common enough for men to ford here on their way northward and I have no power to question or delay them.'

'Well, it might still be that the man is this Eustace fitzRobert, whom you know and loathe. That he would seek my death for his own reasons, let alone at the instruction of William fitzAlan, is quite possible. I will be wary, but you alone of my vassals are able to fulfil this task.' A little pressured praise seemed the best way forward, in de Mortemer's mind.

'I will do what I can, my lord, though the King's Forest could hide an army, not just one man. But I will alert all my people, and do whatever I can to ensure your safety.' It was tantamount to saying he had no hope of success, but de Mortemer knew there was only so much one man might do, and nodded a gracious acceptance. 'What should I do if I do find him?' The question was posed a little tentatively.

'Do? Why, you kill him. It would be useful, I grant, if you could get him to give you details of fitzAlan's plan to ruin me, but I accept you have few men and the Bellême bastard is clearly a dangerous man.'

'My lord, whatever is suspected, even believed, he was never declared outlaw. Under the Law I cannot—'

'The Law is limited in this. If he is found here then that in itself proves his guilt, for the chances of him being in the area by innocent chance do not exist. He is a killer, and a direct and patent threat to me. Killing him will not have de Beauchamp or his men dragging you in chains to Worcester, and if they ask questions, well, you came upon him and he, knowing he was recognised, attacked you. You defended yourself.' De Mortemer did not think there was any moral issue, but could see de Ribbesford was wavering. 'I value your service, de Ribbesford. It is for that reason I arranged the very advantageous marriage for your son.' He paused. 'And now, what can your cook provide me to eat?'

William de Beauchamp's temper had ameliorated a little with the departure of Hugh de Mortemer from Hartlebury, and an unexpected arrival during the latter half of the afternoon actually gave him cause to smile, wryly, though it was the skills of Bishop Simon's cook that put him in a good mood before he retired.

When Bradecote, Catchpoll and Walkelin arrived the next morning, a little after he began breaking his fast, he held up his eating knife, with a piece of cold mutton impaled upon it, and halted them even as Bradecote began to relay what they had learnt.

'It does not really matter now, Bradecote, whatever you discovered. Eustace fitzRobert is dead.' This was said with a flourish and William de Beauchamp was delighted with the genuine shock on the faces of his men.

'Dead, my lord? How? When?' This might make all they had discovered merely an irrelevance.

'The body of a Templar knight was brought in yesterday after you left for Astley. A traveller upon the road south from Bridgnorth came across him and a broken stirrup leather, not far from Ribbesford, so had you looked north for the man you would have saved a lot of time. The neck was broken, so it seems he came off his horse in his haste to leave the scene of the killing.'

The disbelief upon the three faces altered slightly, as doubt replaced simple surprise.

'My lord, is the road from Bridgnorth so little used that nobody else came across the body the day we arrived in Ribbesford?' Bradecote posed the question, knowing it would not please his superior.

'Well, perhaps the body was not completely in the open and was missed.' It did not sound convincing, even to the lord

Sheriff's own ears, but, not having thought of the problem, de Beauchamp was not going to admit he had jumped to an erroneous conclusion.

'And the person as found the body came 'ere, my lord?' This was Catchpoll.

'Yes, because they did not think they would get much further upon the road to Worcester by dark, and seeking shelter for themselves and a corpse would not get a welcoming answer at some assart cott.' De Beauchamp was swift to respond.

'Have you seen the body, my lord, and did you recognise it as Eustace fitzRobert?'

'I saw the body, Bradecote, but I do not recall ever seeing the man alive. However, the idea that any other Templar would be within a mile of Ribbesford defies belief. It must be him.'

'Might be best we looks at 'im, my lord, just to be sure.' Catchpoll sounded soothing, but in reality was wondering why the lord Sheriff did not feel this was all too tidy.

'But you never met fitzRobert either.'

'No, my lord, but we 'as a description of 'im.'

'Very well, view the body if you wish.' De Beauchamp waved them away, as he might a pestering fly.

'Thank you, my lord.' Bradecote was equally suspicious. 'I take it the traveller has not yet left?'

'I have no idea. It did not interest me.'

'Walkelin, go to the guest hall and find out. If he has gone on, you are to follow him and bring him back.' Bradecote spoke urgently. 'Catchpoll and I will see the body.'

They left William de Beauchamp to his cold mutton.

* * *

The body had been left upon trestles in the chapel, and although it had been stripped, Catchpoll was relieved to find that as yet it had not been washed and shrouded. There had been, it turned out, some dispute as to who ought to do this, and so the decision had been delayed until morning. He turned back the covering cloth and both men sighed.

The corpse before them was of a man of about the right age to be Eustace fitzRobert, but his chin was merely stubbled, as though he had not shaved for a day or so, not bearded, and for the second time in only a few days, a bandage covered where the lids would have been closed over the eyes, if the eyes had remained. The physique was not of a man used to riding, or with skill at arms, for the muscles of thigh and arm were not developed.

'So the carrion-seeking ravens found him too, and our Templar has left the Order it seems, Catchpoll.' Bradecote knew this was not Eustace fitzRobert.

'Indeed, my lord, and be very keen we ends searchin' for 'im. Must 'ave taken a bit of a struggle to get a dead-weight body into a coat of mail.' Catchpoll felt the neck and had no difficulty in ascertaining that it was broken. 'Taken by surprise, 'e were, and the neck snapped.'

'This is clever, but not nearly clever enough, if we were on his scent, Catchpoll, and a coat of mail is an expensive thing to leave. I wonder whether he took this man's clothing or had "ordinary" garments with him.'

'Mayhap those as does what we does elsewhere, those as 'e came across, would see little chance of discoverin' 'im and be content to give out that the search be ended.' He paused for a moment. 'Like the lord Sheriff. If Eustace fitzRobert waited, still within the shire so that this death would be reported to the lord Sheriff of Worcestershire, and needed a victim to come by, close as might be to 'is own looks, well, *wyrd* meant that none came, and 'e were waitin' too close to the place of the murder to be safe. I would guess this poor bastard were a victim taken in desperation.'

'True, and that also accounts for why the body was only discovered yesterday morning. I do not believe it was missed for several days, which means the man died the day before yesterday, at the latest, though it is a wonder it was not discovered within hours.'

'Well, some folk might come from Bridgnorth on the other side of the river, my lord, since it be fordable at Quatford, just before the town, and some folk would just hurry on by and not want to get involved or be delayed. They would say they could do nothing, for the man were dead. and it were nothin' to do with 'em.' Catchpoll accepted that a considerable proportion of the population would look the other way when he would be eager to ferret.

'That is fair. It does mean Eustace fitzRobert was close by only two days ago.' He sighed. 'Perhaps the lord Sheriff was right to question why we did not look north.'

'No, my lord, that be foolish thinkin'. When we found the body we knew the killin' were the day previous, and the killer might 'ave gone in any direction and be likely long gone. Dashin' about like chickens without 'eads would 'ave been senseless. We did what were best, try and discover the man's name and 'ow 'e died, first. And if the bastard stayed to kill another to get us off the scent, 'e wants to stay close, not run far, which means we 'as more chance than we thought to get 'im.'

'But we have another unknown dead man as well, Catchpoll.'

'We does, but as long as 'e gets a decent burial, we will find out soon enough if someone comes to Worcester and reports a man missin'.'

'Only if he came from the shire.'

'And if 'e came from far away, nothin' we can do, and God will keep 'is name.' Catchpoll was the complete pragmatist. 'What you does now, my lord, is annoy the lord Sheriff by provin' 'e were tricked as the killer intended, and we carry on with our plan to visit Mitton and Sudwale.'

'Thank you, Catchpoll. I note how the first task falls just to me.'

'Duty of command, my lord.' Catchpoll kept a straight face, but turned as they heard footsteps upon the stone flags and Walkelin's voice, clearly trying to reassure another.

Walkelin had been contemplating another ride, keeping him from the centre of the investigation, but he was in luck, as the man who had found the body had taken advantage of the generous hospitality offered in the lord Bishop's guest hall, and being the centre of curious interest, which meant a certain feeling of celebrity. After an unsettling day, and having accepted a goblet of wine, to which he was unused, he had slept late. He gave his name as Eadward, a miller from Tenbury, who had been to visit his brother, a secular canon at the college in Quatford, to tell him of the death of their mother. He had borrowed an ass for the journey, since he felt it would be quicker than walking and not far to fall off. Walkelin felt sorry for the ass, for though the man was not tall, he was stocky, and possessed the upper body muscles of a man who heaved sacks of grain day in and day out. He was on the return journey when he came across the body of the Templar knight. He looked fearful when Walkelin announced who he was, and became even more flustered when brought before the lord Undersheriff of Worcestershire. Even before Walkelin made the introductions he blurted out his innocence.

'All I did were find the poor man. I swears my oath on it. You must believe me.' The miller's voice shook and he clasped his big hands together before him in supplication.

'My lord, this be Eadward Miller of Tenbury, as found the body.' Walkelin was ignoring the man's protestation.

'Fear not, Master Miller. We do not think you killed this man and have a fair idea who did, but would ask you questions in case you can give us more information.' Bradecote tried not to be too lordly but still a voice of authority.

'I knows nothin', my lord.' The miller's voice was at odds with his frame, being quite soft and mild.

'We will see. Now, where exactly did you discover the body, and where were you travelling from and to?' Bradecote thought these very reassuring questions, but the miller trembled, nevertheless, and it was several moments before he could speak, and he wrung his large hands together as he did so.

'On my way back to Tenbury I be, my lord, from takin' the sad news of our mother's death to my brother, who is one of the clerks at Quatford.' A touch of pride entered his voice for a moment at his brother's elevated position, but then fear took over again. ''Twere about noontide and I were sweatin' a bit, for the ass takes a deal of persuadin' to more than dawdle along, especially when goin' uphill.' The man clearly had not considered that the beast might simply be struggling to carry his weight. 'I 'ad crossed the brook that marks the shire boundary, and were comin' slow up the track that then drops down to the ford at Ribbesford, though I were a-goin' to turn west afore that, on the little track that heads to Tenbury.'

'And did you pass any man upon a horse that morning?'

'No, my lord. There was a few folk on foot, goin' north to Bridgnorth, and an ox cart, but no rider.'

'Thank you. Go on.'

'As I got about a third of the way up the slope, I saw somethin' white, just a mite off the trackway, and when I got off the ass and went to look, well, it were a cloth surcoat, and there were this knight, quite dead and cold. At first I feared outlaws, my lord, but then thought if 'e were stone cold they would be long gone.'

'Describe the scene, friend.' Catchpoll joined the gentle interrogation. 'Did you see the 'orse too?'

'No, that were odd, to my mind, but then I supposed the beast galloped away, frightened by whatever it were that made it throw the poor man.'

'And how did you know that was how he died, Master Miller?'

'My lord, there were no blood, but for a slight old smear of it on one side as though 'is 'and 'ad wiped against it, and the angle of the neck were unnatural. Clear broke, it were. And then one foot were still in a stirrup, and the leather must 'ave snapped for you could see the break. Must 'ave toppled off when the animal tried to bolt, and 'e put pressure upon that strap. I thought about goin' on by, but you can see what the birds and beasts 'as done already, and it did not seem right to leave the man. So I pulled him onto the ass and came 'ere.'

'Why did you not stop in Ribbesford and give the body to the priest there?'

'Ah, I spoke to the priest there, but 'e said as you, my lord Undersheriff, was lookin' for such a man, and was 'ere, and I should bring the body to you. And there be a cross upon the knight's chest, so buryin' the poor man where the lord Bishop 'as a nice chapel and priests, well it turned out quite fittin', to my mind.'

'That is not the reason that passed to the lord Sheriff.' Bradecote looked curious more than judgemental over the lie.

'Ah, well now. When I arrived and asked for the – you, my lord, I were told the lord Sheriff hisself 'ad come and you was gone somewheres else. I thought if I did not say I were on my way to bring the body all the way to Worcester to 'im 'e might be angry.' The man winced as though imagining that anger. 'Mind you, if 'e saw the ass 'e would know it would be another two days afore I would manage to reach Worcester with a man dressed in mail slung over the beast, and me with a bunion.'

'But did you tell him what you have told us?'

'Me? Speak with the lord Sheriff? God be thanked, I were not asked to. I offered up prayers in gratitude that 'e looked at the body but did not ask to speak with me.' The miller's relief was patent and genuine. 'I were surprised that you wanted to speak with me, and if you 'ad been later, I would 'ave set off back to Tenbury and my mill.'

The three sheriff's men exchanged glances. That the lord Sheriff had not sought any information directly from the finder of the body offended the 'serjeanting sense' that they each possessed.

'Well, what you have told us has aided us, Master Miller, so you may go on to Tenbury now, knowing you have done your duty to the dead man and to the Law.' It sounded a bit pretentious, and Bradecote did not say that the corpse did not belong to a knight at all, but Bradecote thought it would give the man something to speak of with pride to his neighbours, and he had put himself out when others might not have done so. It seemed fair recompense.

Chapter Ten

William de Beauchamp scowled at his undersheriff when his men returned to make their own report on the body of 'Eustace fitzRobert'. Whilst Bradecote made sure his words did not overtly say that his superior had fallen into the man's trap, there was no getting past the fact that this was the truth of the matter. Bradecote therefore hastily moved on to what had been discovered at the priory in Astley. De Beauchamp quizzed all three of his men on why any of this added deception might have taken place.

'Why should it not be that Ivo de Mitton killed his family, after all. He went to Astley, for the good of his soul, and then to Mitton, and yes, the second rider was fitzRobert, but it was simply that they argued at the place the murder was committed.'

'It is possible, my lord, and we will be asking more probing questions in Mitton tomorrow. Yet this also seems very neat, and suddenly presented to us.' Bradecote carefully avoided saying 'you'. 'And I cannot see fitzRobert loitering in the undergrowth while Ivo de Mitton made his peace with his remaining brother.'

'And another thing.' De Beauchamp was not yet convinced. 'Sending a false message to ruin de Mortemer's name makes sense, and planning to sacrifice one of the messengers would achieve the aim, though it might be that William fitzAlan just left the details of how the document would be discovered up to the messengers. All this going off to Astley and making some confession, well, it is merely a distraction. Ivo de Mitton was killed so that I, and thus the lord King, would think Hugh de Mortemer traitorous.'

'But this very "distraction" seems designed to remove any suggestion that fitzRobert was involved in those murders in Mitton, and even to want to point the finger of guilt for Ivo de Mitton's death at his brother Simon.'

'Whom fitzRobert has not seen since he was a small boy not worthy of notice? I think that hardly likely, Bradecote.' De Beauchamp was scornful of the idea.

'I know, my lord, but why else particularly tell the monks that he, "Ivo de Mitton", was going to see him?'

'It was just another way to delay the message reaching me and giving him more time to reach de Mortemer, and Ivo de Mitton clearly did not know he would never complete his task.'

'Perhaps, but the whole point was that the message should come to you and not de Mortemer. It is a tangle, my lord, and so we will go back to Mitton and also visit Sudwale.'

'You will get no sense there.'

'Why, my lord?'

'Because the lady of Sudwale breathes but is otherwise lost to the world. The steward has kept all in order and I long ago removed the need for any service from that manor. Her mind began to wander more than five years past, and last I heard she was also now almost blind. I think Simon de Mitton is already taking some of the decisions, and it cannot be many years before he inherits as her nephew and the last of her sire's grandsons.'

'He is the heir to Sudwale?' There was both surprise and a touch of horror in Bradecote's voice.

'Of course he is. He is the remaining grandson of Raoul de Cotigny. Who else is there to inherit?'

'Raoul de Cotigny is the name that Ivo de Mitton used at Astley, my lord. The prior thought they gave false names to protect their mission, which he said was to their Order in Cheshire.'

'Well, they were both related to him, Bradecote.'

'It seems a little daring, since there might be someone at Astley who would have a memory of that name, my lord.'

'Why so? The monks come from Normandy.'

'But the lay brothers, my lord, come from this part of the shire.'

'Yes, but they are only the lay brothers, and he would not think of those.' De Beauchamp said it in a way that suggested lay brothers were certainly beneath his own consideration.

'And Eustace fitzRobert used the name Geoffrey fitzGuimar. Can you think of a reason he did so, my lord?'

'Ha!' The exclamation was accompanied by de Beauchamp slapping his palm upon the arm of his seat. 'Guimar was the name of his grandsire's brother, who was shunned by the family after he sided with Robert de Bellême against King Henry. The man left England with him and was never heard of again.'

'I wonder whether Eustace and Ivo de Mitton went to him, the older exile, when they made their escape?' Bradecote was fitting this new information into the puzzle. 'And if Simon de Mitton were removed and Eustace fitzRobert returned, exonerated from blame for all that happened in the past, there is one very clear heir, my lord. It gives a good reason to place the blame for Ivo de Mitton's killing upon the brother who would have every reason to wish him dead, for past crimes and because he might try and take back the holding.'

'But that would mean Eustace fitzRobert knowing these things.'

''E would know 'em, my lord, if, being in England again, 'e went back to Sudwale afore and found someone as never took agin 'im.' Catchpoll was several steps ahead of the lord Sheriff, but then that was not uncommon. 'And it might be 'e 'eard of Simon de Mitton hisself, and did not know Ivo de Mitton 'ad been told also. Sounds the sort of bastard who could think up a plan quickly, one that might leave Sudwale free for 'im again. I grant it sounds strange, my lord, and we 'as not found the answer as yet, but we will.'

'Prove it, Catchpoll, and then I will take this all seriously.'

'And will you remain here, my lord?' Bradecote wondered about his overlord enjoying the unknowing hospitality of the lord Bishop of Worcester.

'While there is still the remains of the haunch of venison presented to me for dinner last night, I will.' De Beauchamp smiled at last. 'The stomachs of bishops are filled with the choicest of meats for all that they cry abstention and simple fare. It would be a pity for such good meat to go to waste upon his servants.'

It was not a very good reason for remaining, but then the lord Sheriff of Worcestershire did not need a reason.

* * *

As they made their way to Mitton, Catchpoll, who had clearly been preoccupied, made a suggestion.

'I knows we is seekin' answers to the killin' of Ivo de Mitton, my lord, but it strikes me as it would be useful to find out more about what 'appened all those years back also. Some things be clouded, and if we knew more it might aid in the 'ere and now.'

'Indeed, and what happened to the Mitton healer who was involved in the casting out of Rohese de Mitton has been in my mind. The priest, it was said, was replaced shortly afterwards, perhaps even in the short time before Olivier de Mitton was killed, but nothing was mentioned about her.'

'And did she offer up 'er knowledge or did Ivo de Mitton force 'er to say as she did?' Walkelin had also pondered on the healing woman's role.

'And if Simon de Mitton denies any contact with his brother Ivo, other tongues in Mitton might be less tied. It should prove whether the "confession" was purely to exonerate Eustace fitzRobert or if Ivo de Mitton returned to explain he did not murder his own family and that he had killed the man who did. I admit the latter seems more and more unlikely, since nothing of what we have been told about Ivo indicates he was a man inclined to craftiness, and the killing of the man beyond Ribbesford, and dressing him as a Templar, seems part of greater planning than we would imagine from him. I will deal with Simon de Mitton, therefore, and you can both ply your craft in collecting information from everyone else. I think you may have the easier task.'

In fact, Bradecote could get nothing from Simon de Mitton, because he was not within the manor, and he had to discover what he could from the steward, overseeing the manor threshing, and who was not inclined to give up anything. They stepped out into the sunshine and away from the dust and noise within the barn, so that the conversation was private, but the steward was not eager to assist. Even when asked where his lord had gone, he prevaricated.

'Not my place to know or ask, my lord.'

'But surely he would tell you if he expected to be away all day, at the least, and did he ride out or walk?'

'I did not see my lord leave, but 'e might well 'ave taken out the new 'orse as 'e bought yesterday.'

'Describe the animal.'

'A chestnut with a white star, and quite a lively beast. Should not be my place to say it, but the lord does not ride as well as 'e imagines 'e does, and somethin' less mettled would 'ave suited better.' The steward sighed.

'Did he buy him in Worcester or Bridgnorth?' Bradecote tried to sound only casually interested, but was worried.

'Bridgnorth, my lord, for 'e said as 'e bought the animal from Thurstan the Horsweard, and that is where Thurstan trades. I dares not think what it cost and the 'orse that were sold would not 'ave fetched so much, bein' past its prime, though better suited to the lord's 'orsemanship.'

'So he does tell you where he is going.'

'If it be for a full day, aye.' The steward looked resentful, feeling he had been tricked.

'And was his decision to go to Bridgnorth and buy a horse sudden?'

'I knows not, for the lord does as the lord wants.' The steward hunched a shoulder and closed his mouth tightly, intimating that would be all that the lord Undersheriff would get from him, but Bradecote was not put off.

'Do you know whether he crossed the Severn and went up the western bank, or remained this side until he reached the Quatford crossing, and from which direction and at what time did he return?'

'Them's a load o' questions, my lord, and I cannot give answers to all of 'em. I does not watch 'im like a cat with one kitten.' The steward realised this sounded impolite and tried to make amends. 'I can tell you the lord came back late in the afternoon, and I think rode up from the ford, for when 'e showed me the animal the legs was still darker where wet.' He paused, and frowned. 'For all 'e were proud of the beast, 'e looked – not worried, but like wrestling with a problem, and when I reported to 'im first thing, I would say 'twere not yet solved.'

'Thank you. Now, I am sure you will not mind telling me how long you have been steward here.' Bradecote sounded very reasonable. 'Come now, that is not giving information on your lord.'

'Fifteen year come Candlemas, after my father died.'

Bradecote judged the man to be near his own age, which would mean he would have been of full age when the hall had been burnt down and its occupants murdered.

'And so he was steward when the lord Olivier de Mitton and his mother and sister died. It must have taken a good steward to keep the manor working after such a tragedy. It speaks very well of your father.' A little flattery might achieve what outright questions would not.

'That 'e were, God rest 'is soul.' The steward crossed himself.

'But you were old enough to assist him, no doubt.'

'I did what I could.'

'And did he send you to Worcester with the news of it?' It was a guess, but even if incorrect might still elicit something.

'Aye. Never been to Worcester afore nor since.' The man said this quite proudly.

'So you will have had to know everything about what was found.'

'Not somethin' a man forgets, my lord.' The steward looked suddenly grim. 'Not the sight, and not the smell neither. The lord Olivier were not so many years older 'n me, and a good man.' There was something in the tone that Bradecote felt implied Simon de Mitton did not quite match up to his brother.

'Yes, I too have seen a burnt corpse, and it is indeed not something you forget. How bad was the fire when it was noticed?'

''Twere night time and dark. The alarm were raised by the beasts in the stable makin' a noise in fear and rousin' the ploughman as lived next to it. By the time we all was awake and could fetch water, roof were all alight and then caved in over the main chamber. We, Father and me, broke the shutters to the solar window and 'e lifted me up to see within. 'Twere all smoky, but you could see the bodies where they lay, and Father always 'ad a soft spot for the lady ever since she 'ad been kind when our mother were ailin' and died. Tied a wet cloth about 'is face 'e did, and tried to climb in and reach 'em, but the smoke were too bad and 'e only managed to get the lord Olivier's little sister as were closest afore we 'ad to give up. That were when we saw 'er throat were cut. Wicked thing to do.'

'And the other bodies were recovered after the fire died?'

'Aye. Dark and shrivelled and . . .' The steward shuddered. 'We reckoned as the lord Olivier were made to watch as . . .' He shook his head.

'And everyone believed the killer was Ivo de Mitton.'

'Who else but 'im would 'ave wanted such a thing? Never liked the man, though not my place to say it. The lord Olivier were like 'is own father, but Messire Ivo were nothin' but a serpent in the bosom of 'is family.'

'And how might he have done it, since he had been cast out?' Bradecote wondered how much of the antipathy postdated the events, but it certainly showed that the steward, at least, still considered the man guilty of the heinous crime.

'Wicket gate in the palisade about the 'all were never latched, not in Mitton. No threat 'ad there ever been, and the land were more peaceable than these days when all manner of bad things goes on.'

'And the hall would not be barred from within at night?' Bradecote dropped the latch in his solar without thinking about it, but then he was a man with a wife.

'Well, the lord Olivier complained the latch bar in the solar were cracked and weak and wanted it replaced. Even told off Messire Ivo for not takin' care of the manor in 'is absence afore what 'appened with Mistress Rohese. A shoulder to the door would have got it open, and if them in the solar slept, I doubts it would 'ave been a noise to waken 'em.'

'And was there anything else that pointed to Messire Ivo being the killer?'

'Father said the ring were missin' from about the lady's neck. Belonged to 'er mother's father or some such, and she always said it would eventually go to Messire Ivo. Seems 'e wanted it sooner.'

Bradecote did not say that the maternal grandsire was also that of Eustace fitzRobert. The man had clearly made much of his Bellême lineage, but he might either have wanted it for himself or to keep it to use in the future. The fact that a gold ring had been mentioned in the 'confession' was, the undersheriff felt, significant. Had Eustace placed it on the dead hand of Ivo de Mitton just as he had placed the man's sword in his hand, or had de Mitton really obtained one upon pilgrimage to Santiago de Compostela and always worn it since?

'I see.' It was suitably noncommittal. 'And was it the lord Simon who had the new church built? The wood is not much weathered.'

'No, my father asked permission of the lord Sheriff, the last one, to build it where they died. All the men of the manor aided in the buildin' of it, out of respect, and the lord Sheriff allowed wood to be taken from the King's Forest. We was grateful for that 'acos we felt their spirits would not be at peace otherwise. When the lord Simon grew to man's years and took up the manor, 'e said 'e would see a stone church replace it, but thus far no mason 'as even come to look at the ground. But then, times is difficult – and now silver goes upon new 'orses.' The steward sighed.

Bradecote, who had seen four good harvests in a row fill the granaries of his holdings, and had excess to sell in Worcester, wondered why they were difficult here, but did not pursue farming matters.

'Has anyone other than us come to the manor to see your lord in the last two weeks?'

'No, my lord.' The answer was swift, perhaps too swift. The steward looked uncomfortable, and avoided the lord Undersheriff's eye.

'You are a poor liar, which does you some credit. I ask a second time whether anyone came to see the lord Simon this last week?'

'The lord of Ribbesford.' It was mumbled, guiltily, though it surprised Bradecote.

'When?'

'Four days afore you came, must 'ave been, my lord, in the forenoon.' The steward clearly did not think this was information he ought to hide, and then added, 'And this forenoon, though I told 'im the lord were out ridin', and so 'e could not see 'im.'

This meant William de Ribbesford had come across the river before he had decided to go to Rock and check upon his son's management of the harvest. He and de Mitton had not seemed close when they had both been viewing the body, so what had been the reason for that visit and why did he now want to see him again, so soon after? There would be questions for de Ribbesford when they returned to his hall, and instead of clarifying matters, Bradecote felt that although they now had more information, it was information that befogged their way to the truth. He hoped Catchpoll and Walkelin had fared better.

Catchpoll and Walkelin had decided to deal with the past and present separately, with Catchpoll delving into the tragedy of decades ago, and Walkelin ferreting in his seemingly innocuous way into recent events. In part this was because Catchpoll could claim his aching knees needed something to rub into them from the Mitton healer. He thought she would be very useful in finding out about one who had gone before her. He was in luck, for although she was still young in the craft and had only been the manor folk's source of salves, potions and advice for three years, she was a voluble young woman, who had clearly decided that talking as she did whatever she did would keep her patient at ease. It was therefore not difficult, once Catchpoll had described the 'mortal bad' ache in his knees when he had had to ride several days in a row, to set her off on the right path and then words flowed like a brook in spate.

'Oh yes, Aldith as cared for everyone afore me, well, she were Mitton's 'ealer a score o' years, and like me, came to it afore she expected. Poor soul, woke up one morn and could see nothin' at all, and me barely ready to deal with things alone. I asks 'er advice on the quiet, but not so as folk thinks I rely upon it. Understandin' she be, since she were little older 'n me when the time came for 'er to take up the responsibilities, and she could not ask questions, for the 'ealer afore 'er drowned in the river. Afore I were born that were, but my oldmother used to say that she chose the river, not that it took 'er, but them as thought it kept it from the priest so she could rest in blessed earth.'

'Why would she 'ave done such a thing?' Catchpoll sounded suitably shocked.

'Ah, well, years and years back somethin' terrible took place right 'ere. Our lord, the lord Simon de Mitton, well, 'e be the only one of 'is blood as lives since that time. Folk does not speak of it, but 'is brother, mother and sister perished, they did, in a fire set by 'is other brother.'

'But that would not make the 'ealer feel guilty, surely?'

'No, I suppose not, but . . .' The young woman frowned, and had clearly never thought beyond this point. Catchpoll therefore decided he needed to speak with the blind Aldith, and when his knees had been fully anointed with the unguent of the healer's preparing, he thanked her and went, quite spryly, to the cott she pointed out as her predecessor's.

The chamber was very gloomy within, since lamps would not aid the woman and in fact be more of a risk of fire, and the hearth had been provided with iron stakes at each corner and rods laid across to form a tangible barrier so that Aldith did not blunder into her only source of heat and cooking. Catchpoll announced himself and was open about what he sought to learn. The blind woman, who was, in Catchpoll's view, not old, being somewhere in her early forties, was not the sort who now sat and bemoaned her fate. As his eyes adjusted to the darkness, he saw that everything in the little dwelling was placed exactly, so that Aldith would know her way around easily and not mix things up or trip over anything. He thought she would be open with him and was not disappointed.

'Godgifu knew the craft well, and did much good, but she could be weak. She admitted as much to me afore she died. Afraid of sayin' no to some folk – some men – and it be better that we' – Aldith spoke of all her sorority of healers – 'fears nobody and tells and does true. Now, the men she feared most was, I grant, nasty men with cruelty runnin' in their veins like blood, but even so . . .' She shook her head. 'And the price paid was death.'

'Tell me about Rohese de Mitton and what happened to her.' Catchpoll did not command, but posed the question politely.

'Ah, you knows that much, then. A lovely girl she were, full of joy, and only a few years younger 'n me. When our lord Osmund died, the eldest son Olivier succeeded, and were a good young lord. Pity it were that the next brother, Messire Ivo, were as different as could be. When the lord Olivier went to complete 'is father's pilgrimage, Messire Ivo were left in control, and a bad day that were for Mitton. So keen to act "I am lord and none will say me nay" 'e were, and under the spell of that devil from Sudwale.' Aldith crossed herself. 'The priest says we was made in the image of God, but not 'im.' She paused, and then continued slowly. 'There be some men as dislikes women so much they takes 'em as punishment, not for desire. The lord of Sudwale were like that. There were tales from Sudwale, whispers. Mistress Rohese 'ad no time for the man and showed it. The lord of Ribbesford, over the river, were goin' to marry 'er, and both seemed pleased with the match. Mayhap the lord of Sudwale did not like their 'appiness, I does not know, but one summer's day, when the maid went to the river to cool 'er feet, 'e went also and not only left 'er no longer a maid but tried to kill 'er. This I know, for Godgifu told me, as Mistress Rohese eventually told 'er. She were brought to us, for I were Godgifu's apprentice then, most part drowned, and 'er face so broken as nothin' could make it good. Godgifu did all she could, and if she 'ad possessed less craft then the poor soul would 'ave died.' She paused for a moment. 'I knows it sounds wrong, 'specially for an 'ealer to say, but I sometimes thought afterwards it might 'ave been better she died after all. Could not even try and speak for weeks, and even swallowin' were a trial. Never beheld a face that broken, Serjeant, nor would I again even if my eyes could see. What were left of 'er face were no face at all one side, and if children 'ad seen it they would wake at night screamin'.' She shook her head at the memory as if to dispel the image within.

'But surely a brother would seek out any man as did that to 'is sister?' Catchpoll was still acting the shocked listener.

'You would think so, Serjeant. Once 'er wits was back and she could at least try and speak, which were many weeks later, she named the lord of Sudwale as the man as beat 'er, though she 'ad no memory of what else occurred and we 'ad seen from the other injuries. Sometimes, when things is too bad, the mind shuts 'em out, you understand?'

Catchpoll nodded.

'Messire Ivo said it were a madness and she were possessed of the Devil to besmirch the lord of Sudwale's good name. Ha, good name! The only name 'e deserved were Devil's Bastard, on my good oath and 'ope of 'Eaven. A bare few days later what had been foisted upon 'er came away very early. I would 'ave kept it quiet, but Aldith said 'er mother ought to know, and that were when Messire Ivo overheard and demanded to see the "proof". Now, we women sees things as men does not. If a woman loses very early, what comes be not a babe, but a tiny, strange thing as God must turn into a babe later, when the belly swells and the child quickens. Master Ivo said it were a dragon's seed, then a devil, and demanded Godgifu say as much. She ought to 'ave stood 'er ground, but she dared not, and then the messire went to the priest, who were a man with as much understandin' as my neighbour's rooster, and 'e saw it as a devil too. I thinks then Messire Ivo realised sayin' she were whored by the Devil would damage the family name too much, so 'e picked upon the rash on the back of the poor soul's hand and said it were leprosy. Serjeant, many a child gets a rash in the crease o' the elbow or knee, on the back of their little 'and, and 'tis nothin' dangerous. Seems worse for some if they is worried or upset and what more upset could the poor girl 'ave gone through? It were not leprosy, but the lord of Sudwale told Godgifu that if she did not say it were, then 'e would say that she were a witch and 'ad procured the Mistress Rohese for Satan, and they would both be drowned in the river. She gave in. You knows the poor young lady were declared "dead" by the Church and cast out?'

'Yes.'

'A short while after, the lord Olivier returned and Godgifu and 'is mother, who should 'ave spoken but were too cowed, spoke up. Then the messire were the one cast out, and a message sent to Worcester about what the lord of Sudwale 'ad done, but the messire returned and killed all 'is kinfolk in a fire. Godgifu felt the weight of all those deaths and blamed 'erself. Well, I says she bore some, but nothin' compared to the men as did the deeds. Preyed upon 'er it did, and a few weeks later she went to do the washin' at the river's edge, but not when any other woman went, and – the body were found caught beneath a willow bough. The bank were not steep, nor slippery there. None ever came to fall in, yet she did. So she drowned 'erself, as the lord of Sudwale 'ad threatened 'er with, and I came to my full duties earlier than I expected. That be the whole of it, Serjeant, and every word true.'

'I have no doubt of it, mistress. You know that Ivo de Mitton is now dead, by violence?'

'Aye, and I says 'tis *wyrd*, and also God's Will, though too late for the good souls as perished 'cos of the man. May they rest in peace and Ivo de Mitton burn in the fires of Hell itself, alongside the lord of Sudwale when 'is time comes to be judged.'

'And none would say otherwise, mistress, me included. Thank you.' Catchpoll went to the door, but then asked a final question. 'You may not see now, but your callin' means you noticed more'n most folk. Do you recall anything about Messire Ivo, in the look of 'im?'

'Never looked lordly to me, Serjeant, for all that 'e made much of 'isself. There were a scar on 'is fore'ead, and 'e disliked it so much 'e grew 'is locks long at the front to disguise it, though it flopped about and did not cover it much. Looked quite funny, the way 'e kept pullin' it forward, though none dared laugh at it to 'is face. In truth, Ivo de Mitton were forgettable, and that is what I were glad to do once 'e left.'

'Then again thanks, mistress.' Catchpoll opened the door and stood for a few moments, blinking in the sunlight as his eyes readjusted. Whilst not much of what had been learnt was new, it corroborated what they had been told before, and painted a more detailed picture.

Walkelin had begun his enquiries very much in 'just a man-at-arms' mode, since he sensed that acting as a shrieval officer might well make simple folk reluctant to speak up. He was met with blank looks when he asked if any lordly men had visited the manor in recent days, other than the woman who said that the lord of Ribbesford, who rarely came to see the lord Simon, had come a few days past.

'I suppose 'e does not like to come to Mitton, for brother-close 'e were to the poor lord Olivier, God rest 'is soul.' The woman crossed herself piously, and sighed. Upon further enquiry, she said that she could not say which day he came, 'But 'twere in the last week for sure.'

Walkelin was pleased that he would have at least something of interest to report. It then occurred to him to speak with the priest. A priest knew his parishioners well, and whilst the sanctity of the confessional was always paramount, in other things priests were inclined to be open and forthcoming. They were also not as ordinary manor folk, and not subject to the lord, or the steward.

Walkelin was in luck, for the incumbent was in the garden of his home next to the wooden church. He looked up from weeding his onions when Walkelin hailed him.

'Can I help you, my son?'

'I 'opes so, Father.' Walkelin had been pleased to see the man was far nearer Catchpoll's age than his own, so it might just be that he had information on the past as well as the present. 'I am Walkelin, the lord Sheriff's Underserjeant, and we are seekin' the truth about the killin' of Ivo de Mitton, found dead across in Ribbesford woods. We wondered if 'e came back to Mitton afore crossin' the Severn.'

'I never saw Ivo de Mitton, though I know of the tragedy that occurred here, of course. I was sent here by the lord Bishop, when my predecessor, er, decided to return to the cloister.' The priest looked a little embarrassed. 'I was newly ordained, and

200

was surprised at the faith he had in me, coming to a parish that had suffered and where trust, even belief, was shaken.'

'Yet you is here still, Father, so it seems the trust were well founded.' Walkelin smiled at the cleric, and his open, honest features drew a smile in return.

'Yes, I suppose that is true, Serjeant.' The priest elevated his rank, which sounded odd, but, Walkelin realised, only slightly.

'You would not 'ave recognised the man, but did any lord come to visit the lord Simon this last week, a Templar knight mayhap?'

'I saw no Templar here, only going towards Sudwale, when I returned from giving communion to the poor lady there. Her mind, alas, is much clouded and her sight is so poor as to be almost nothing, but it does not mean she should be prevented from partaking of the Holy Sacrament.'

'Sudwale be part of this parish?' Walkelin was genuinely surprised by this.

'Indeed. I do not think it was ever a prosperous manor where the village about it would grow, and when it lost its lord and his lady mother had the ordering of it, I think it lost its way as she did. I believe now that it has been settled that in God's good time, the lord Simon, as nearest kin, will inherit, and it may then change. It has been trapped in the past, if you understand me.'

'Yes, Father, I do. What can you tell me of this Templar, and how many days past did you see him?' Walkelin kept the eagerness from his voice, though it was not easy.

'Let me see. It must be the better part of a week. I was on my way back, and had gone there shortly after Sext and spent some time with the poor lady, so it must have been a little after the time for None. I had left the track to pick some plump blackberries.' He paused, and frowned. 'I do not think that was theft, Serjeant, was it? I mean, did the berries belong to the lady of Sudwale? They were wild fruit.'

'I am sure they was just God's bounty, Father.' Walkelin had no idea if that was legally true, but he did not want to distract the priest, and he knew that hedgerow fruits around Worcester were considered as belonging to none.

'Yes, that was my feeling, and I gave thanks for them even as they stained my fingers and the brambles pricked and scratched my hands.'

'And the Templar knight?'

'Not one knight, Serjeant, but two. They were riding towards Sudwale, and I am not even sure they saw me, for I was among the bushes and they were deep in speech, a little heatedly, I thought, and not much aware of what was not immediately before them.'

'Can you describe 'em, or even the 'orses?'

'I saw them in profile only, you understand. The one nearer to me had a neat beard, brown, and his nose was straight. His horse was chestnut, and a fine beast. The other horse was a bay, and did not move very easily. I could not see the rider beyond he wore the same garb as his companion. They wore cloaks, but had them cast back over their shoulders, it being quite warm that part of the afternoon. I was quite hot in my habit.' He smiled, then continued. 'Of course they need not have stopped in Sudwale, and might have turned as easily towards the other manors of Kidderminster.'

Walkelin, thinking the chance of any other Templars being in the area at the time was nil, doubted that was the case.

'And can you say for sure how many days ago you went to Sudwale?' Walkelin was already able to make a very likely guess, but wanted corroboration.

'Let me see.' The priest paused, and counted the days upon his bony-jointed fingers. 'Yes. It was six days ago.' He said it triumphantly, as though a feat of arithmetic and memory.

'That has aided us, Father.' Walkelin smiled, and a Walkelin smile was a very genuine thing. 'I would ask one thing more. You said your predecessor returned to the cloister. Do you know where?'

'Oh yes. I think it was a poor decision for him to have been sent here, in truth, for his English was still – lacking. He returned to Astley Priory, where the brethren, the choir monks, come from Normandy. Poor Father Julian. I am sure their prayers and fraternal bond healed him, but I think he went back to Normandy some years ago.'

Walkelin tried not to look jubilant when he met with his superiors, but he certainly felt he had discovered something potentially very important.

Chapter Eleven

The discovery that the lord Undersheriff had also found out that William de Ribbesford had visited Mitton, and also on which particular day, did not diminish Walkelin's exuberance, since he knew his other information was far more important. The only difficulty was not rushing his words as he presented his finding, and it was clear from their expressions that his news was well received.

'So they did not visit Mitton but went on to Sudwale and Eustace fitzRobert must 'ave seen the poor state of 'is mother, and learnt that Simon de Mitton will take over the manor on 'er death, if'n Eustace be thought long dead and gone. Doubt that would please 'im, my lord.' Walkelin successfully kept the jubilation from his face but not his voice as he explained what the priest had told him.

'Oh, I am pretty sure that would anger him mightily, Walkelin.' Bradecote paused, thinking. 'Which also gives us a reason why Eustace might have decided to kill Ivo at this point, even if he had not done so before. It makes "here" even more reasonable.'

'But now there would be Simon de Mitton in 'is way, my lord.' Walkelin looked a little puzzled.

'I think the plan changed a bit.' Catchpoll's eyes glinted. 'We 'as to go back. Avoidin' this side o' the Severn would 'ave been wise if they was simply on their way to the lord de Mortemer at Wigmore, and fitzRobert probably just thought at some point 'e would do the deed and kill Ivo de Mitton so that the plan worked. And the lord Sheriff would find out about the "plot". Also, Astley Priory would be a good place to spend a night in comfort rather than in the open, and the monks would not talk of their visitors. But some word of 'ow things lies in Sudwale must 'ave reached Eustace in the priory, so 'e made a plan, a clever one, for the confession would take away bein' accused of foul murders and means 'e could, at least one day, return to Sudwale. 'E then suggested they visit Sudwale, which might be the reason they was arguin' on the way there, and I would guess Ivo de Mitton were left feelin' they was wastin' time, while Eustace were with the lady.'

'Except there was the accusation of rape and great violence upon Rohese de Mitton, Catchpoll.'

'True, my lord, but that were so long ago, and the lord Sheriff be different and 'e could say 'e knew nothin' of it and 'ad just gone away from choice, and none could prove otherwise. 'E could not know Rohese de Mitton would still be alive.'

'Fair enough. And so Eustace sees the frail state of his mother and knows time is not with him. Taking the manor back from Simon would be harder than inheriting from her.' Bradecote had worked it through to the end now. 'He kills Ivo de Mitton, the "confessed" murderer. There is, he believes, no way that it can be proved he murdered the de Mittons and set fire to the hall. If he now appears, all innocent as the prodigal son, returned after years atoning for the sins of his youth, he could make his claim with ease.'

'Except the *Hrafn Wif* would be able to make the accusation of rape and an attempt to kill 'er, my lord.' Walkelin raised the caveat. 'So she would be in danger.'

'Yes, but he does not know such a person even exists, and if he did hear of her, as Catchpoll says, why would he think that it was Rohese de Mitton still living? Only William de Ribbesford knows her identity, and the last person he would ever tell would be fitzRobert. Even if the man reclaimed his position and honours, would she, after all the years alone as a wild thing, avoiding being seen by people, be prepared to go to Worcester and accuse him before the Justices? She seemed reluctant even speaking with the two of us, so I doubt it.'

'That may be, my lord, but we looks too far ahead. What we needs to do is take up Eustace fitzRobert for the killin' of Ivo de Mitton and the man killed to be dressed as the Templar, for which 'e will dangle, assuredly. And all of this plan means Eustace fitzRobert needs to remain close by, which be good for us. We will catch the bastard.'

'And, Holy Virgin, it will be bad for Simon de Mitton! He went to Bridgnorth yesterday and bought a horse, a chestnut horse with a white star upon its forehead, and has gone riding today. You often speak of *wyrd*, Catchpoll, and I have an awful feeling that *wyrd* will have meant that horse is the one fitzRobert was riding the day he killed Ivo de Mitton. Even if he did not recognise Simon de Mitton as a man grown, he would know the horse if he has come "home" and saw it, and that alone might well lead to a killing, let alone if de Mitton recognised him and saw himself as an avenger upon the man who led to his family's fall. We need to find Simon de Mitton. It takes priority over visiting Sudwale. The steward was not helpful about his lord's whereabouts today, but if he knows he is in danger he might be more forthcoming.'

Without waiting for any response, Bradecote turned and headed back to the barn, with Catchpoll and Walkelin almost running to keep up with his long stride.

When it was made clear that his lord was in mortal danger, the steward gave up all he knew, but it was precious little.

'My lord, I can only say that the lord Simon most often stays this side o' the river, and does not ride out for long, if just for exercise. In truth, I were beginnin' to wonder if the animal 'ad thrown 'im, and, bein' new, it would not come back to its stable as the old 'un did the time 'e tumbled from it.'

'What do we do now?' Bradecote ran his long fingers through his hair and looked at Catchpoll. 'We might split up and try different directions, but there are more than three ways he might have gone, and he need not even have kept to the trackways, now the harvest is in. He could go across country.'

'I still think we goes to Sudwale, my lord, or leastways in that direction. If fitzRobert came back, why would 'e want to go beyond Sudwale? We said 'e would want to remain close by, and that means as long as de Mitton did not ride north, or just break 'is neck fallin' off a beast too lively for 'im, all will be well.' Catchpoll did not look as though he really thought all was well at all. 'But you can't avoid *wyrd,* and so much of all this 'as been *wyrd* so far, I would not wish to say it does not steer things still.' He shook his head.

'My lord.' The steward, seeing the grim expressions upon the faces of the lord Sheriff's men, spoke up again. 'The threshin' be important, but this be more so. I will get every man of Mitton that be fit and able, and send 'em out in pairs, if it might aid you.'

'Well, the more pairs of eyes and ears the better, and tell them that they look for their lord, and not necessarily the horse, for it might have run away or been taken away. They look foremost for a fallen rider.'

'Aye, my lord. I will go and tell 'em right away.' The steward went back into the threshing barn, and Bradecote heard his voice raised and the beating of the wheat stalks cease.

'So let us hope we find nothing on the way to Sudwale, and a manor that has not seen its lord in many years. Come on.' Bradecote almost ran to the stables.

William de Ribbesford was an unhappy man, and it was definitely not because his overlord's presence had meant another night sleeping upon the dais in his own hall. He was a dutiful vassal, and also respected his overlord, but felt he had been commanded to undertake what was a task with very little chance of success, and, if he did encounter Eustace fitzRobert, a man who must have had ample killing experience in the Holy Land and had never had qualms about taking life, he was not entirely certain he could defeat him. Even if he did so, he was not sure de Mortemer's assurance that it would not have consequences held true. Several days with Hugh Bradecote and the lord Sheriff's serjeants under his roof had shown him men who took the Law very seriously indeed, and were not simply going to accept anything they were told. He had even wondered if he would have to inflict some injury upon himself to support his claim of self-defence, and then faced the unpleasant reality that he would probably not come out of any encounter with Eustace fitzRobert unscathed anyway. William de Ribbesford had always been a man by nature quiet and peaceable. Depressing and worrying as this was, it was not the thing that made him most unhappy. He felt honour bound to go to Rohese and tell her that the man who was believed to have killed her brother was the man who had ruined her life, that she must have been within feet of him, and that he might yet be in the vicinity. He was not sure how she would react, for he felt she had grown more and more a wild creature of instinct, and, if he was honest, perhaps even a little mad, which was hardly surprising. She always mentioned her 'friends' the ravens, as if they were family, and sometimes he felt she took a moment even to recognise him. Might she lose her wits completely at the revived thought of Eustace fitzRobert?

Having spent a very uncomfortable night in more ways than one, it was a tired lord of Ribbesford who saw his overlord and his men-at-arms make their preparations and depart well into the September morning. He watched them until they disappeared from his view, and then went first to the threshing barn. He was not going to have work cease for some hunt through the woods as though beating for boar, since the lives of everyone on the manor depended upon the harvest and the grain being stored for the year to come. However, he did announce that everyone should report to Herluin the Steward any men who were unknown to them, whom they saw pass through

Ribbesford or cross the ford. He received puzzled looks, but he thought it better than making them even more frightened. The killing of Ivo de Mitton had been the first violent death any had ever heard of within the manor boundaries, and he could sense the disquiet and nervousness. Having discharged at least this duty, he shut himself in his solar, staring into space and trying to work out how best to tell Rohese that her remaining brother now knew she lived, and that the cause of all her woes was likely to be in the vicinity and meant her life was at risk. His failure to find Simon de Mitton at home the previous day had been, in his own mind, a good thing, although he knew it only delayed the meeting, and he had felt Fate had played a trick upon him when he had encountered him about to cross the ford. The exchange, mounted, was more brief and to the point than he had intended, but trying to reach the 'confession' in a roundabout way would not work when the man was heading homeward and upon a horse that was new to him and clearly impatient with its unknown rider. Now he was facing the harder task. He went to the church to hear Father Laurentius say Matins and then remained in the cool silence alone, praying for guidance. It was thus not long before noon when he walked up the track at an almost funereal pace and then turned off into the woods. Rohese was not at the cave, but then he heard the ravens down towards the river, so followed the sound down the slope and across the narrow swathe of flatter land towards the riverbank. It was then the ravens announced his presence, and so he called, lest she think some stranger approached.

'Wait. Stay back.' The female voice was urgent. He coloured

though none but one of the ravens, now peering at him accusingly from an alder bough, saw the blush. Rohese would not have sounded so urgent if she had merely been collecting water from the river. He waited obediently, and a few minutes later the black-swathed figure emerged from where willow gave way to birch.

'I am sorry.' He almost stumbled in his apology. 'There is something you need to know. My lord commands me to seek, around this manor, the man who killed your brother, as the agent of William fitzAlan of Oswestry and . . .' Now the time came to say the words, they half choked him. 'And that man, the one who killed Ivo, could well have been Eustace fitzRobert.' There, it was said.

For a long moment there was silence, then came a long drawn-out hiss.

'No. Not after so long. Why would they be companions still and then one kill the other? And I did not recognise them. I only knew it was Ivo – afterwards.'

'If you saw no faces, nor heard a voice, why would you, after all this time, and with it so unlikely either would return? I am sorry. You had to know, and also be warned. Eustace is dangerous.'

This was met immediately by a cackling laugh so like the gurgling croak of a raven it was as if she had learnt their 'speech'. William de Ribbesford could hear why it had been so easy to have the inhabitants of his manor believe in a shape-changer. Even he found it slightly unnerving.

'You tell me, *me*, he is dangerous, my lord?' There was a pause and the familiar sucking sound. 'Of all people on God's earth, do I not know this every second of my life?'

'Yes, of course, but – I meant that if he should be at large and return this side of the river, you are at risk – again.'

'I am glad to be warned, but not out of fear.' The dry, rasping voice dropped several tones, and made what sounded to William de Ribbesford not a threat but a promise. 'If I see him before he sees me, do not look elsewhere for the Devil's Spawn.'

There was another pause, and the voice reverted to its form of normal. 'And remember your own words, my lord. I have wondered, many times, whether he did what he did out of lust, or also spite. Sometimes in dreams, I think he mentioned your name. Perhaps that was half the reason, to take what would be yours, William, so be careful.' She rarely used his name, and it caused a wave of reminiscence to flood over him. They had both been so young, and if not in love with her, he had been teetering on the edge of that emotion. She had possessed beautiful eyes, a soft voice and a ready mind. She was very pretty, and always so vibrant. It had all shrivelled into this black, faceless form that was but an echo of the Rohese de Mitton he had been about to wed. Such a tragic waste, and had it had something to do with him, and the animosity that had existed between him and Eustace fitzRobert? He had loathed him, but yes, also been jealous of the charisma he exuded. William de Ribbesford knew he had never possessed that. He was always the sort of man people paused when recalling and then said 'Ah yes' in a vague way. Nobody had ever said that about Eustace fitzRobert. So had the terrible things happened to Rohese because they had become betrothed and he had been happy? It made his heart grow cold at the thought, and if, in that moment, Eustace fitzRobert had appeared before him, there would have been no indecision about taking his life as forfeit for the past.

'I am sorry, Rohese.' It was heartfelt, but seemed of little worth, for it could change nothing.

She looked at him through the thin black veiling that kept her face from the world, and saw in that moment the young man he had been all those years ago, when they had a future together and it seemed bright and positive.

'You have nothing to be sorry for.' Her voice was tired and flat. 'I should not have told you.' She sighed, though it was more of a hiss.

'I wish I could have done more for you.'

'You have done as no other would have done.' Her hand brushed away his wish. 'And have kept me secret. I know that.'

De Ribbesford's guilt increased, and he bit his lip. He could not face telling her that he had encountered her brother Simon the previous afternoon and revealed that she still lived.

'Thank you for the warning.' It was a dismissal, though gently given, and she turned away, calling the ravens to follow her.

He walked back along the riverbank towards the ford, but then cut up before the track across the stubbled field to reach his hall. He thought again about his encounter at the ford with Simon de Mitton on his new horse. Deep in thought, having built himself up to revealing Rohese's existence and then finding de Mitton away from home, he was so surprised to see him right there before him that the chestnut, with its white star, had not registered in his mind as the description of one of the horses ridden by the men now known to be Ivo de Mitton and Eustace fitzRobert. It registered now.

De Mitton would have been happy just to show off his horse, and felt rather put out when he had halted him before he had even got into his stride. All the ways he had planned to lead carefully to his revelation disappeared, and he had simply said there was something very important that de Mitton should now know.

'Which is?' Simon de Mitton had scowled at him, and so he had declared, without preamble, that his sister lived.

'Why tell me such a lie? She was buried with my mother and—'

'Not Iveta. Rohese.'

There had been silence, broken only by the untroubled cooing of a wood pigeon on a nearby bough.

'Oh, I know that she was declared "dead" falsely. I was told that long, long ago.'

'No, not that she was alive, but lives still.'

'If she had been anywhere near Mitton she would have returned when Olivier came back. She and Olivier were always close. She did not, so she was far away, and if she was forced to live with lepers, real lepers, then most likely it passed to her and she is long in the earth or so crippled by the disease as to make even the thought of seeing her unbearable. Leave her dead and be sure I pray for her soul.'

'You do not wish to know how she has managed? I have done what I can and – she is your sister.'

'She *was* my sister.' It had been said with finality, and Simon de Mitton had urged his horse into the water and splashed across, setting off at a canter the other side as if to put as much ground between him and Ribbesford as possible.

Perhaps, de Ribbesford told himself, as he entered his hall, if Simon de Mitton refused to acknowledge the revealed secret, then telling him had not been not such a betrayal of Rohese after all.

'Who do I deceive other than myself? Every time I see her I will know I did what she would not want. I was strong enough not to tell Olivier all that time ago. I should have been as strong now.' Yet a voice in his head reminded him it had been done because others already knew. It did not help the guilt. He sat alone for some hours in his solar, gazing into space, his brow furrowed and his lips compressed, and finally resolved to go to Father Laurentius. After all, telling him, within the constraints of the confessional, was not like telling another living soul.

Father Laurentius had been the priest of Ribbesford for eighteen years and was a good judge of men. None were perfect, including himself, and some in Ribbesford had been lambs that had strayed at times, but he accounted William de Ribbesford an honest and godly man, and a fair, even thoughtful, lord. His sins were the commonplace sins of every man, and when he made confession it was genuine but never an ordeal. When he came to the church as he prepared to say None the man was before the church door, looking distraught, almost in tears, which shocked the priest.

'Good Father, I must speak with you.'

Father Laurentius opened his mouth to suggest that he say the Office with him, but then decided that whatever burdened William de Ribbesford so heavily should be heard immediately. He felt sure that God would consider he had made the right decision.

'Come into God's house, my son, and relieve your soul. I will listen.'

'In part it is advice I need, but I would ask it all be considered within the sanctity of confession, Father, for another's sake.'

'Then it shall be so.' The priest exuded calm, and, once within, took the lord by the arm and pressed him to rest against the little ledge that the most ancient and frail sat upon during the services. He then sat quietly at his side.

'How can I help you?'

William de Ribbesford took a deep breath, and began. If Father Laurentius was surprised to learn that a woman had lived a feral life within his parish all the years of his ministry there, he did not show it, nor did he show his distress that her seclusion meant that she had not received the benefit of the Sacrament in all that time. He had been swift to carry the cross to protect those who went to collect the body of the murdered man, but had he himself been guilty of preferring to think of all the whisperings and warnings of the *Hrafn Wif* over the years as mere tales, and not had the courage to make efforts to find out if there was a kernel of truth within them and a soul to give succour? Even lepers, though they might not enter the church building, had access to the Mass. He consoled himself with the thought that she would have been kept from many temptations and most of the sins of the everyday, stemming from lust, greed and jealousy, and he hoped her faith remained. That she had not given up in spirit and cast herself into the Severn long ago inclined him to think that it might.

The torment of William de Ribbesford's guilt was a different matter.

'My son, that you feel this weight upon you shows that your conscience is strong within you, which is a good thing in all men, but you have thought too much in this case. In many moral situations the path is not clear, and none seems a perfect answer, so what we can do is our best. You only went to tell the lord of Mitton about his sister when you knew he might hear of it from strangers, and with less knowledge of her, and when the secret was no longer intact. You did this thing even though it pained you to do so, for a good and godly reason. Your guilt, which you assign to the deed, comes from your conscience telling you that you should reveal to her whom you have aided and protected as best you could for all this time, what you have done. It is that "cowardice" that besets you, and so it can be alleviated by taking courage and doing so.'

'But she will be disappointed in me, and may even refuse further contact, Father.'

'It might be her immediate reaction, but even a little time would mean that changed, for she knows that what you do is done from love.'

'Father!' William de Ribbesford sounded shocked. 'I never—'

'Ah no! I do not mean the lustful love between man and woman, but the love of one soul for another, which is a more glorious and Christ-like love, untainted by anything of the flesh. You have come to love her.'

William de Ribbesford made a sound somewhere between a gasp and a sob, realising that it was true and that he had kept the thought from him because he could not process it as the priest had done. The acceptance of it flooded him like a crashing wave.

'Yes. When first she came to me, all those years ago, I acted out of charity and because I felt a responsibility as the man to whom she had been betrothed. Little by little it has become because I truly want to protect her and give what little I can to a life lived without comforts. I offered once to have a cott built in the woods, saying it was for an anchoress, so she could still be apart and private, but she said no to that.' He gave a choked laugh. 'And her reason? She said her "friends" would not like to live in a place enclosed with a door. Her only "friends" are the ravens. She has names for them, and the oldest, the one she found fallen from its nest many years ago, it has learnt to laugh as she laughs, or perhaps she laughs like it does, and makes a sound that is almost "Go!".' He shook his head. 'I do not know if it is the loneliness or a gentle madness that binds her to birds of death, the battlefield searchers.' He paused, and then said slowly, 'We meet no more than once in a month, few words are said, but there is a bond as close as blood between us. I would defend her with my life and I could not bear to see that weakened.'

'That is not quite so, for you are her friend also. The bond of which you speak, to be so strong, has to be mutual, my son, and so you being honest with her will not weaken it. Do what your God-directed conscience tells you, and be at peace with yourself and her.'

'Thank you, Father. I will.'

When the church door closed, Father Laurentius said None, for better the Office be said late than not at all, and then he prayed, most assiduously, for a lady whose only friends were ravens, and the lord of Ribbesford.

* * *

Rohese de Mitton, though she barely felt herself named at all any more, other than with the sound the ravens made that she was sure was their 'word' for her, sat upon the rudimentary bed in her cave with her head in her hands. One of the ravens, perched upon the hedge-like partition, cocked its head on one side and watched her silently. She did not weep, or make any sound beyond the frequent sucking, sniffing noise as she tried to hold back the constant drip from her nose, where the damaged sinus leaked permanently. Even had it stopped, the action had become habitual. She had not thought of Eustace fitzRobert, or her other life, at all in many years, until she had seen the raven-ravaged face of her brother Ivo, since to do so was pointless, and it had become a vague dream that no longer contacted reality. What she had said to that dead face in the church had been true, for she felt that his death where she might know of it had been a gift, but afterwards she realised that in fact it came at a price, because it brought the distant past back into focus. She had even been so foolish, one night, to lie and dream what life might have been like if Eustace fitzRobert had not found her paddling in the river that day. The son of which William de Ribbesford was so proud might have been hers, the adventurous little boy she had glimpsed once or twice in the woods as he grew up, the young man she had espied upon his horse now that he was full grown. There would have been family, and love as she had felt it as a child herself. From that thought also came the recollection of mother, father, sister and brothers, though the memory was so vague they were but the sound of a laugh, a comforting hand, a voice that sang, and they vanished like the smoke from her hearth. There had been tears then. At no point had she thought of the physical advantages of living in a hall, for her mind had rejected all memory of such comforts.

Seeing Ivo was one thing; knowing Eustace fitzRobert was close by, and had been within her vision when she had seen the two knights, made her feel sick, not with fear, but with frustrated anger. He had taken her life, the life she would have had, and all her family, even Ivo, and there had been no justice. She rocked silently to and fro, and imagined him before her, close enough for her to achieve it at last at the tip of her knife, which had never done anything more violent than gutting fish. The reality was that he would be far stronger than her, and would almost certainly kill her, but it was good to feel it was possible, though Father Laurentius would have shaken his head over it.

Chapter Twelve

Eustace fitzRobert still hoped to reach his manor before noon, though for the last mile or so the bay had been nursed along at walking pace, and if he did not have to dismount before Sudwale and lead the beast in lame, it would be a miracle. He vowed that when he had resumed his lordship and next went to Worcester, he would sell it with pleasure, even at a cheap price. Returning to the horse dealer in Bridgnorth would not be wise for some time, not if he was riding his chestnut again. The bay had been Ivo de Mitton's, and the man had ever been a poor judge of horseflesh. FitzRobert had not enjoyed riding the bay that day to Astley, but it had been important that he had been seen upon it to reinforce that he was Ivo de Mitton, since he was sure that questions would be asked of whoever took the 'confession' to the lord Sheriff. It needed to tally with any sighting of Ivo thereafter. That Ivo had not even questioned why he had said that they should swap horses, upon the excuse that it was showing signs of lameness and he was marginally the lighter man, had never been in doubt, for even after all these years Ivo was still the 'loyal hound', willing to do anything for his master's approval. Long ago it been amusing and useful, and Eustace fitzRobert had assumed that it would eventually diminish, but it never had. Ivo the obedient fool would say yes to any suggestion, obey any command. Perhaps he had simply stopped thinking for himself. No, that was not quite true, because on that last day he had been – different. There had been a tension in him, from the moment they left Astley, and he had been unusually tight-lipped until they skirted Mitton but took the diversion to Sudwale. Then he had complained about the delay, questioned Eustace's decision and even argued out loud with him, and he never did that. Only later, at the end, had Eustace discovered why.

When they had first fled England, it had been Eustace's idea that they go to France and see if their great-uncle Guimar was remembered in Bellême, since that would mean them being treated better than being 'unknowns from nowhere'. The ideas were always his. As it turned out, Guimar had indeed been remembered, but for all the wrong reasons, and the familial connection had proved awkward. It had then been his idea that they should go to Santiago de Compostela, which Ivo had assumed was because their grandsire had done so, and had sighed, repeatedly, over the fact that he ought to have inherited his grandsire's pilgrim ring. In reality, Eustace had seen having pilgrim credentials there would be a good way to earn trust in the future, since someone who could describe the shrine had not simply taken someone's token. Rather than make the gruelling pilgrimage from France, they had taken a ship from Bénodet in Brittany, and crossed the Bay of Biscay, most uncomfortably, to Ferrol. Not only did this save many days of arduous walking, it was the route usually taken by pilgrims from England. It was the shortest pilgrim trail on Spanish soil, but then the English pilgrims would have walked from wherever they lived in England before taking ship at the south coast. Eustace, however, had no intention of wearing out shoe leather, or worse, going barefoot, for the good of his soul, so they rode to just beyond Sigüeiro, which was generally the last place pilgrims slept before the final few miles to the fulfilment of their vow and the glories of the resting place of St James the Apostle. They found an accommodating widow who was prepared, at a reasonable cost, to stable their horses during the following day. They thus walked virtuously into Santiago de Compostela as if devout souls filled with joy at the end of a long and tiring pilgrimage and bought, with every appearance of legitimacy, shell badges and various mementoes that would advertise their piety to the world thereafter. Eustace had actively encouraged Ivo to buy the thin gold ring that would remind him of his lost inheritance, simply because he liked the idea that Ivo would never know the actual ring of their grandsire hung in the little bag about Eustace's neck, where he said he kept a trinket that Robert de Bellême had given to his mother as a keepsake, and which was too small to be worn. That he had torn it from about the neck of Ivo's mother just before he cut her throat added a certain extra thrill to it. He glanced down at his left hand. It still felt 'new' wearing it now, and he was inclined to play with it, turning it upon the little finger, where it was a little loose, since it had felt uncomfortably tight on its neighbour.

There had been no long-term plan all that time ago, but the pair had eventually ended up in Outremer where they spent years adventuring, 'protecting' travellers, whether merchants or pilgrims, and accepting gifts of gratitude, or quietly stealing their silver if nothing looked forthcoming. If they killed a Saracen, his horse fetched a fine price, and his sword even more. It was a life living just dangerously enough to be exciting, and then, some months back, he had decided they should return to England. He still did not know why he had come to the decision. Perhaps it had been homesickness after all. The sun was suddenly too hot and the travellers not generous enough and too wary. England, damp, green England, with its fertile fields and dappled woods of oak and ash, would be better than the heat of the Levant, and the past was so long ago buried it would not be remembered anywhere beyond that little area on the eastern bank of the Severn. What was more, the political turmoil of the last few years would mean opportunities for those not too scrupulous but of good birth. Rumours and news were always months old by the time they reached the Holy Land, but the final thing that had made them head homeward had been when Eustace learnt that the fortunes and influence of William fitzAlan, lord of Oswestry, had risen with the Empress Maud, and that Bridgnorth, the place he always felt at heart should have belonged to him, had been given some time since by King Stephen into the custody of the lord of Wigmore. The de Mortemers and fitzAlans had long been rivals in the Marches, and Eustace fitzRobert began to see a way forward.

When they landed back in England, he and Ivo de Mitton had sought out William fitzAlan, presenting themselves as men who had cleansed their souls upon Crusade and now sought to aid good King Henry's daughter in taking her rightful throne. They could speak of the right people, and the right places, and were perfectly plausible. It had then been easy to offer a way in which the lord of Wigmore, though it was the son of the one Eustace remembered, could be toppled from royal favour once and for all and to the advance of fitzAlan. Only two parts of the plan were not set out in detail, the first of which was how the damning document would be 'lost' so that it would find its way into the hands of William de Beauchamp, lord Sheriff of Worcestershire. Eustace had assured fitzAlan that he would find a way that could not fail, and left it at that. The second thing was that the pair would be travelling in the guise of Templar knights. This was because Eustace became aware that fitzAlan was much inclined towards the Order, and was already talking of making grants of land to the Templars when he regained his estates. He was unlikely to approve of the deception, but Eustace had seen the respect and even deference accorded to a Templar who had been on the ship that brought them from Vigo to Falmouth, and saw it as a way to put themselves above suspicion and also to put them in plain sight until the time they chose to remove the disguise and 'disappear'. In the end FitzAlan, who liked the idea but had more important matters claiming his attention, happily dictated the message, set his seal upon it and then forgot about them within three days of their departure.

Eustace fitzRobert prided himself on his ability to adapt and to think beyond the simple next step. He had not set off with the idea of murdering his companion, but it had occurred to him that if the message was found upon a body, which would have to be reported to the lord Sheriff, it guaranteed that the plan would work. It was as they drew closer to places they had once known that Ivo's repeated bemoaning of how life had been unfair to him had driven Eustace (thereby putting the onus of blame upon Ivo de Mitton) to consider the idea that the body should be that of his long-time companion, and once the seed was planted, it grew quickly. He was an incubus he needed to cast off.

They had chosen to cross the Severn at Tewkesbury and keep to the western side of the river, avoiding Worcester, and by the time they spent the following night at Malvern Priory, he had already decided Ivo's fate, and that he would die so that he would be buried close to Mitton, since he went on about the place so much. What then struck him as inspired was that he could ensure that all possible blame for the Mitton murders was once and for all placed upon Ivo, and he would be free to reclaim his overlordship of Sudwale. The accusation of rape would have been forgotten like Rohese de Mitton herself. It had not seemed of any great importance when he was two and twenty, but now – Sudwale was his manor and he wanted to be Eustace fitzRobert of Sudwale again. The feeling only increased when they made the very small diversion to visit the manor hall. Ivo had seen it as a waste of time, and been vocal about it. Eustace considered killing him then and there, but dismissed the idea as one that might too easily remind people of the link between them. There was somewhere close but less obvious, and where the corpse would be less likely to be discovered for some time, so he curtailed the urge for action and was patient.

Eustace had never been a loving son and had not thought of his mother in years, and he had no high expectation that she would still be living. It would not have concerned him if she had been dead and buried, but finding her mostly blind and deranged of mind shook him a little. The steward, after initially disbelieving it could be that his lord was returned after so long a time, was convinced by his revealing past events only he could know, and had then been eager to tell him how hard he had laboured in caring for lady and manor. In truth, the steward had lived a good and indolent life for the last few years, but knew that when the lady Adela died, Simon de Mitton would be in control, and the lord of Mitton did not like him. Reverting to being steward to a lord who ought to be grateful for all he had done was much better. The steward had clearly forgotten a lot about his lord's character.

Simon de Mitton . . . Eustace had forgotten all about him, the little boy whose nose had always seemed to be running, who had cried too easily and been squeamish, and had been a spoilsport who told tales. That he should hold Sudwale was unthinkable.

When Eustace had seen the man who purchased the chestnut from Thurstan Horsweard, there had been no reason to associate him with the irritating child. There had been something vaguely familiar in the man's face, but his resemblance to his brother Ivo was not strong, and Eustace assumed it was just that he shared some features with someone he had known a little in the Holy Land. When he discovered his name, he realised that Simon had more of the look of his oldest brother Olivier, whose face had been forgotten for over twenty years. His first thought was exultation, since 'his' horse would be within easy reach. It would be perfectly understandable that he would be seen in the vicinity since he held the adjacent manor, and if the wicket gate at Mitton was still left unbarred, 'collecting' it would be simple enough. However, that idea lacked a certain neatness.

What had occurred to him as he lay in his bed in the guest hall at Quatford, his hands behind his head, dreaming of the future, was that it had been ordained by Fate that he should destroy the line of de Mitton. He had already come so close, and, forgetting the child Simon, had considered that he had done so. It irked him that he had not, but now he could set that right. He had fallen asleep with a smile on his face, thinking of Simon de Mitton's expression when he realised who he was, and what he would do. That smile returned now, as, somewhat to his surprise, a very familiar chestnut with a white star upon its forehead came trotting towards him, and whinnied as it recognised both the bay and its rider. This was so easy.

Simon de Mitton was not a man who liked to admit his mistakes to himself, let alone anyone else, but he was coming to the conclusion that he had been too easily swayed by the chestnut's good looks and the horse trader's patter, which had both extolled the animal's finest points and drawn the picture of how he would be widely admired upon its back, and complimented upon owning such a horse. The return journey from Bridgnorth had not been without incident, and he had nearly been thrown twice as the chestnut took exception to a blackbird's alarm call in the undergrowth and then a fox trotting across the track. He told himself this was not indicative of his poor horsemanship, but simply of horse and rider not yet being used to each other, which would take a little time. He had decided to ride today to establish a better connection to his new mount, but his mind was preoccupied and the horse took advantage of his distraction and played up, even more so when he began yanking the reins and jabbing at its mouth in a half-hearted attempt to establish his dominance.

What William de Ribbesford had told him the previous day had given rise to a confusion of emotions, predominant among which was guilt. Simon de Mitton found it far easier to think of his sister Rohese as long dead, like the rest of his family. That way he could keep them all in a casket of grief that he could leave closed in his memory. It was tidier, and for most of the time kept the ghosts at bay and the feeling that the whole family was cursed towards the back of his mind. The idea that Rohese was alive ought to fill him with joy that he was not alone after all, but the thought of seeing her, and what she must have become after all these years hiding from the world, living like some forest creature because she was too awful to behold, filled him with horror, and then the enormous guilt because he wished she was dead for his own sake, not hers.

He had not registered that there was a horseman coming towards him until the chestnut raised its head, ears flicking forward, called to them and broke into a canter. He hauled hard on its mouth to restrain its disobedience, and in retaliation it bucked. This threw de Mitton off balance and its second, even stronger, attempt saw him thrown from its back, to land winded and facing up at the sky. He tried to take a breath and found it impossible, and for a brief moment felt he was dying. Even though that was fleeting, struggling to take a breath took all his concentration, and only as he filled his lungs fully at last did he become aware of the face looking down at him. He did not instantly recognise it, but there was something about the smile that was unsettling.

'I would have asked you to dismount from my horse, but you need not have done so in such a spectacular way.' The voice was amused, not sympathetic.

Simon de Mitton gathered his wits, frowning as he did so.

'Your horse?' He took another deep breath. 'You mistake.' He could not manage more than a few words at a time, and his head was spinning a little.

'No. It is definitely my horse. He even recognised me.'

'Bought him in Bridgnorth.'

'I know. I saw you do so.' It was said silkily.

The unsettling smile grew broader, and de Mitton closed his eyes for a moment both to focus his thoughts and stop seeing it.

'But – not following me.'

'Oh no, de Mitton, I had no need to follow you, for I knew where to find you. I admit I had not thought that you would come to meet me. How – helpful.'

Simon de Mitton felt slightly sick, and it was not from the fall. This man knew who he was. He opened his eyes again, and squinted up at the face. There was something in face and voice and – whatever colour was returning to his cheeks fled.

'Holy Virgin!' Recognition filled him with dread. 'Eustace fitzRobert.'

'I am flattered that I have not altered so much. You, of course, have, but at that time you were just in the way. Interestingly, you are again, but it will not be for long.'

Simon de Mitton swallowed hard, and fitzRobert began to

really enjoy himself. He liked seeing fear in others, and torture was not simply about inflicting physical pain.

'Why have you returned?'

'Oh, you know.' FitzRobert shrugged. 'I did wonder if it was all this' – he waved the hand that was not holding the chestnut's reins to indicate the surroundings – 'English greenery, but in fact it turned out to be finishing something I began a long, long time ago. What you begin, you really ought to finish, I am sure you will agree.'

Simon de Mitton nodded, though he knew he should not. It was as though he were a coney mesmerised by a 'dancing' stoat.

'Of course I did not remember you, so I thought I had completed the task when I killed your brother Ivo. You know the English have a word for Fate; they call it "wurd" or something very like that. I have to say it has proved very strong of late. I mean, when you think that Ivo followed me faithfully for over a score of years and never even knew about what happened in the hall at Mitton, and yet discovered it only a few hours before I ended his life, that must be Fate at its most active.' FitzRobert watched the full import of that sink in, and de Mitton's eyes widen. 'Oh yes, everyone has blamed Ivo for that, though he had no idea, and they will blame him still. I have ensured that. I really am quite clever.'

'You are Devil's Spawn.' The words came out in a hoarse whisper.

'Thank you for the compliment. I am glad I am recognisably my father's son and am very proud of my bloodline. Now, where was I? Ah yes, the death of Ivo. What I find humorous is that when we halted early for the day, it seems he was planning to kill me, just as I was planning to kill him, or at least he ranted that he wanted to kill me, but then it was just anger. Death is always dealt better when done without anger, for it gets in the way of things. Ivo was so consumed with the need to tell me what he had learnt of the Mitton fire by chance at Astley Priory, and I think he expected me to deny it, which is odd. He did not expect me to tell him everything, every little detail of how they died – sanctimonious Olivier, your whimpering sister, your fool-blind mother, who kept saying "This cannot be so" right up to the moment that I slit her throat. Ah yes, Ivo had the same look on his face that you have now.' FitzRobert laughed, and Simon de Mitton, rage briefly overcoming fear, scrabbled for his knife, only to have fitzRobert kick him hard in the ribs and then, as he gasped again for breath, take it from him.

'Well done. You at least made the attempt. Ivo just stared at me. I think that must be because he was struck by the realisation that he had followed me like a dog all that time, and even, once or twice, risked his life for me, and I had killed them all. So I took off my gauntlet, and showed him the final proof.' He held up his hand with the golden ring upon it. 'He had worn a more paltry version for over twenty years, because the one he ought to have inherited was lost to him, and I had it in my possession all along.'

Simon de Mitton glanced at his own hand, where Ivo's thin gold pilgrim ring shone upon his ring finger and fitzRobert suddenly saw it too.

'Oh dear, did you think that it was this one? What a shame. As he stared at it on my finger I stepped close to him, and drove my dagger up thus.' He mimicked the action under his own chin.

'He did die within a moment, which is a shame really, but now I have one last de Mitton to dispatch, and I will have fulfilled the task.'

Simon de Mitton stared at him. The man was mad as well as evil. He remembered the coney that had been tortured before it was killed. He had to struggle to speak, for his mouth was dry.

'But I would not be the last.'

'Do not say your loins are fruitful and your hall full of snivelling children.' FitzRobert turned up his nose at the thought.

'No. But Rohese lives.'

If Simon de Mitton wanted to see Eustace fitzRobert thrown off balance, he was granted that wish.

'That is a lie.' It had to be a lie.

'It is true. I thought her dead too, until yesterday. William de Ribbesford told me she lives, if you can call it living. He has aided her all these years.'

'You lie.' This time it was not as much an assertion as a fervent hope. FitzRobert reached down and grabbed de Mitton by his tunic at the throat and jerked him up, even as be bent closer. 'She is dead.' He shook him.

'Was declared so, but lives, I swear it.'

Eustace fitzRobert wanted to think it the lie of a desperate man striving to live just a little longer in the hope some Heaven-sent stranger would trot along the trackway and save him, but the mention of William de Ribbesford's name gave him reason to doubt. If Olivier de Mitton had been sanctimonious, de Ribbesford had been 'worthy', a young man who tried to do the right thing, but so quietly none might notice him. In this he had been quite successful. He never had a bad word about anyone, except Eustace, and by association, Ivo de Mitton. He had always looked contented and calm and that had been the reason, besides lust, that fitzRobert had, upon the impulse of a moment, attacked Rohese de Mitton when he discovered her by the river. The thought had occurred to him like the brief flash of a shooting star in a moonless sky, that deflowering the man's bride-to-be would wipe the serenity from William de Ribbesford once and for all. That the foolish maid had tried to fight back, and had made him silence her with a stone first, meant the rest had been her fault, and he had been right. De Ribbesford had been horrified, outraged and unable to do anything. At least that was how it had seemed, but the man was the sort who would genuinely seek to help if she had gone to him, for he was all about duty and honour. He ought to have thought of that when he had tried to find her and silence her back then. He growled his displeasure.

'So if she lives, tell me where and I will end this the quicker. Your choice.'

In a tear-filled voice, Simon de Mitton, without any thought that he was placing his sister in mortal danger, whimpered that he only knew it was in the woods about Ribbesford.

'Not good enough,' growled fitzRobert, taking a step back and kicking de Mitton hard between the legs. De Mitton made a sound, half squeal and half grunt of pain, rolling and drawing his knees up. He then vomited on the grass. FitzRobert watched impassively, and gave him a few moments. 'Try harder.'

'I – I do not know, I swear it. That was all he said. Ask him, de Ribbesford, for I do not know and cannot tell you more. I have done you no harm. I will say nothing to anyone. Better still, I will say I saw you this side of the river when Ivo was killed, and none would believe that I would say that if it was not true.' Simon de Mitton was gabbling now, panic in his voice. 'You can have your horse. Please.' He begged for mercy, which was a pointless thing to do with Eustace fitzRobert, who had also decided that de Mitton had not earnt a death as swift as his brother.

When it was done, fitzRobert, a little breathless, regarded the crumpled heap that had been Simon de Mitton and experienced a feeling of regret, though not for the man he had just killed. He realised that he had let himself act more for pleasure than from good sense. When Simon de Mitton did not return to his hall after a ride, he would be sought. If that were just by worried peasants and thereafter a pointless hue and cry were raised, there was no problem, but by now it was possible that the lord Sheriff had men in the area, and the murder of Simon de Mitton, so soon after another violent death, might mean a more realistic man-hunt than peasants stumbling about trying very hard not to find anyone dangerous. He bit his lip, thinking. Taking two horses everywhere was pointless, and he had had enough of it over the last few days. Going back to Sudwale was taking a risk, but then he was a risk taker. The best thing he could do would be to conceal the body, and make sure the bay horse was taken not to the stable but a less obvious place, at least for a few days. Then he would cross the river and find William de Ribbesford, though he would have to do so when the man was alone. Thereafter, well, he had proved how persuasive he could be, so he would find out exactly where Rohese de Mitton hid herself. He looked down at the limp form of her youngest brother, sighed and proceeded to lug the corpse away from the trackway and among a jumble of scrubby bushes. By his reckoning, at first only Mitton men would be looking for him, and so if he rode quietly to Sudwale and should encounter any lord-seekers on the way, he could say that he had found the chestnut running loose, with no sign of a rider. They would not recognise him and he was taking it to the nearest manor, in case it came from there. It meant riding the bay again, and the chestnut gave him a look that might almost be reproach and disappointment.

Chapter Thirteen

The manor of Sudwale was one that Bradecote would have instantly said lacked a lord, or at the least an industrious steward, for he acknowledged that many manors that were not the caput of their lord's honours were visited rarely by them and run almost independently by that individual. The point was that the lord should ensure that his steward was honest, hardworking and fair. Sudwale did not look a manor that had ever prospered, for the soil thinned as the red sandstone high ground grew out of it, with the knoll at the northern extent. It was cliff-sided nearest the Severn, bare but for stunted trees lodged precariously in the crevices and the pockets of earth within them, and dominating the eastern bank of the river. Yet the manor's tired air owed nothing to that. It gave the impression that there was no plan to its cultivation, no determined ploughing or planting or harvesting, and in the great field there were still bent-backed peasantry collecting stooks when elsewhere all were already threshing. Even a few days could make a great difference with a harvest, and each new one saw the risk of the weather changing for the worse. An attentive steward would have been like Herluin at Ribbesford, and the steward of Mitton, and had everyone working as long as back and arm had strength and there was light to see by. Aching limbs might be grumbled at, but every man, woman and child understood the urgency, and a good steward encouraged but did not need to berate. Yet here was Sudwale, late with the harvest.

They rode into the field, for that was where Bradecote would expect the steward to be, overseeing the labour. Workers straightened and gazed at the riders, but nobody asked who they were, and simply stared in a bovine way until he called out that he needed to speak with the steward. A chorus of voices responded that he was back in the hall. Bradecote frowned. Was this a steward who acted as though he were the lord, and thought himself above the day-to-day? He himself had, on one or two occasions when the weather had threatened to turn and there was a rush to get the last of the harvest safely under cover, helped his workers load the last wagonloads, and he would certainly put in an appearance each day of harvesting to show he was involved and was taking an active interest.

The hall itself also had an odd feel, for the hearth in the main part of it had no fire laid ready for the evening, and looked as if none had burnt there not just for months but years, though it had been swept recently, and the rushes upon the floor were not so old as to have rotted away. There was no lord's seat upon the low dais at the far end, and only one lonely bench against a side wall. There had been neither judgement nor feasting in the place for a long time, and sparrows twittered in the eaves as though to say they had taken full seisin of it. The chamber had lost the woodsmoke smell of an inhabited space, and it was strangely disturbing. Bradecote knocked upon the door of the solar, since this must be where the lady of Sudwale now remained, or was perhaps kept. After a few moments the door was opened, and a sharp-faced woman, clearly a retainer from her garb, opened it, but did not stand aside to let them enter. She looked squarely at Bradecote, and, assessing his rank, adjusted her challenge, which was delivered in a low tone, barely above a whisper.

'Who are you and what brings you 'ere, my lord? My lady is not well and cannot receive visitors.'

'I understand that this is so, but seek the steward, and was told that he was here. I am Hugh Bradecote, Undersheriff of Worcestershire, and these' – he indicated Catchpoll and Walkelin standing behind him – 'are the lord Sheriff's Serjeant and Underserjeant. If the steward is not here, then can you tell—'

'I am 'ere.' A voice, very even and also quiet, interrupted the question, and the woman stepped aside so that Bradecote could see a short, stocky man, older than himself but certainly much younger than Catchpoll. The man folded his arms before his chest in a gesture that did not suggest he would be eager to assist them.

The shutters of only one of the two narrow solar windows let any light and air into the sparsely furnished chamber, and it smelt strongly of herbs and lavender. It contained little more than the curtained lordly bed, a chest, a brazier and two stools. There was a woman in the room, seated straight-backed in what looked like the lord's seat removed from the hall, her thin fingers gripping, talon-like, the curving ends of the arms, and her head, at odds with her upright posture, bent forward as though she sought something that had dropped into her lap. She did not move, or show any sign she was aware that there was anyone in the room with her. The steward saw Bradecote take this in, and his words were more warning than explanation.

'The lady Adela must not be disturbed and agitated.'

'I do not seek to do either.' Bradecote spoke calmly, but a little louder than the steward.

'My son!' The lady's head jerked up, and one hand was lifted from the oak arm and extended towards him. 'You are returned once more.'

The steward cast her a glance that was a mixture of frustration and anger. Bradecote's eyes were upon the lady only, and whilst he was aware that her utterances might be less than trustworthy, he was conscious of hope that where the steward would be guarded, she would be open.

'Not Eustace, my lady, not today. Has he come often of late?'

'You cannot take anything she—' The steward's words were a rushed and vehement whisper, and Bradecote held up a hand to silence him.

'He comes every day, to see the mother that can, alas, barely see him any more. He is a good son.' It was said with confidence, and joy, in an almost child-like sing-song voice.

'Since when, my lady?'

'As long as I can remember. He is a good son.' The answer sounded not confused but wondering why the question had been posed at all. 'And every evening he comes to wish me a good night and kisses my cheek.' She was nodding her head now, agreeing with herself. 'Will it be night time soon?'

This then was just the delusion of a lonely woman whose grip on reality had been lost, Bradecote realised. She 'saw' her son because she wished above all things to do so, and it must give her comfort, and he would not say anything to give her doubt.

'Not yet, my lady.'

'I shall wait for him.'

'Yes, that is a good thing to do.'

She smiled, a slightly vacuous smile, and then her head drooped back towards her thin bosom and she became as a thing of stone again.

'My lord, 'tis all imagined,' the steward whispered. 'The lord Eustace went from England many years past and 'as never returned.'

'You would swear your oath to that?'

'Aye, my lord.' The answer came swiftly, perhaps a little too eagerly.

'Even though he was seen within the manor boundaries only six days ago?' The words were said softly, so as not to disturb the lady again, but had a core of steel. 'We have not come to listen to lies.'

'My lord, that cannot be true. The lord Sheriff' isself knows this manor lacks a lord, and stood it down from service years ago.'

'Indeed, but that does not mean Eustace fitzRobert has not returned unexpectedly.'

'Only his poor lady mother thinks 'e lives, but that be 'cos 'er wits fail.' It was as good as saying anyone who believed he had returned was mad.

Bradecote wondered if the steward was trying to distract him by being insolent, and did not rise to the bait.

'The person who saw him had no cause to lie, and we have

241

other, most compelling, reasons to know that he is very much alive and within a few miles of Sudwale, even as we speak. He will not know that we seek him, so there is no reason to think he would not come here.' If the last part was not guaranteed, it was very probable. 'You were steward when he left England?'

'Aye, my lord, for just one year back then.'

'So you are loyal to him.'

'I *were* loyal, my lord, and now be loyal to my lady.' The steward was clearly not going to break easily.

'We will not disturb the lady further, but will search all the buildings, and speak with all who live here.'

The steward did not say anything, but Catchpoll, who had been watching him closely, thought he breathed a little faster. The shrieval trio went out, followed by the steward, who closed the door behind him. The chamber was quiet again, and the servant woman went back to her darning where the light shone best, and after a few minutes the lady Adela asked in a plaintive voice, 'Will my son come back soon? To wish me good night?'

The steward was, in part, relieved, since he knew that his lord would not be discovered within the manor, but he was trying to misdirect the lord Sheriff's men as much as he could, making it very clear he did not like the idea of them going to the stable, just so that they would be sure to do so. It would mean they were not looking in the direction of the barracks where once the lords of Sudwale had housed their men-at-arms, and he held on to a vague hope that after a cursory look at a few buildings, the trio would shrug and go away. It would have been easier if the horse had been left in the stable rather than hidden, since he could have said it was kept because it had been the lady Adela's and it felt wrong to sell it while she still lived. He tried to make an excuse to leave them so that he could quietly set a groom to get the animal out of the enclosure altogether, but the lord Undersheriff said that he must remain on hand. The lord Sheriff's men split up, with Walkelin going to the stables, Bradecote to the building where the sound of female voices indicated the kitchen, if it was anything like his own, and Catchpoll first to the byre where the plough oxen were chewing cud and looking lethargic before their autumn labours. The steward's sense of impending doom increased.

Walkelin came running back to Bradecote, who was now outside the kitchen, where he had been met by cooking smells but blank faces when he had asked about their lord, or any man unknown to them and seen that day within the palisade.

'My lord, the steward 'ere runs this manor, and does not look a man as rides. The lady cannot ride, and if she ever owned an animal for ridin' it would 'ave been sold long since. So there be no 'orses in the stable, nor signs of any, and yet I saw a saddle, and bridle also.' Walkelin cocked his head a little on one side. 'I doubts they ride the pigs.'

'Well done, Walkelin. So, do you think yourself so much in control of this manor that you ride like a lord, master steward, and if so, where is the animal?' Bradecote turned on the steward.

'Saddle and bridle were not sold when the 'orse were sold, my lord, and 'as been – forgotten.' Even as he spoke, the steward realised this would ruin his idea of saying the horse was the lady Adela's.

'The same way a bay horse 'as been "forgotten" in your barrack room, eh?' Catchpoll's voice made the steward jump. Catchpoll looked not angry but implacable. 'Or does you give shelter to poor lame beasts that wanders past the gate?'

'A lame bay, you say, Catchpoll?' Bradecote did not look at the serjeant, but kept his gaze upon the steward. 'Strange, then, that Ivo de Mitton rode a bay that was unsound, and whoever killed him took the horse.'

The steward's worry became fear. He had little idea about laws, other than to break them was a bad thing if you wanted to thrive. If his lord had committed murder, would he be arraigned because he had concealed and lied for him?

'It were found runnin' loose, my lord. I knows I should 'ave reported it, but with the grain still to be brought in, I 'ave been that busy . . .' The steward said the first thing that came into his head.

'So this horse, frightened when its rider was murdered, did not just gallop away, but swam across the Severn first?' Bradecote's expression hardened to match that of Catchpoll. 'The truth now. Nothing less.'

'I must be loyal to my lord, my lord.' The man was desperate.

'To a murderer.'

'He would not . . .'

'Oh, we both know that he would. So all of it, now.'

The steward crumbled. His shoulders sagged and he sighed.

'The lord Eustace returned about a week past, though never did any in Sudwale expect to see 'im again. The lord de Mitton's brother came also. We thought them both long dead and gone, truly we did.' The steward was keen to be inclusive of all in the manor, as though spreading the knowledge meant less blame fell upon his shoulders alone.

'So you saw the bay was Ivo de Mitton's horse, and yet have concealed it today, when it is known the man was murdered.'

'We did not know, not in Sudwale, my lord.' The steward did not look the undersheriff in the eye, for such shocking and surprising news had spread from Mitton and Ribbesford to the neighbouring manor as ripples from a stone falling into water.

'That is a lie and I have told you I will suffer no more of them. I lose patience. When did Eustace fitzRobert ride in today and did he walk from here, or was there another horse?' A thought had occurred to Bradecote, and it was that the hunt for Simon de Mitton was assuredly the hunt for a corpse.

'He rode his chestnut as before, my lord, and led the bay, which showed a little lame.' The one thing the man was unlikely to know was that the chestnut had been bought by Simon de Mitton. He would assume the man was still in possession of his former companion's mount. 'He went to 'is mother, barely more than to give good day, and asked that the bay be kept hidden in case – in case anyone came seeking it. Then he rode out.'

'How long before we arrived, and in which direction?'

'Not long, my lord. My lady's serving woman came to me to say she seemed unsettled after 'is visit, which she were bound to be, and I went to try and calm 'er. I 'ad suggested to the lord Eustace that seein' 'er again would upset the poor lady, and so it did. I 'ad just done calmin' 'er when you came. I did not see which way the lord went, I swears my good oath on that.'

'Not that your word, upon oath or not, counts for very much

at this moment.' Bradecote was not in a forgiving mood. 'When this is concluded, I will speak with the lord Sheriff, who will decide whether you also should be taken before the Justices.' He decided that, at the very least, the man deserved some sleepless nights, and the steward's blanched cheeks showed his words had had an effect. The man was apologetic, but the undersheriff waved away his protestations and turned to Catchpoll and Walkelin, while the quaking steward took his chance to remove himself from the disapproval of the Law.

'I think we have to assume Simon de Mitton is dead. I do not see fitzRobert leaving him merely injured, though it is possible he still draws breath, and by mistake. We need to find him, and we need to find fitzRobert. But where has he gone now? Where would he hide and for how long? Do we even seek to aid a man probably past saving before we hunt our murderer, who has the blood of the de Mittons all over his hands?'

'My lord, it must mean that Simon de Mitton rode right into fitzRobert, and even if the bastard did not recognise 'im, 'e would 'ave known 'is own animal. It means 'e sold it in Bridgnorth and *wyrd* decided Simon de Mitton would buy 'is dead brother's 'orse.' Catchpoll had thought it through.

'So fitzRobert was riding south and met de Mitton riding north, and before fitzRobert reached here. We therefore look upon the way that goes northward, and I doubt it will be very far, but I hope he did not take too long concealing the body. Speed is important.'

'But will fitzRobert now leave the shire for good, my lord, if'n 'e thinks we will name 'im as a murderer? Will 'e not gallop away on the chestnut and be beyond our takin' within the hour?

The Staffordshire and Shropshire borders be both close enough.'
Walkelin frowned.

'If that is his course, we have probably lost him already.
But he could have done that as soon as he had killed Ivo de
Mitton, and yet he did not. Something drew him home, and it
was not, I would swear, mother-love.' Bradecote was frowning
in thought. 'What if he still thinks there is a chance we will not
come this way and be too curious, and have believed the lie of
the "dead Templar companion" brought in by the miller? There
is a chance he might consider himself still "innocent" enough
to return, and he is a man who has taken chances all through
this. But he might have gone in any direction to lie low for a
day or so.'

'My lord, if 'e thinks straight, fitzRobert will realise if we
finds the bay we will know 'e rode that from where 'e sold the
chestnut – Bridgnorth. Would be crafty to go back northward,
mayhap to where 'e spent last night. We might go to Bridgnorth
to prove things, but it would get us no closer and be too obvious.
So Quatford would be a likely place, and the guest 'all there.'
Catchpoll could be crafty thinker too.

'A good thought, Catchpoll.'

'My lord, this Eustace fitzRobert 'as cut down all the family of
de Mitton – but for one. I asked afore, but ask again, be Rohese
de Mitton's life at risk?' Walkelin had a 'serjeanting feeling' about
it. 'You said the steward at Mitton reported the lord Simon
were not in the good mood 'e expected for one with a fine new
mount. What if the lord de Ribbesford came across the river
in the forenoon to tell 'im about 'er, and left when 'e were not
there, but they met as de Mitton rode back from Bridgnorth.

Learnin' that would make de Mitton a thoughtful man.'

'There are many "if"s in that, Walkelin, but it might be the case. The only way to find out is to ask William de Ribbesford. Go back across the river, find him and ask him. When we find de Mitton I doubt he will able to tell us any more than the dead always tell Catchpoll. If he said nothing, she is safe enough, but ask after the chestnut, and guard the fording place until we join you or send to you.'

Walkelin just nodded, and rushed off to get his horse. With only marginally less urgency, Bradecote and Catchpoll returned to their own horses and rode out to the north, keeping an eye out on either side of the trackway for anything out of the ordinary. About a mile north of Sudwale they were hailed by a man waving his arms, and beckoning them. As they drew close they saw he had a small and rather unkempt terrier dog at his side.

'There be a man dead, terrible to see, lord.' He had gauged Bradecote's status and thought perhaps the other man was a man-at-arms, since he had a sword at his side. 'My dog ran from me and began to bark when 'e found 'im. Must 'ave smelt the blood, and – first 'e found an ear by the track, and it were not bitten off by a beast, but cut off, and then there be the body that-a-way.' The man looked quite distraught, and pointed. The little dog sat quietly, and had the ear in the grass before it, guarding the prize it still hoped it might be allowed to chew.

Bradecote and Catchpoll dismounted. Catchpoll told the man to hold the dog, and went and picked up the ear, holding it in his palm and inspecting it without any sign of distaste. He also reported the blood still fresh and staining the late-summer grass. Then, leading their horses, he and Bradecote followed the man, who did not get too close, but pointed to where a body lay half-concealed, lying face down. Catchpoll stepped forward and turned the corpse over. Simon de Mitton stared up at them, not surprised or accusing, but with death-dread fixed upon his much battered face.

'Who would kill a man and then cut off 'is ear?' The distraught man, at least relieved that someone more important and with authority had come along, began to actually think about what he had found. He crossed himself and shook his head.

'Well, the ear came off first, then 'e died, and it were probably a relief.' Catchpoll was matter-of-fact. 'Otherwise there would not be so much blood alongside in one place, and the beatin' took long enough for 'im to bruise bad. Still quite warm, my lord, so not dead for long, not at all. I reckons as 'e were kicked mostly.' His hands ran over torso and limbs, prodding and pressing. 'Ribs is broken, and one lower leg, both bones together, but to get that, well, it would be from bein' stamped on. You would think this were done in a red-mist rage, my lord, but the ear be a cold-blooded thing to do.'

'You think he was tortured, and then killed?' It was what occurred to Bradecote.

'It looks as if that were the way of it, but there be some bastards, as we knows, who just likes to inflict pain.'

'So was he kicked to death because he did not reveal what was sought?'

'As I says, from what we knows of fitzRobert, the bastard could as likely done it for pleasure, my lord.'

'True enough. But if it was torture, what could he hope

to learn from Simon de Mitton?' Bradecote paused, and then his voice became more urgent. 'The obvious answer is that de Mitton did, as Walkelin suggested, learn his sister was alive, and tried to use that to barter for his life. Even the possibility means that we have to assume that was the case and get to her before he does.' Having ignored the man with the terrier, he turned to him. 'Were you heading south, and did a rider on a chestnut horse pass you before you reached here?'

'Set off from Trimpley I did, my lord, and saw none but an oldmother pickin' berries. For sure no rider passed me this morn.' The man, slightly calmer now, showed no doubt.

'Then we know fitzRobert has not gone further north, and if he has crossed the river we need to get to Ribbesford woods, Catchpoll.'

'My lord, the weather 'as been good for the 'arvest and the river be low enough for a man on an 'orse to cross further up this way and not really need to use the ford, if'n 'e does not mind gettin' 'is feet wet.' The terrier owner was trying to be helpful. 'I would reckon your grey would not even need to swim to get across if you goes west to the river afore it loops above Ribbesford. Mind you, you would need to take it steady for there be shallows and then depths. Used to fish a lot in that stretch as a lad, see, and—'

'Thank you.' Bradecote held up a hand to stop the description of good fishing. 'There are people from Mitton searching for their lord on foot and they cannot be far behind us. I am the Undersheriff of Worcestershire and would have you wait here with the body until they reach you and can take it for burial.'

'As you wish, my lord.' The man, now even more in awe,

was also relieved that the instruction clearly meant that his involvement would end at that point and he did not have to worry about making any report to authority, since authority had come to him. 'I will pray for the poor man and keep bird and beast from the body till then. If *hrafn* or *earn* 'ad reached the body first, the ear would 'ave gone for sure.'

'Yes. Do that.' Bradecote was already mounting his steel-grey horse, and, following the man's pointed directions, he and Catchpoll headed west to cross the Severn as soon as possible. It had occurred to Bradecote that fitzRobert might have remembered the river was crossable and taken the same route, but he hoped that he had been so long from Worcestershire, and seen so many places, that the knowledge was lost in the depths of the past.

There was no track or path, but the man had told them that as long as they kept the red sandstone outcrop well to their left, the descent would be easy enough for the horses at the riverbank. Bradecote just hoped the man's estimation of the depth of water was accurate and their horses could wade across, since the Severn had already once nearly cost him his life, and he gave up silent thanks that when they reached the edge it did not look treacherous, and the flow ought to mean a horse could keep its footing even if the water was well over its hocks. Even so, they crossed with caution, and kept their feet out of their stirrups in case their mounts stumbled, or suddenly had to swim. At the other side they were water-splashed but relieved, and followed the bank southwards, as much as the tangle of willow and alder would allow, until they could see the woods rising to the low ridge where Rohese de Mitton hid from the world.

'If she is "at home" it will be both easier for us, but also more dangerous for her, if fitzRobert ever knew of a cave up there, and recalls it. He would know she would need somewhere dry and safe.'

'Or he might think the lord de Ribbesford 'ad a place built for 'er, my lord, if 'e does not know all the *Hrafn Wif* tale. Depends on 'ow much de Ribbesford would 'ave told de Mitton and then 'ow much de Mitton told fitzRobert.'

'True. Either way, we must pray we reach her before he does.'

Chapter Fourteen

Walkelin urged Snægl across the ford, praying that the lord of Ribbesford would be in his hall, but although he was honest and devout, his prayer was not answered. He did not even bother to tether Snægl in the deserted bailey, but simply dismounted and ran into the hall. It was empty. Disappointed, he came back, looped his mount's reins through a tethering ring and went to find the steward. Herluin was still overseeing the threshing, and could only shake his head and say he had not seen his lord since 'early' but that he seemed preoccupied with something. Walkelin went back to the hall and checked the stable, fearing that this preoccupation had been with his son and Rock, or even his overlord. If he had ridden out, then there was almost no chance of him being found quickly, and perhaps not even this day. He sighed with relief, since William de Ribbesford's horse was lipping at its hay in a bored manner.

'Well, leastways 'e must be somewheres close.' Walkelin spoke out loud, and the horse's ears twitched. 'And if 'e were bothered by somethin' it might be to do with the *Hrafn Wif*.' He set off on foot up the track and turned off just below the ridge line, remembering the location of the cave as it had been described to him. It did not take him long to discover it, but like the hall, there was nobody there. He emerged, wrinkling his nose, for the cave had an unpleasant smell to it. He wondered if the *Hrafn Wif* shared it with the ravens.

William de Ribbesford was a man still burdened of mind. He had gone from the church the previous afternoon, bracing himself for Rohese's reaction when he divulged his 'betrayal' of her secret, but he was unable to find her, which perplexed him, since she rarely went far, and he knew her favoured places. He spent a fruitless hour, and then became worried. What if Eustace fitzRobert, purely by chance, had returned to the clearing where he had killed Ivo, perhaps looking for something he had dropped, and encountered her? No, that was a foolish thought, for if he had then her body, or just possibly Eustace's, would be lying waiting to be found. It did remind him of his commitment to his lord, and he apostrophised himself for coming out without at least a dagger. When he returned to his hall it was without any ease of mind, and he ate so little of his evening meal that the cook wondered if he was sickening for something.

The night had been no better, and he had been wakeful more than he had slept, and even then his sleep was tormented by nightmares. Eventually exhaustion had claimed him, and he slept well past dawn, rising still jaded. He went to the threshing barn to show his face as a good manorial lord should, and commended the workers for their labours, even though it was in their own interest to have all the grain bagged and stored safe from rats for the year. Such little things made a manor run more smoothly, and made folk more willing when tasks were irksome. Then he went into the woods and back to the cave, hoping that Rohese had not gone foraging further away, which he told himself was, after all, the most likely thing for her to have done the day before. Perhaps she knew of a good place for blackberries, beyond the woodland but away from people. He repeated his search from the day previously, working his way back and forth down the slope to the band of flat land before the river's bank. He considered calling her name, but he rarely did so other than at the mouth of her cave, where it felt the same as knocking upon the door of her chamber. He hoped that he was not being watched, and that she was intentionally hiding from him. He reached the clearing with the fallen ash, though he did not know it was the place where Ivo de Mitton had been killed. To him it was just the place where Rohese very occasionally came and sat upon its trunk and let the summer sun warm her. He was so focused upon her and what he would say that he did not register the sound of a horse brushing through the twiggy undergrowth until it was in view and within ten paces of him. He was startled, and then horrified as he recognised the rider.

Eustace fitzRobert had been contemplating his meeting with William de Ribbesford from the moment he left Simon de Mitton's body. That the man would be less willing to comply with the demand for information was neither an issue nor a problem, and in fact part of him rather hoped it would take a lot of 'persuasion' before he gave in. However, torturing a man in his own hall without anyone being the wiser might prove difficult, and fitzRobert was at first undecided. He knew that killing de Ribbesford would mean so much shrieval interest that his idea of taking up his lordship of Sudwale was probably out of the question, at least for some years, but then he could return to William fitzAlan with news of success, and a tale of danger where his friend was, alas, killed, and then link his fortunes to those of the Empress Maud.

He found a place where the chestnut could cross the river, and avoided joining the trackway running south from Bridgnorth, but instead kept within the woods, following a narrow path made by those who came along the Severn's bank to fish. Once, long ago, he had found Rohese de Mitton by water, and since Fate had shone upon him already this morning he felt it might do so again. The path broadened out and he realised he was reaching the clearing he had visited only a week past. He certainly did not expect to see William de Ribbesford before him, and where none would hear what might happen between them. Fate was definitely on his side and determining what he should do. He laughed out loud, which struck William de Ribbesford as ominous in the extreme.

'Just the man I wanted to see.' FitzRobert sounded delighted.

'Whereas I would rather meet any other man in England.' De Ribbesford's heart was pounding, but he knew Eustace fitzRobert liked to see fear, and this was his opportunity both to fulfil his overlord's command and also avenge Rohese and his friend Olivier. It gave him courage where courage might have been lacking. He planted his feet squarely, making it obvious he barred the way, not that fitzRobert wished to avoid him, and drew his dagger from its sheath at his belt.

'Ah, so have you grown a spine in all the years since last we met? How surprising.'

'I never lacked one, just an inclination to violence, you Devil's bastard.'

'Oh, if you answer my very simple question, there will be no need for violence.' FitzRobert did not add that necessity was not the only reason to inflict it. 'You see, I have something I need to finish, and you hold the key to it.'

'The only key I would offer you is the key to Hell, and invite you to open the door.'

This seemed to amuse fitzRobert even more, for he sensed the man was fuelling his own wrath in an attempt to make himself more courageous.

'I think, no, I know, that I can persuade you to change your mind. All you have to do to avoid unpleasant, very unpleasant, consequences is give me my answer. I would say you could ask Simon de Mitton how unpleasant, but he is no longer able to give an answer to anyone.' It was said silkily, but with great menace, and he saw the colour drain from William de Ribbesford's cheeks. He assumed it was simply fear, but in reality it was shock and horror, for de Ribbesford now knew for certain what the question would be. 'You see I was always destined to destroy the house of de Mitton, in more ways than one, and, since I had forgotten even the existence of "the child" Simon, I thought I had done so. I admit it was rather a shock to discover otherwise, but it is easily corrected. Now, where is she?' FitzRobert did not need to specify who 'she' was.

William de Ribbesford glared at him, his mouth closed tightly, and now a genuine fire in his eyes, which, combined with his aquiline nose, gave him the look of the eagle, but then the eagle was facing the wolf, and the wolf snarled.

'Where is she? You will tell me – in the end.'

William de Ribbesford shook his head, gripped the dagger more tightly, and said nothing, and that almost calm implacability both surprised and annoyed Eustace fitzRobert. He set his spur to the chestnut's flank and it jumped forward and came directly at the man to its front and looked about to run him down. De Ribbesford had no time to step fully out of the way, but just as it seemed certain he would fall beneath the hooves the horse swerved slightly, and fitzRobert, who had kicked his foot from his stirrup, sent de Ribbesford flying with his boot. It was a trick he had taught his mount after he won him in a game of chance in Malta, and one very useful for a man who lived by his wits and his sword. Had he wished to kill him, he could have drawn that sword from its scabbard, hanging upon the saddle, but he did not want anything so final, not yet.

De Ribbesford, half-winded, lay sprawled in the grass, with the dagger now some feet from him. FitzRobert very ostentatiously drew his own dagger, letting a shaft of sunlight catch upon the well-honed blade.

'If you do not loosen your tongue I will be forced to remove it.' He smiled, but as he made to dismount there came a drawn-out cry, half scream and half command, more animal than human.

'Nooo!'

From somewhere behind fitzRobert's right shoulder, a black shape crashed out of the undergrowth, and at the same time, three ravens, one almost echoing the cry, swooped down to mob horse and rider. The chestnut was spooked, and fitzRobert could barely spare even the one hand to try and wave away the black birds with their dangerous beaks and flapping wings. The black creature rushed to stand protectively, arms outstretched, before the stricken de Ribbesford. The tattered black cloth of the all-covering garb gave the appearance of wings, and for one terrifying moment fitzRobert wondered if the shape was human at all.

The ravens wheeled about and came in again, and although there were only three of them their wingspan alone meant the clearing seemed full of furious birds. Even as fitzRobert batted one away, a second caught at his scalp with its talons and pecked viciously, and the sharp pain was followed by the feeling of warm blood in his hair. The third raven pecked at the horse's ear and it reared, so that with one foot already loosed from the stirrup, fitzRobert was flung sideways from the panicking animal, and it careered from the clearing, not caring where it might go other than away from the birds. As it did so a flying hoof caught de Ribbesford in the shoulder as he struggled to sit up, throwing him back onto the grass groaning in pain.

FitzRobert's dagger left his hand as he fell and spun away into the grass, and the black shape lunged forward and claimed it with a strange gurgling sound of triumph. Then Rohese de Mitton did something she had not done in over twenty years, and dragged the veil from before her face. FitzRobert, slightly disorientated, shook his head, sat up and then his eyes widened. Even a man who had no fear of gore or wounds recoiled at what was before him.

'Yes.' It was a sibilant hiss. 'You shall not harm him and I have so much to repay.' The words were slurred, but he was not really listening. All he could register was that face, or the bizarre gargoyle that approximated to a face. The right-hand side of the pale visage was that of a woman, fiery-eyed, snarling with anger, but the left side was as if a face had melted into something more horrific than those of the souls in torment in a Doom painting over a chancel arch. The left eye did not look at him, or at anything in particular, but was cast up and skyward to the left, which made it seem even more as though that side had nothing to do with the other. The face sagged, unsupported by the structure of cheekbone and upper jaw, and excoriated red channels ran deep beside the nose from eye to mouth, where the unremitting flow of salty tears from the eye had eaten away the flesh. The mouth turned down, and the skin above the mouth was raw from the constant dripping from the nose where the sinus leaked. The image robbed him of the power of thought, until pain brought him to his senses as one of the ravens landed upon his left hand and bit off a finger. He screamed, and Rohese laughed hysterically.

'Feast, friends!'

'You are mad!' fitzRobert yelled, and tried to protect his face from the avenging beaks with his other arm. Panic would not help him, and he fought to overcome it. The ghastly face came closer, and he looked at Rohese de Mitton with appalled loathing but not one iota of remorse. Her grip upon the dagger tightened, and she stepped near enough to wield it, but that was his chance. He kicked out his leg in a scything motion and it caught in her skirts and took her off balance. She was a slight thing, and only a woman, he told himself, but he knew he was fighting for his life. Now she was on the ground, rolling away, but the dagger had been dropped. Without the onslaught from the ravens it would have been easy, even with the blood now running down his forehead and into his eyes, but they complicated matters. He too rolled, and scrabbled on all fours to grab the hilt. From the ravens' view it looked like two slithering animals upon the forest floor, and then they entwined and rolled and Eustace fitzRobert was uppermost.

It was all happening so fast, and William de Ribbesford was struggling to catch up whilst dealing with the sickening pain in his shoulder. Rohese and her ravens had come seemingly from nowhere, and a small part of his brain still wondered if she had been watching him but using woodcraft to avoid him seeing her. Yet she had clearly sought to protect him above even thoughts of revenge upon Eustace fitzRobert, though now it looked as if she must surely become his victim. She had been facing away from him, so he could not see what had shaken fitzRobert, and the attacking ravens further confused the scene. If he got too close they might strike him by mistake, but that was not important. What mattered now was that Rohese was in dire need. He scrambled to his feet as best he could, swaying slightly, taking a few frantic seconds to find his weapon in the long grass, and stumbled more than ran the few paces to where fitzRobert was about to deliver the fatal blow. He knew he would be a fraction too late.

'Holy Virgin!' FitzRobert had not been prepared for the foul stench of Rohese's breath and it almost made him gag. It delayed him for a few moments and Rohese, one hand trying to reach up and claw at his face, used it well. With her left hand she reached among the black rags of her garb and took the knife that did everything from cutting garlic to striking a flint for her fire and lived in a sheath at her waist. It was not a long blade, and a slicing one, not a dagger, but if it could gut a fish . . .

FitzRobert mastered the desire to vomit.

'A thing like you is better dead.' He spat the words, preferring not to breathe too deeply.

He heard de Ribbesford cry out and then other male voices shouting. He could not afford to wait, to enjoy even a few moments of power over life and death. He thrust the dagger in, just below the sternum, but even as he stabbed, intending to strike up towards the heart, he felt an icy pain as her knife skidded over a rib and entered his chest low on the right side. It meant his own thrust went straight, hilt deep, and as he let go of the weapon and rolled away, yelling in pain, he knew that he had struck a mortal wound. He managed, with an effort, to raise himself on his elbows. Breathing was so hard.

'I win,' he managed, though it emerged as little more than a whisper.

'No, the Law wins.' A hand gripped his shoulder so hard he felt the muscles bruise, and Walkelin's voice, cold, hard and totally unlike Walkelin the friendly man of Worcester, growled in his ear.

Walkelin had heard the eldritch scream, and was already crashing his way down the slope, risking a fall from the tangling tree roots, as he heard the second cry. He had neither time nor room to draw his sword, and emerged into the clearing as Eustace fitzRobert, gasping and swearing as much as possible with a lung no longer functioning, rolled away from the crumpled heap that was Rohese de Mitton. His first thought was that she must be dead, and that he needed to secure fitzRobert as his prisoner, for this was a man who deserved to hang many times over.

'Rohese.' William de Ribbesford's voice broke. He ignored both underserjeant and murderer, and dropped on his knees beside the fallen woman. The knife hilt alone told him the inevitability of death, and he did not need to touch the increasingly blood-soaked black cloth of her tattered gown. He looked her in the face, a face in which the one eye that could move at will looked at him in an increasingly hazy expectation of his recoiling, but he did not do so. He did not even see the ruination, just the unblemished side that was the Rohese he remembered as a girl, grown older and more life-battered. His hand went to stroke the pale cheek, and she twitched, for no human hand other than her own had touched her skin for so long that she had forgotten what it felt like. 'Still beautiful,' he whispered, and he meant it.

'God's mercy is granted at last.' The mangled voice was surprisingly calm. 'Will he die?' The question was to William de Ribbesford, on whose face she was trying to focus, but the answer came from another.

''e will die, lady, if not now from your wounding, then by month's end struggling in a tightened noose, because of you.' Walkelin sought to give reassurance with his promise.

'Good.' The voice was weaker. 'William?' She was drifting now, almost as if soaring in the blue sky with the ravens.

'I am here. I will not leave you.' De Ribbesford was weeping quite openly.

'I am ready. Living . . . has been so hard. Dying . . . is so easy. Promise me . . . you will be kind to . . . my friends.' One hand was raised with great effort from the grass, and she made a soft call. The ravens had circled, unsure what to do at the last, but one now dropped to the forest floor and came to her hand, clearly expecting a caress.

'I promise.'

Rohese de Mitton smiled as much as her face would allow, tracing a finger softly down the back of the raven's jet-feathered neck, and then the hand slipped to the grass.

Bradecote and Catchpoll arrived too late, and to a scene that could not be instantly deciphered. Rohese de Mitton lay dead, and William de Ribbesford was beside her, holding one of her hands and praying audibly.

Eustace fitzRobert, and although they had never seen the man before, it had to be him, also lay incongruously among the late summer flowers, but Walkelin was not praying beside him but rather pressing a cloth made from the man's own sleeve to his chest. Bradecote registered that there was no horse, and wondered how all four had come to meet in this small clearing.

'Is it a fatal wound?' Bradecote hoped it was not.

'I think not, my lord, with luck.' Walkelin was pressing hard still.

'And did you—'

''E killed the lady Rohese, but she stabbed 'im with 'er knife, and knew 'e will meet the noose afore she died. The other wounds I did not see.'

'That was her ravens' work. And she came to protect me.'

William de Ribbesford broke off from his orisons.

'Tell us what happened.' Bradecote moved from the living to the dead, and if he was shocked at the face of the dead woman it was not visible in his expression.

'I was seeking her, to confess that I had told her brother Simon that she lived. I felt he should know now that you did. I – I could not find her yesterday afternoon nor even this morning. I was still looking when he appeared, as if from nowhere. He has killed Simon de Mitton.'

'We knows. We saw the body.' Catchpoll looked grim.

'So he wanted to kill her too, the last of the family. He said Fate had decreed he should exterminate them all, and he thought he had until he heard she lived. Simon must have told him. I would not tell him where she was and – he knocked me down with his horse and would have killed me, but for her coming with her ravens.'

Bradecote had by now noticed three silent ravens in the branches of the tree nearest to her body. Normally, having humans so close would have such birds vocal in their alarm, but these seemed almost subdued and mourning as de Ribbesford mourned.

'She stood between him and me, and the ravens attacked him and his horse until he came off and the horse bolted, and kicked me as it fled.' De Ribbesford grimaced and reached to his left shoulder. 'He had a dagger, but dropped it as he fell and she, she was so brave, she went and took it up, but he kicked her down and then – he was much bigger and stronger than she was, and I was not fast enough. He must have thought it would be easy, but as he stabbed her she used her little knife and thrust it into him also. Then your underserjeant arrived and – she said living had been hard but dying was easy. I will not have her taken to Mitton, Bradecote. She was betrayed too often by brothers there. She will find her rest in Ribbesford, where she sought refuge all that time ago. They may call her the Raven Woman, but none will begrudge her remaining where she spent more than half her life.'

'It seems fair, and there are no other family.'

'"Other family". Yes, she was as family to me, only to me, and to her raven friends.'

'We needs to get this bastard to the 'ealin' woman, my lord,' Walkelin interrupted. 'I sees no reason for 'im to be eased, but best we be sure 'e does not go and die on us.'

'Indeed. Get him on Catchpoll's horse'. He was about to offer his own grey to bear Rohese de Mitton, but decided against it, since it seemed undignified for her to be slung across it, and even if it was only after death, the lady deserved some dignity restored to her.

'Shall I carry her, de Ribbesford?'

'No, I will bear her, but could you help me lift her from the ground? My shoulder pains me.'

Bradecote respected de Ribbesford's wish to carry her himself, even though it would be slower. Helping to lift her meant he felt how light she had been. 'Like a bird' would have been the description of many. As he followed de Ribbesford with his black burden, Bradecote wondered if it would have been better to have arrived in time. Having seen that destroyed face, the life she had been forced to live by the acts of Eustace fitzRobert and her brother, and what she had said to de Ribbesford at the end, their failure had enabled her to leave life knowing justice, however belatedly, would be served, and to set down that weight of living. He knew Catchpoll would say it was *wyrd*.

William de Ribbesford carried the body with the reverence of a holy relic, though he had to concentrate not to stumble, and his arms ached so much by the time he reached the church he feared he would collapse with the strain in them. He had covered her face, out of respect for her as much as not to frighten any manor children who might see their arrival, and stare and be haunted by it.

Eustace fitzRobert was, with some difficulty, got up onto Catchpoll's horse, where he slumped like a sack of grain, and Walkelin then mounted up behind on the horse's croup to both ensure he did not fall off, and keep pressure on the wound as much as he could. Catchpoll went to the horse's head and led it at the snail's pace of William de Ribbesford's walk. They did not want their prisoner to suffer further injury, though they cared nothing for his groans of pain.

The ravens followed the slow moving cortège, wheeling silently above it as it made its way down to Ribbesford church. As it reached the cluster of buildings about the manor barns, Hugh Bradecote went ahead to seek Estrith the Healer and the priest. William de Ribbesford was adamant that he would not have Eustace fitzRobert under his roof, even to be tended, so at the churchyard gate Catchpoll and Walkelin manhandled the wounded man, now barely conscious, from the horse and to the church itself. Walkelin managed to open the church door for de Ribbesford, and then he and Catchpoll dragged fitzRobert within and laid him, less than gently, upon the stone floor. The black birds now settled in a yew tree, though only they knew if they were waiting, and saw Father Laurentius, his sun-bronzed tonsure slightly shiny from above in the bright sunlight, hastening to attend both the dead and the bereaved. The churchyard was quiet, and after a while one raven lifted into the noontide sky, peacefully blue and in contrast to the death and darkness below, and flew, very purposefully, back to the clearing, where it landed and strutted about until it found exactly what it sought.

Chapter Fifteen

When Father Laurentius entered, he was startled to see the man bleeding upon the floor of his church. For a moment he assumed he had also been called to administer the Last Rites, and wondered why the lord Undersheriff had not mentioned so important a task, but de Ribbesford called him to the chancel, and Catchpoll almost shooed him away.

'My son?' Father Laurentius had heard the tears in the lord's voice. De Ribbesford was kneeling beside a body, though it appeared little more than a collection of black rags upon the floor.

'God looks generously upon those who have suffered in this life, Father?' There was a hint of doubt in William de Ribbesford's question.

'Assuredly, He does.'

'Then her place will soon be with the angels.' There was relief now, and his whole body sagged.

The priest placed his hand upon the man's shoulder, and was surprised that he flinched at it. His mind, which was quick, made the right assumption about the identity of the deceased.

'So this is the *Hrafn Wif*.'

'This is the lady Rohese de Mitton, falsely declared dead to the world over twenty years past, whose great suffering is over.' De Ribbesford announced it as if it were her official title, and with a trembling hand, uncovered the distorted face. Father Laurentius took a sudden intake of breath at the shock of what he saw, but composed himself almost immediately, clasped his hands together, and knelt beside the lord of Ribbesford.

'Indeed. Great suffering. We will pray for her, and at the resurrection the godly shall be raised unblemished from the grave and rise to Glory.'

Estrith the Healer was not a tall woman, and she actually had to trot along to keep up with the lord Undersheriff. Bradecote had been directed at the threshing barn to a small cott where she was tending an old man's arthritic hands, and when he said she was needed to deal with wounds, she asserted she had to return first to her own home to collect what she would assuredly need. She was quite pink of cheek when she followed him into the church, and frowned at her patient being laid upon the bare floor without even a folded cloth beneath his head.

'We needs you to keep this man alive, if you can, mistress.' Walkelin greeted her.

'Well, 'e would do better given some comfort.' Estrith shook her head at the foolishness of men.

'As little comfort as possible, and we just wants 'im livin' long enough to get to Worcester and so the Justices in Eyre can condemn 'im to the rope after Michaelmas, so 'e need not make a full recovery.' Catchpoll's tone and expression told her even more than his words.

'Ah.' She nodded her comprehension, and, being aware out

of the corner of her eye of the lord of the manor and priest beside a body in the chancel, she made the correct guess that her patient was a killer. 'Nevertheless, roughness now will not give what you want, and the craft demands I does nothing less than my best for any man, woman or child. I take it 'e possesses no weapon now?' It was safest to check.

Catchpoll gave the confirmation, and the woman knelt down beside Eustace fitzRobert, who was only semi-conscious. The wound to the hand made her wince, for she understood how painful it would be, but it was far from a mortal wound unless it later festered. The bleeding from the scalp and cheek she also dismissed, though they bled freely as head wounds always did, but her ears immediately told her the source of the man's debility from his breathing. She tutted. Collapsed lungs took their time to heal, and other than ensuring no more air got into the chest and giving relief for the pain, it was a case of waiting to see if there was any fever that came. That was always the caveat with wounds, so she would make no guarantee the man would live, but she was pretty sure he would not die so fast that it would be in her care, whatever happened.

The healer spent some time dealing with Eustace fitzRobert's wounds, and she treated him with the same care and the same calm voice she would have used with an innocent child, for until he was taken elsewhere by the Law, it was her duty to do the best for him. She even ensured the concoction she gave to ease the pain and aid sleep was not weakened so that he should suffer the more, for that suffering might influence his ability to recover. She did not see her time as wasted, even if the man was going to be hanged. When she finally rose from her knees, she dusted her hands upon her skirts, and sniffed.

'He will do, and unless the wounds go bad, which be as God wills it, he will be fit to take with you to Worcester, though I doubts 'e will possess the strength to ride for some days. If you wants 'im there the sooner, put 'im in a cart.'

'Thank you, mistress.' Bradecote, who had watched her ministrations, quietly directed her to the chancel, and in whispered tones, forewarned her of what she would see.

'Poor lady. 'Tis a pity in some ways that she did not succumb all those years past, and the Mitton 'ealer knew the craft almost too well, but God decides, in the end.' Estrith had been a healer long enough to know that success was never guaranteed, and that the thing that gave sleep at nights was knowing she had done all she could but that a higher authority decided the outcomes. It made seeing little lives lost just a bit more bearable.

She went before the altar, genuflected and crossed herself, and then knelt on the opposite side to where lord and priest still intoned prayers with bent heads. When the next prayer reached its 'amen', she spoke up, though gently.

'Leave the lady with me, my lord, just for a bit, and I will see all made right for burial.'

He looked up, his expression slightly surprised, as though he had been apart from his surroundings.

'Yes, but I will bring the best cloth from my bed to cover the shrouding until she is laid in the earth, and I want it to be here, where she spent more than half her life. She will remain with us.' He got up off his knees.

'I will come with you, my son,' murmured Father Laurentius, laying a hand upon William de Ribbesford's arm, 'and we can pray in the quiet of the hall until the cloth will be of use. Come.' He got up, very easily for one of his years, for the decades of doing so many times a day meant that it had become a natural action. Then he led the lord of Ribbesford, unprotesting, from the church. Bradecote accompanied them, for there was nothing for him to do within its walls.

'It almost feels wrong that a man could kill so many but die only once. Eustace fitzRobert murdered all the issue of Oswald de Mitton, so that none shall inherit by blood, and he shall face damnation for the deeds, but there is but one rope.' De Ribbesford sounded regretful.

'He will certainly be presented before the Justices for all five deaths, and all that he inflicted upon the lady.'

'Yes, but hanging will be too easy a death.' It was almost wrung from de Ribbesford.

'Not that easy if the rope is not so tight, and it takes longer. That is the skill of the hangman, as I have learnt these last few years. There are some who face a death from an act of the moment, almost a madness, and they die more swiftly and the crowd keeps silent, for they realise it could be something they might do in such a case. Men like Eustace fitzRobert die slowly and the crowd will cheer every choking breath and writhing.'

Father Laurentius frowned, for he thought that taking pleasure from any death, even a judicial one, was bad for the soul of the onlooker, though he understood that for the family of victims, forgiveness and prayers for the departing soul were possibly too much to expect.

Estrith, having dismissed the men, said a little prayer of her own and then slowly lifted the head and drew away the bedraggled black cloth that had been both veil and coif. She sighed over the ravaged visage of Rohese de Mitton.

'You poor soul,' she whispered, and touched the damaged side of the face. 'You poor, poor soul. No more sufferin', my lady, not any more.'

Walkelin was sent to Hartlebury to inform the lord Sheriff of the deaths and of the taking of Eustace fitzRobert, and to tell him that it was the lord Bradecote's intention to remain in Ribbesford until after the burial of the lady Rohese de Mitton the next day, and that fitzRobert would be brought slowly by cart thereafter.

'I will remain here until he comes, then, and as long as we can reach Worcester in a day, will escort the accused myself, for his crimes are many and will not easily be forgotten.' De Beauchamp said this sombrely, but Walkelin was wise enough to realise that in fact the lord Sheriff wanted his own name to be associated with the successful taking of such a dangerous and evil man of rank. It did not matter to the underserjeant, as he knew it would not to the lord Undersheriff or Serjeant Catchpoll, for it was not about them and praise, but about the Law, and its being executed properly. He returned with this information to Ribbesford, as darkness quietly supplanted day to the accompaniment of a hooting owl, and saw Catchpoll smile at it. Then he went to the healer's dwelling for the night, since although Eustace fitzRobert should be too weak to do anything, even to himself, it seemed right that Estrith the Healer should not be his only guardian through the hours of darkness.

'O' course. There be times when the lord Sheriff likes to show everyone that the lord Sheriff does not just collect the lord King's taxes and make folk's lives more difficult.' Catchpoll had not expected anything else.

'And if it means I need not stay in Worcester, but can go home the faster, I see it as a good thing,' added Bradecote, with a small smile, but then it faded and after a pause he continued. 'There have been five deaths, excluding that of the de Mittons in the past, Catchpoll, since I think we can be pretty sure that it was Eustace fitzRobert that killed Brother Albanus as well, but I do not think we could have prevented any of them.'

'No, my lord. I grant that usually the lord Sheriff would complain at so many, but in this case we could not 'ave done anythin' different from what were known and when it were known, and the lord Sheriff will see that.'

'Even though he does not see he should speak to whoever finds a body?' Bradecote raised an eyebrow and the faint smile returned.

'Well, my lord, that be where being lord Sheriff differs from bein' like us. We does not consider the great matters of England and who 'olds power where, and the lord Sheriff leaves the "ferretin'" and seein' the Law works to us. I would not want 'is life, nor 'e want mine, which be right and proper. The other lord Undersheriffs afore you, well, they wanted to act like the lord Sheriff.'

'And you think I want to act like you, Catchpoll?'

'In most things, no, my lord, for which 'eaven be praised, but in the Law and the craft of serjeantin', yes.'

'You are right.'

'Oh, I be nearly always right, my lord.' Catchpoll helped himself to another wedge of cheese.

The manor hall was, this evening, a very melancholy place, and they were the only two within it. William de Ribbesford had that said he would fast until the burial and had returned to the church with Father Laurentius to remain there until after Compline. He had arranged for food to be provided for the lord Sheriff's men, and spoken briefly and privately with Bradecote.

'I will have her buried outside the east end of the church, beside my wife, and with room betwixt them for when my time comes. I never loved her as a man loves a wife, but over the years the bond has become so strong, stronger than a friendship, that it has become different but equal. She would have been my wife, so . . .' He paused. 'I feel guilty.'

'Why?'

'Because I am glad it is over for her, and yes, you will say that all should feel that, but also because I feel relief. I was responsible for her, and yet could never do enough, never enough.'

'You did all that she would permit, de Ribbesford. For all the hardship and things she missed, she did have some ordering of how her life was lived. You did not override that.'

'I suppose so. She was – a remarkable being.'

'Yes, I think you are right.'

When Bradecote slept he did so without any interrupting nightmares to disturb him, nor unanswered questions to keep him wakeful at the points where he surfaced, briefly.

The following day dawned bright and with a whisper of

breeze that trembled the leaves that were just upon the point of losing their moisture and replacing sighing with rustling. The earth was neither wet nor summer-hard, and the gravedigger and his assistant had been excused from the barn and were at their labours from the moment they could safely see where they set their spades and before the sun had crept high enough over the sandstone outcrops on the eastern bank of the Severn to cast its rays upon them. By a little after Matins they had cut a grave of suitable depth, and William de Ribbesford had every soul within the manor come to the church, even abandoning the threshing, for although none of them knew the woman who was to be interred, he wanted them to know that the *Hrafn Wif* was not some malevolent spirit and was deserving of their prayers. He also did not want any tales to arise that meant that part of the churchyard would be avoided, or superstition arise over it. So before the service for the dead began, he stood before them all and gave a eulogy that had some of the women wiping their eyes by its end. He spoke of the young woman who had been destined to be the lady of Ribbesford but who had instead been disfigured beyond imagining at the hand of Eustace fitzRobert, cast out from her kin, and yet condemned to keep living. She had harmed none in Ribbesford, for all that there had been fear of her. He asked, and did not quite demand, that they keep her in their prayers and made it clear that in Ribbesford the ravens should be treated with kindness and not scared away. Then Father Laurentius spoke of suffering, and the infinite grace of God, and after that the Latin service commenced.

When the body was carried to the grave, some could still be heard sniffing, though they might afterwards say it was just that good Father Laurentius said the service so movingly.

A yew tree stood close to the eastern boundary wall of the churchyard, and not so far from the east end of the church. In its branches three ravens perched silently, unnoticed until the first handful of earth was cast into the grave, and then they rose into the air, their dry, rasping croaking a corvid requiem. Some of the people below crossed themselves at that, but Father Laurentius told them that the ravens were God's creatures too, and should be left in peace.

The crowd dispersed quietly to return to the threshing. William de Ribbesford lingered a little, and the lord Sheriff's men did not intrude. Only when he finally turned away and the gravediggers began shovelling back the earth they had so industriously removed a few hours previously, did they approach him with the practicalities of departure.

'We would borrow your ox cart to get fitzRobert to Worcester, though one of the lord Sheriff's men can drive it from Hartlebury. We will ensure it is returned to you quickly, but you should not have urgent need of it now the harvest is gathered.' Bradecote did not make a refusal an option, but was quite surprised that no objection was raised at all. Instead, de Ribbesford asked a question.

'When exactly are the Justices due in Worcester to hear cases?'

'The week after Michaelmas, as I have heard, though sometimes they are a little delayed. As a witness to the death of Rohese de Mitton, the attempt upon your own life, and with your knowledge of the past, you will be needed and sent for in good time.'

'Even if that were not so, I would come so that I might see him pronounced guilty and be there when he is hauled up at a rope's end. I want him to see me as he dies, representing her and all her kin.' He glanced back at the filling grave. 'I think that is the final end to all this, after so many years.'

'Then we will leave you as soon as the cart is ready and travel to Hartlebury this afternoon, so that your ox-driver may return by nightfall.'

'Thank you, my lord Undersheriff.' De Ribbesford was very formal.

An hour later, Bradecote, Catchpoll and Walkelin splashed across the ford behind the ox cart bearing the blanketed form of Eustace fitzRobert, whose ankles were bound beneath the covering, and took the track that crossed the western extent of the manor of Sudwale, which would be the last time Eustace fitzRobert would be upon his own land, though he did not notice it as he lay staring up at the sky. All three officers of the Law agreed that the lady of Sudwale, in her darkness and clouding of mind, did not deserve to be told the evil deeds of her son, nor the penalty he would face in Worcester. Better she should remain in her own world where he came each evening to kiss her good night. In time there would be a new lord of Sudwale, and, like Mitton, they would have no connection by blood to those who held it before.

In the churchyard in Ribbesford the soft, reddish earth of the grave formed a mound over Rohese de Mitton. Everyone had gone, and the only sound was the distant angry chatter of a disturbed jay. A raven dropped from a bough of the yew and landed upon the grave, hopping to the churchward end, its feet leaving slight imprints in the soil, and in its beak something shiny glinted. The big black bird leant forward as though to peck the earth, but instead pressed a gold ring into it, a ring upon which, faintly etched, was the design of a shell. It bobbed its head three times as if in final homage, and then flew away with a mournful croak, to join its companions and seek new carrion.

Author's Note

The inspiration for this story was one of the three Anglo-Saxon 'beasts of battle', the raven, white-tailed eagle and wolf, which were immortalised in Old English poems because they were the prime scavengers of the battlefield when the living moved on and the dead alone remained. The wolf was driven to extinction in England centuries ago, and the white-tailed eagle is just being reintroduced, but the raven has remained. Ravens are remarkable birds, highly intelligent, able to recognise those who are their 'friends' and those who have behaved as enemies, capable of imitating human sounds, and, when used to one human from an early age, faithful companions.

I sought expert advice on the disfigurement and damage that severe blunt trauma to the maxilla and zygomatic bone would cause, if not surgically repaired, and Rohese's disability reflects that, including the severe halitosis, the nasal and lacrimal drip, and difficulty with speech.

Hugh de Mortemer, lord of Wigmore, was a powerful Marcher lord of the twelfth century and ancestor of the Mortemers who played such an important part in the politics of England in the following centuries into the Wars of the Roses. The attributes I have given him are those that were recorded at the time, though of course the attempt to discredit him with King Stephen is, like Eustace fitzRobert, a plot invention of my own.

The House of Bellême was, however, genuinely regarded at the time as tainted, and their history is as I have related. That they were regarded as connected to the Devil because of their deeds, in an era when violence and betrayal was part and parcel of being powerful as a lord, shows how far beyond the acceptable norm of their time they were thought to be.

The topography around Ribbesford has been slightly altered by the embankment of the A456 bridging the Severn and neither Bewdley nor Stourport existed in the mid-twelfth century. Ribbesford today is little more than a beautiful little church with a highly decorated arch over the north door, in the 'Kilpeck' style, a farm and a couple of houses, a later grand hall and an access road that is much later than the original and on a different alignment.

To discover more great books and to
place an order visit our website at
allisonandbusby.com

Don't forget to sign up to our free newsletter at
allisonandbusby.com/newsletter
for latest releases, events and exclusive offers

You can also call us for orders, queries
and reading recommendations on
020 3950 7834

SARAH HAWKSWOOD describes herself as a 'wordsmith' who is only really happy when writing. She read Modern History at Oxford and first published a non-fiction book on the Royal Marines in the First World War before moving on to medieval mysteries set in Worcestershire.

@bradecote
bradecoteandcatchpoll.com